T0150727

Praise for the wor

Virgin Territory

A classic rich woman, poor woman tale, White's story brings together wealthy and successful Elise with her chauffeur Jan, who is from the poorer side of the tracks. Both main characters are great—they each have their flaws, and Jan in particular carries a secret that keeps her quite distant from Elise at times. Elise's attempts to get closer to Jan, and to get her to admit she wants their romance as much as Elise does, are rather poignant in places. I liked that Elise is in her forties—it's refreshing to read a romance featuring a woman older than thirty-five. White's writing style is good—just enough detail and background to allow me to delve into the characters, and great pacing.

-Rainbow Book Reviews

Simple Pleasures

When the storm is over, the difficulties of recovery are just beginning... Read it to experience empathy and hope, resiliency, and triumph over adversity—and second chances at love, because in the end, love is the most important simple pleasure of all.

-Lambda Literary Review

Taken by Surprise

Kenna White is one of the mistresses of lesbian romance. She definitely knows how to write a love story that grips its readers from start to satisfying finish. *Taken by Surprise* does not disappoint her readers. In this story set in Aspen, with wonderful descriptions of both the charming town and the beautiful Rockies, White has given us two very lovable characters. ...A great fireside read, which lets you enjoy the mountains, beautiful women, and a great romance while snuggled in your chair.

-Just About Write

Body Language

Kenna White has developed a reputation for writing satisfying romances with strong characters. *Body Language* may be the best she's written so far.

-*Just About Write*

Confessions of a Dreamer

Other Bella Books by Kenna White

About the Author

Lambda Literary Award winner for her contemporary romance, *Taken By Surprise*, and best-selling author, Kenna White, resides in Southwest Missouri and enjoys travel, creating dollhouse miniatures, her family and writing with a good cup of coffee by her side. After living from the Rocky Mountains to New England, she is once again back where bare feet, faded jeans and lazy streams fill her life.

Confessions

of a Dreamer

Kenna White

BELLA
BOOKS
2020

Copyright © 2020 by Kenna White

Bella Books, Inc.
P.O. Box 10543
Tallahassee, FL 32302

All rights reserved. No part of this book may be reproduced or transmitted in any form or by any means, electronic or mechanical, including photocopying, without permission in writing from the publisher.

This is a work of fiction. Names, characters, businesses, places, events and incidents are either the products of the author's imagination or used in a fictitious manner. Any resemblance to actual persons, living or dead, or actual events is purely coincidental. The publisher does not have any control over and does not assume any responsibility for author or third-party websites or their content.

Printed in the United States of America on acid-free paper.

First Bella Books Edition 2020

Editor: Medora MacDougall
Cover Designer: Kayla Mancuso

ISBN: 978-1-64247-195-3

PUBLISHER'S NOTE

The scanning, uploading, and distribution of this book via the Internet or via any other means without the permission of the publisher is illegal and punishable by law. Please purchase only authorized electronic editions, and do not participate in or encourage electronic piracy of copyrighted materials. Your support of the author's rights is appreciated.

Acknowledgments

A sincere thank you to Mari-Beth and Sharon for their expertise and sharing it with me. And to all those who stayed at home, washed, sanitized, kept their distance, and wore masks and gloves against the pandemic we all long endured. The fight is not over. Thank you from the bottom of my heart.

Dedication

This book is dedicated to MM, a dear friend who is deeply missed and will be forever remembered with love.

CHAPTER ONE

Ros McClure finished her speech welcoming department members to Carla Sweeney's retirement reception. As Mrs. Sweeney's assistant it was her job to lavish praise on her accomplishments and years of service to the university. That didn't mean she had to like doing it. Giving speeches wasn't the issue. Accepting a new boss was. When Dean Chang stepped to the microphone to welcome Steve Hansinger as the university's new chief internal auditor Ros moved through the crowd and out the door into the hall. She had done her duty. She didn't need to stay for punch and appetizers. And she certainly didn't need to stay for the inevitable questions about her status with the university and how long she had been with the department.

Carla was an intelligent, dedicated, demanding at times but charming woman. And a pleasure to work for. When Ros came to the university, fresh out of college herself, Carla was already a force to be reckoned with. When she became head of the department she had been the one to recommend Ros for the job as her assistant. Now she was leaving and the entire department would be the lesser for it.

Ros walked to the end of the hall, pressed the elevator button, and waited for it to whisk her to her office on the eighth floor. A few hours of work would hopefully return her jovial mood and put this day behind her. If nothing else it offered a safe haven from the anger she felt.

"Come on, come on, come on," she muttered under her breath and pressed the button again. Ros wasn't a drinker but if there was ever a time for a stiff one, this was it. She would now have to answer to someone with little to no experience with internal auditing, someone the university seemed to think was the man for the job.

"That was fun," a woman said, joining Ros to wait for the elevator.

"Yeah, fun."

"The buffet was nice," the woman said after an awkward silence.

"Yes, nice." Ros clenched her jaw.

The door opened to an empty elevator. They stepped in and pressed the six and eight buttons. Distant refrains of "For He's a Jolly Good Fellow" could be heard until the door closed and they started up. It was a slow ride to the sixth floor accompanied only by the hum of the motor and the chime of the passing floors. When the door opened the woman stepped out, but before it could close she reached out to stop it.

"Ros, I'm really sorry. It's not fair," she said with a pained expression. "That job should have been yours."

"Thank you," Ros said with quiet reserve. She pressed the button for the eighth floor as if signaling her to release the door.

Once at her desk, Ros sat staring at her computer screen. She usually left her office door open to encourage the circulation of fresh air, but doing that today meant she would be able to see across the hall into Mrs. Sweeney's office. Or rather what would soon be Steve's office. No, she wasn't ready to think of him as Mr. Hansinger. He hadn't reached that pinnacle. He would be her boss and she'd show him respect. But he had been promoted despite Ros's obvious qualifications and experience to the job she assumed would be hers.

He needed to put in two more years at the university to pad his pension and Social Security and the good old boys network found the perfect place to hide him until his retirement. He had been assistant to the assistant in the Student Financial Aid Department long enough. Carla Sweeney's retirement had provided the solution. Carla had told Ros how much the university appreciated her work ethic and knew she'd carry on that tradition. Meaning Ros would be assistant to a man who knew nothing about the internal auditing department, her workload would increase, and he would take credit for everything that went well.

A tap at her door brought her back to reality.

"Did you know Dean Chang has a long hyphenated name? Beson-Thorpe-Chang or something like that. Can you believe it?" a young woman said as she entered Ros's office with an armload of papers. "I wonder if I should put a couple of hyphens in my name."

"I beg your pardon." Ros was trying to read an email.

"I could be…" She thought a moment. "Laurel Marie Anderson-Rink," she announced and placed the papers on Ros's desk. "My mother's second husband was John Rink. I didn't like him, but she seemed to. That's why I just use Anderson. But hey. If a hyphen gets me attention, why not?"

"You can add that to your résumé for your next employer," Ros said without looking up at her. Laurel seemed to read the disapproval on Ros's face as she tried to concentrate and returned to her desk without another word.

"Ros, are you in your office?" a male voice called.

"Yes, I am," she replied without much interest. She was busy.

"There was a call for you. They called twice. No, three times, but didn't leave a message." When she didn't reply, he added. "It was a woman. Older woman, I think."

"Did you get a name?" Ros stepped back into her shoes and headed to his desk in the office lobby. She had been nursing a stress-driven headache for three hours and didn't feel like playing twenty questions with a graduate student more interested in texting his friends than doing his job.

"Uh, I don't remember. Barbara? Betty? Brenda?"

"Rick, the key to answering a phone call is to get a name, a message, and perhaps write it down. Now, let's try again. What did the woman say?"

"Okay, she sounded sort of, you know, frustrated and a little, you know, scatterbrained. When I told her you weren't here she wanted to know where you were and when you'd be back. I wasn't sure that was any of her business so I said I didn't know."

"Was it someone on campus?"

"I don't think so. I got the idea it was someone out of town. She said something about a different time zone."

"And you didn't think to ask who it was?" Ros rubbed her fingertips across her forehead at the twinge of pain vying for her attention. "Could it have been Bonnie?"

"Bonnie? Yeah, yeah, it could have been," he agreed, pleased with himself for the revelation. "Yeah, I'm pretty sure it was Bonnie."

"My Aunt Bonnie from Kansas? Do you remember what she wanted?"

"Ya know, I don't think she said. She was a little aggravated you weren't here. I remember that."

"Did you ask her what she wanted?"

"I'm sure I did."

"So, my Aunt Bonnie called three times, didn't leave a message, and seemed upset about something."

"Is she the one who sent the five pounds of buffalo jerky for Christmas?" he asked through a chuckle.

"Yes." Ros returned to her office.

"If she calls again, do you want me to ask what she wants?" he shouted.

"Absolutely." But she was already pressing the contact button on her cell phone. After several rings the voice mail picked up. "Aunt Bonnie, this is Ros. I'm sorry I missed your call. I was in a meeting. You should have my cell phone number on your phone if you want to call back. I'll be in my office until six thirty today. That's five thirty your time. Again, I'm sorry I missed you."

Ros was always sorry when she missed one of Bonnie's calls although sometimes her timing was lousy. The reasons for her call could be anything from world apocalypse to spilt coffee grounds on the carpet, but Ros felt a pang of guilt nonetheless. There was no doubt Bonnie would call back.

It was well past six thirty when Ros shut down her computer and decided to call it a day. She hadn't been as productive as she intended, but between the retirement reception, Bonnie's fruitless attempts at contacting her, and the headache small accomplishments were better than none. The office was empty when she turned out the light and closed the door. Most of her coworkers who attended the reception hadn't returned to work that afternoon. It was just as well. She accomplished more when she wasn't bothered by incessant questions and banal chitchat.

As she waited for the elevator she contemplated calling Bonnie again. She'd probably be eating dinner. It was Friday. She'd be with her friends at the Welcome Home Café on the south side of town having the senior chicken fried steak plate with mashed potatoes. It was tradition. Four women, all retired and widowed, sharing a weekly get-together to gab about weather, local events, and family.

Ros slipped her phone in her jacket pocket, resigned to calling Bonnie later. They had talked twice this week and about nothing urgent. Bonnie had been trying to decide on a new trim color for the front porch and vacillating between white walls with sage green trim and yellow walls with white trim. Ros didn't know why her approval was needed.

Ros stepped into the elevator and pressed the button for the lobby. As always, it would be a slow methodical descent to the ground floor. She normally considered it wasted time, but on stressful days like today, it gave a few moments to gather herself together and decompress. She closed her eyes and rubbed her forehead as her headache deepened. Home. That's where she wished she was. Home, in her baggy sweatpants and T-shirt, curled up in her chair with a cup of herbal tea. Before she could finish the thought, the lights blinked and the elevator jerked to a stop. She braced her hand against the wall as it gave another jerk.

"Oh, come on. Don't do this. Not today," she grumbled, tapping the lobby button repeatedly. "I've got places to go and things to accomplish and they do not include being stuck in an elevator." She pressed the button again and held it, but the elevator didn't move. "I don't have the patience for this today." She waited a moment, expecting something to happen. But there was only silence.

"Damnit," she shouted as if someone could hear. "Damnit, damnit, damnit," she repeated systematically pressing every button on the panel. When still nothing happened, she opened the door on the control panel, expecting to find an emergency phone connected to the campus police or fire department. But there wasn't one. She pressed the red emergency button, expecting to hear an alarm. Nothing. She pressed it again, assuming it sent a warning signal to the powers that be. "Okay, this isn't fun anymore. I'd like to be rescued," she called out. "Today, if possible."

She pulled out her cell phone, pressed the main number to the campus switchboard, and listened to the automated system offer her choices.

"Campus Security," she said and listened while the system connected her call.

"Security, Damon Stewart speaking."

"Mr. Stewart, this is Ros McClure. I am stuck in the elevator between the sixth and seventh floor. Would you please notify the campus fire department so they can extricate me?"

"You're in an elevator on your way to the seventh floor?"

"No, I'm stuck in an elevator. Elevator number two."

"Where?"

"On campus. I work in the Auditor's Office. Could you please get me some help?"

"What building?" The man seemed overwhelmed with too much information and it was adding to Ros's exasperation.

"Mr. Stewart, how many buildings on campus have more than five floors?"

"Oh. Just the Maxwell Administration Building I guess."

"Correct."

"And you want me to call someone to get you out?"

"That's right. Very good. Now, I'm going to hang up so you can use your phone to call the fire department and get me some help. How does that sound?" she said, unable to hide her sarcasm.

"Is there a fire in the elevator?"

"No, Mr. Stewart, I am in the elevator. The fire department is trained for this kind of rescue." This man's ineptitude was eroding the last of her tolerance for the day.

"I'll get this reported right away, ma'am," he said but without much conviction. He hung up. Ros would have been more reassured of a timely rescue had he asked for her phone number so she could be kept apprised on what to expect and when.

Thirty minutes had passed with no word. No tapping on the wall. No shouting from the elevator shaft. No reassuring communication of any kind. Ros wasn't surprised but still frustrated. She was poised to call Security for an update when an incoming call flashed across the screen. She didn't mean to answer it, but her finger pressed the Accept button.

"Hello, Aunt Bonnie."

"Hello, honey. I got your message. How are you?"

"I'm fine. How are you?" She'd give her aunt two minutes to find out what she had called about earlier, in case it was important. Then she'd excuse herself and hang up.

"My daffodils are blooming like crazy. I love yellow flowers in the spring."

"That's nice."

"No, it isn't. They're predicting temperatures to drop overnight. It's going to nip those blooms, I'm sure. Do you have any spring flowers yet?"

"Not that I've noticed. My apartment building doesn't have much green space."

"When you are coming to visit, honey?"

"I'm not sure. Things have been busy at work. It may not be until late summer or maybe in the fall." Ros pressed the elevator buttons again for good measure.

"You're coming for the class reunion I assume. Meredith Eason had a thing in the paper about it. She's the editor, you know. She said it's your twenty-fifth reunion." Bonnie gave a wicked little laugh. "I remember you and Meredith had a slumber party and snuck out the bedroom window. You got caught putting toilet paper all over someone's yard."

Bonnie was wafting. And as much as she'd like to entertain one of her aunt's strolls down memory lane Ros didn't have time or tolerance for it while stuck in an elevator after having to congratulate an unqualified man for being given a job that should have been hers. And memories of Meredith Eason and high school weren't anything she wanted to take a stroll with today either.

"Aunt Bonnie, I've got to…"

"What do you think of the color beige?" Bonnie asked.

Before Ros could exit the conversation Bonnie had found a new path that seemed to demand an answer.

"Beige for what?" Ros tried to show patience.

"The house, of course. On my way home from dinner with the gals this evening I drove by that new house out on South Franklin. You know the one with the circle drive. The grass is finally coming in, but they need to plant some shrubs. That yard is as bald as a wheat field in December. Anyway, I noticed they painted the trim a light beige. I always liked beige. I think beige would look good, don't you?"

"Beige is okay. A light sandy beige maybe. Aunt Bonnie, I've got to go."

"Sandy beige. That sounds better. Wet sand. I like that." Bonnie took hold of Ros's suggestion as if it was gospel. "Oh, yes. Wet sandy beige."

"I thought you decided on yellow walls and white trim." Ros wasn't sure why she mentioned it. Being stuck in an elevator was more pressing than arguing over paint colors. She leaned her forehead against the wall, praying for an opening in the conversation so she could end it.

"Yes, yellow and white is so fresh looking. I've always liked yellow with white trim. Maybe you'd like your bedroom painted yellow with white trim. I remember in high school you wanted every wall in your bedroom painted a different color. That was the wildest assortment of colors I'd ever seen."

It was Bonnie who had thought painting each wall a different color might be a fun thing to do, but Ros wasn't going to bring that up. Not now. There was no point in arguing with her.

"Aunt Bonnie, I've got to go. You know how it is when you're busy."

"Indeed I do. I've got a load in the washer, one in the dryer, and clean sheets that won't make the bed themselves. Now you're coming for the reunion, aren't you? It's an important year. You can tell a lot about people after twenty-five years. Remember that boy in your class with the retarded sister? Johnny something or other. Everyone thought he was going to do great things. Well, he's in county jail for stealing a pickup truck."

"John Hock. And his sister wasn't retarded. She had muscular dystrophy. It was great visiting with you, Aunt Bonnie. I'll talk with you again soon. Bye-bye."

Ros hung up before Bonnie could steer the conversation in a new direction. If there was important news, she would have already mentioned it. Beige paint and her high school class reunion didn't warrant further conversation. Later she'd decide how best to tell Bonnie she wasn't attending the reunion. But not today.

She placed another call to the switchboard, asked again for Campus Security, and waited for Damon to answer.

"Security, Damon Stewart speaking,"

"Damon, this is Ros McClure again. I'm the one stuck in the elevator. Remember me?"

"Oh, yes. I reported it to the campus police. They're supposed to be taking care of that."

"Did you call the fire department also?"

"I report directly to the campus police."

"So, no, you didn't." She took a deep exasperated breath. "Is everyone conspiring against me today?" she mumbled. "Okay, Damon, open your computer screen to the telephone registry and read me the number for the campus fire department."

"But I already reported your incident."

"It has been forty-six minutes since I called you and I have heard nothing. So I want you to read me the phone number for the campus fire department and I want you to do it now," she said in a soft but demanding tone.

"Yes, ma'am."

Sure enough, the fire department had only just received notice someone was trapped in the elevator, leaving her to wonder how long Damon had waited before reporting it.

"We'll have someone there in ten minutes, ma'am. Will you need an ambulance?" the dispatcher asked.

"No. No ambulance. Just an open elevator door."

"We can do that, ma'am. Don't worry. We'll have you out of there before you know it. Would you like to stay on the line with me until they arrive?"

"If you mean am I claustrophobic and ready to pull my hair out, no."

"No, Ms. McClure, that's not what I meant," he said with a chuckle. "Although some people do have a problem with tight spaces."

Ros was encouraged by the man's professionalism and attentiveness to her situation. Maybe rescue was on the way.

True to his word, within a few minutes the elevator door had been pried open and several firefighters in helmets and rescue gear were staring down through the gap between the door and the floor above.

"Ms. McClure?" A woman lowered herself through the partial opening. "Are you okay, ma'am?" Another fireman handed down a folding chair.

"If you're here to get me out I am."

"Will you need assistance? We can hoist you through the opening."

"No, you hold the chair and I think I can make it."

Thankful she was wearing slacks and top that didn't make for an embarrassing climb, Ros didn't take long to scramble up and out of the elevator even though she wasn't necessarily athletic. She thanked the rescue team, descended the staircase to the lobby, and crossed campus to the parking lot as the last glimmer of sunlight faded from the evening sky. She started her car, buckled her seat belt, and switched on the headlights, but before pulling out she closed her eyes and rested her forehead against the steering wheel. It had been a long, tiring, and frustrating day. One of those days that curdled her nerves. It dawned on her she'd probably have to climb the stairs to her office on Monday. She shook her head and began to laugh.

"T G I F!" she shouted.

CHAPTER TWO

Monday morning was a rainy, dreary day, perfect for curling up with a good book. But not for Ros. She had meetings to attend and work that wouldn't wait. Thankfully the elevator repair crew had worked throughout the weekend, eliminating the need to climb eight flights of stairs. She had been at her desk for an hour when Carla Sweeney appeared in the doorway with a plastic tub in her hands.

"Good morning," Carla said with an agreeable smile. "I see my team is hard at it."

"Good morning. Let me guess. You're going to spend your last few weeks, while you're training Steve, stealing the stapler and paperclips," Ros teased, knowing Carla wouldn't dream of taking even one paperclip that wasn't hers.

"This is to rescue my coffeemaker from the break room. And because, for some unknown reason, I've accumulated four umbrellas, half a dozen bottles of hand lotion, and the ugliest scarf I've ever owned. It has beer mugs on it."

"Wasn't that your Secret Santa gift last year?"

"Well, Santa can have it back. And speaking of rescue, I heard you had a problem last Friday that required the fire department rescue team."

"Oh, the elevator?" Ros laughed. "Let's just say it was the perfect ending to a perfect day. I'm thankful they got it fixed over the weekend. I wasn't looking forward to climbing all those stairs carrying my tote bag."

"By the way, thank you for coordinating the reception and for your kind words. I noticed you didn't stay to try some of the goodies, though. They were wonderful. How did you know I like baklava?"

"I'm glad you enjoyed it."

"Ros," Carla said, stepping inside the office and closing the door. "I know why you didn't stay and I don't blame you. I would have done the same thing if I were in your shoes. I want you to know it wasn't my doing."

"I know, Carla. I know."

"I have always believed the stars align when we deserve them to. This time they didn't and I feel terrible about it."

Ros shrugged, not sure what response to offer.

"I'm afraid politics played a role in this, although you didn't hear that from me. You're more than capable and qualified. Promise me you won't give up. You're a hard-working assistant and Steve will need your help and support. You never know. Someday your job title may improve."

"Thank you, Carla."

"Now, I have a meeting with the library administrator to discuss how they plan to financially justify their increased staffing expenses. And I have a stapler to commandeer." With a twinkle in her eye, she left Ros to her work.

Ros had finished her lunch and was in the middle of a report that required absolute concentration when her cell phone rang. She usually muted it when she was working but had forgotten. She flipped the mute switch without looking at the screen, muttering figures to herself so she wouldn't lose her stream of thought. It wasn't until she returned from the ladies' room over an hour later that she noticed three missed calls on the screen. A voice message had been left with each call. One was from Aunt Bonnie. The other two were identified only as Potential Spam.

"Ros, can you take this call from Lily in the Business Office?" Carla called from across the hall. "I'm in the middle of something."

"Sure," Ros replied, resigning herself to checking the messages later.

When she finished the call, it was time for a staff meeting. When she returned to her desk, there were two more messages on her phone, both from Bonnie. Two more messages that would have to wait.

"Pick a trim color and leave me out of it," she said, placing the phone in a drawer. "Beige. Chartreuse. Pink with purple polka dots. I don't care."

"Ros." Carla appeared in the doorway with a concerned look on her face. "Are you concealing your whereabouts from anyone?"

"Concealing? No, not that I'm aware of. Why?"

"I just got a call from Dean Chang. Evidently you aren't answering your phone or returning your messages."

"My desk phone hasn't rung."

"Your cell phone. Your personal cell phone. Someone has been trying to get a hold of you all day and has resorted to going up the food chain to the dean of the department, who in turn called me."

"I'm so sorry you got involved in this." Ros retrieved her phone from the drawer. "My aunt has been calling all morning and I was busy. She gets a little impatient sometimes when she can't reach me. I'll take care of it."

"I understand it's not a relative. Do you know a Dr. Smithton?" Carla handed Ros a piece of paper with a name and phone number on it. "I trust you'll take care of it." She gave her a stern glance, then returned to her office.

"Absolutely." Ros called the number and asked to speak with Dr. Smithton. It took several minutes before a man picked up the call.

"Ms. McClure, this is Doctor Smithton at the Citizens Medical Center in Colby, Kansas. We had a patient admitted yesterday, Bonnie Ingram Bartholomew, who asked me to contact you. You are listed as her next of kin. Is that correct?"

"Yes, that is my aunt. What happened? Why was she admitted?"

"She had an accident. Someone found her in her yard. For some reason, she felt the need to be up on a ladder."

"Is she all right?"

"She will be. But it'll take some time and rehabilitation. I waited until we had all her test results back before I called you. She broke her humerus just below the head and dislocated her scapula from the Glenoid socket."

"Oh my God. I'm not a doctor, but that sounds like her shoulder?"

"Yes. She'll be out of commission for several weeks. I understand she lives alone."

"Yes, she does."

"We're preparing her for surgery. I assume you aren't here in Colby. We'd like to have your permission to go ahead and treat her. I got the idea she wanted your approval although she is a consenting adult."

"You have it, Doctor. I'm sorry, but I couldn't get there today. I'm in Cincinnati."

"Does your aunt have any other relatives we should be contacting? Anyone who could be here during the surgery?"

"Is the surgery dangerous?"

"No more than any other surgery using general anesthetic on a woman your aunt's age. Perhaps she has a son or a brother?"

"No, she has no children." Ros hesitated. "There's no one else to call. I'm her next of kin. I'll try to get there tomorrow. Please have someone call to keep me posted on her progress."

"I'll call you as soon as she's sent to recovery."

"Did you say she was admitted yesterday?"

"Yes, late in the afternoon. We couldn't do surgery until we got the results of the X-rays and got her stabilized. She was dehydrated and had some internal bleeding. She's been in a lot of pain, so we've had to keep her sedated."

"My aunt tried to call me several times today. If she's sedated and with those kind of injuries, I'm surprised she could do that."

"She didn't. I understand she gave her cell phone to someone and asked them to call you. I'm guessing you didn't return their calls either."

"No, I'm sorry. I assumed it was my aunt calling me for one of our daily chats. I feel terrible about this. Please tell Aunt Bonnie I love her and I'll be there soon."

Carla was eavesdropping from the hall when Ros finished the call.

"Your aunt?"

"Yes, she fell off a ladder and broke her shoulder." Ros drew a deep breath. "They're prepping her for surgery now."

"Ooo, shoulder. That's not good. Does she live alone? She may need to be in rehab a while."

"Yes and she's not going to like it."

"Is this the aunt you lived with in high school?"

"Yes."

"Then you'll need some time off to go see to her needs." Carla gave a nod.

"I was going to ask if I could take a few days. I know we're coming up on the first quarter report, but there's no one else to do this."

"I'll take care of things here. You go take care of your aunt. It's the least I can do." She started out the door, then looked back. "Not that it's any of my business, but what in the name of blue blazes was your aunt doing on a ladder?"

"I have no idea, but I think I can guess. And it makes me furious to think about it."

"Where do you fly into? Colby, Kansas, can't have much of an airport."

"Denver. It's about a three-hour drive back to Colby. My aunt insists Wichita is closer, but it isn't and the connections aren't as good," Ros said as she scanned a travel site for flight options. "Wow, I like this. One eighty-six roundtrip—if I knew how long I'd be there."

"How long do you want to be there?"

"I have no idea. I think it depends on how quickly she recovers from surgery. The doctor said she'll need to be in rehab a while. I assume they wouldn't release her if she couldn't care for herself at home. My job will probably be to get her to agree to a live-in facility at least until her shoulder heals. I know my aunt. It's not going to be easy. She likes her independence."

"Everyone likes their independence. My mother-in-law fought tooth and nail to stay out of the nursing home. She had a broken hip and arthritis and could barely brush her teeth without help, but she wanted to stay in her home. She was sure visiting nurses could do what she needed. The family had a powwow and made the decision for her."

"Did she hate you for it?"

"No. It took a week or so, but she loved it. She loved the food and playing bingo and the sing-a-longs. She knew half of the people in the nursing home. She said it was like old home week." Carla gave a reflective smile. "You do what you know is right for your aunt. It'll all work out in the end. Take two weeks, Ros. Call it your spring break."

"No, no. I shouldn't need two weeks. And spring break isn't two weeks long. It's one." Ros didn't want to confess that two weeks in Colby was way longer than she wanted to be there, though it had little to do with her aunt.

"Okay, ten days. Take ten days. We'll cover for you here. You have family matters to tend to."

"Are you sure?"

"Ten days and if you need more, take it. The university owes you. I'll be here until the first of the month." Carla leaned in and said softly, "And I can be here longer if I'm needed."

"Then I'm booked. My flight leaves this evening at 8:22, nonstop to Denver." She pressed the confirmation button and waited for the printer to spit out her boarding pass.

"Good. Now you need to get out of here. You've got packing to do. Email me that report and I'll look it over," Carla said as she returned to her office.

Ros finished the last details of her report, forwarded it to Carla, and shut down her computer. She gathered her things and was on her way to her car when her cell phone rang. It was another call from her aunt's phone. She was curious who had the phone.

"Hello?" Ros headed for the elevator as she talked, not wanting to waste any time.

"Is this Ros McClure?" a woman asked. The sound of rushing wind could be heard in the background; it made it difficult to hear.

"Yes. Who is this?"

"I'm calling for your aunt, Ms. McClure. I'm sorry to report she had an accident and is in the hospital."

"Yes, I know. I spoke with her doctor earlier today."

"Your aunt was worried you'd be upset. She wanted me to reassure you she'll be okay."

"She's having surgery and will need extensive rehabilitation. I don't know about you, but I do not call that okay."

"She doesn't want you to worry."

"Well, she's too late," Ros snipped.

"You could have been here if you had answered any of my calls." There was a judgmental tone to the statement.

"I have a flight this evening. I'll be at the hospital tomorrow morning." As if it was any of this woman's business. "Who are you, if I may ask?"

"A concerned neighbor. I'm the one who found Miss Bonnie lying in her yard and called the ambulance."

"The doctor said she fell off a ladder. It that right?"

"Apparently so. She was painting and my best guess is she lost her balance and fell. Fortunately she fell into the yard and didn't hit the porch."

"Oh, good grief."

"Why was your aunt painting on a ladder? At her age you should insist she hire someone to do that. And I'm not sure you know this, but it's not painting weather. It's too damp and too cool for paint to dry properly. It'll bubble up and peel, then need repainting in a few months."

"Well, I didn't tell her to do it. She's not a child. She's seventy-three. And if you know my aunt, you'd know she pretty much does whatever she wants." Ros was losing her patience and was finding it hard not to shout at this woman.

"A seventy-three-year-old woman who had no business being on a ladder. You should have known that," the woman said as if accusing Ros for enabling her aunt's accident. "I like Miss Bonnie. I've seen her around town and she's a nice lady. If she was my aunt, I would certainly make an effort to keep her safe."

"I don't know who you are, but let me straighten you out. I appreciate your finding my aunt and getting her to the hospital, but please don't interfere with my relationship with her. If I could have prevented her from climbing that ladder, don't you think I would have? But that was her choice. Now we have to deal with the consequences. I'll be there tomorrow morning and I'll handle it."

"Let's hope so."

Ros released an exasperated breath, one she was sure the woman could hear. "Thank you for looking after my aunt. You may leave her cell phone with someone at the hospital. I'll pick it up when I arrive."

"Your aunt asked me to take care of it for her. I think I'll hang on to it a little longer."

Whoever this woman was, she was testing Ros's tolerance. She saw no need to argue with her over the phone. She'd deal with her once she got to town. She said good-bye and ended the call. She had just buckled her seat belt when Dr. Smithton called to report Bonnie was in recovery. Surgery had gone well, although he'd discuss the details when Ros arrived in the morning. Something in his short conversation sounded troubling, something he wasn't admitting over the phone.

"Please tell her I'll be there in the morning, Doctor. Tell her I'll take care of everything." Ros wondered if she was deceiving herself. Bonnie wasn't going to go quietly to any rehab facility.

CHAPTER THREE

By the time Ros landed in Denver, claimed her rental car, and drove the 228 miles to Colby, Kansas, it was three in the morning and she was exhausted. She used her key to let herself in Bonnie's house and collapsed on the couch. Dr. Smithton had agreed to meet with her at eight o'clock in the morning to discuss Bonnie's condition and what needed to be done.

As tired as she was, when the alarm on her cell phone sounded at seven Ros was already dressed and ready to leave for the hospital. She left her things draped over the chair in the living room. She'd move them upstairs to what had been her bedroom when she returned from the hospital. From the looks of the downstairs, she suspected her room would also be filled with clutter and knickknacks, something she didn't want to deal with just yet. Aunt Bonnie was a collector of miniatures, salt and pepper shakers, bud vases, ceramic cookie jars, colorful rocks, and souvenir ashtrays, although she hadn't smoked in years. Every doorway had a throw rug over the carpet. The three recliners in the living room, each a different color, each had an afghan folded over the back. The kitchen was large with vintage décor. Not by choice, but because Bonnie hadn't updated anything since she moved in forty years ago.

The two-story frame house was nearly a hundred years old and had a wraparound front porch with a porch swing suspended on hooks. Three bedrooms upstairs, one large bathroom, and a drafty attic were all the things Ros remembered. Little had changed since the last time she visited. It was more than two years ago when Ros had to rush to Colby to help Bonnie straighten out problems with the IRS. Bonnie had ignored the registered letters and that didn't resolve the issues. It took some doing but Ros was able to re-file and minimize the damage. When Bonnie would encourage her to come visit it was easier to buy her a ticket and bring Bonnie to Cincinnati. It was also easier to visit with her away from the small town that held too many unpleasant memories. She loved her aunt. But Colby, Kansas represented a painful past.

Ros gave a quick perusal of the kitchen and saw nothing she could call breakfast. She wasn't that hungry anyway. She'd find something later at the hospital. She locked up the house and headed out. She couldn't help notice the splotch of beige paint on the porch wall along with a patch of beige paint on the grass. That must have been where Bonnie fell and it put a knot in the pit of Ros's stomach.

Bonnie was asleep when Ros arrived. She had an IV in the back of her hand and oxygen tubing running to her nose. Her shoulder was heavily bandaged and secured with an immobilizer. Ros swept a lock of hair out of Bonnie's face and smiled down at her. She kissed her forehead and whispered hello. Bonnie was a weathered woman with short white hair and a round face deeply wrinkled from age and years of enjoying the outdoors. She was paler than Ros remembered from the last time she saw her. Probably from the accident and surgery.

Ros stroked Bonnie's arm softly. She didn't want to wake her, but she did feel the need to touch her, to know she was okay.

She remembered the times Bonnie would cup her hands under Ros's chin and look into her eyes, checking to see if she was sick or upset. "Everything will be all right, sweetie," she would say. "Your Aunt Bonnie will take care of everything." Bonnie's hands had been soft and warm and comforting. Now they were cool to the touch and bruised and dry.

"I'm here, Aunt Bonnie," Ros whispered. "I'm right here and I'll take care of everything."

Bonnie's eyes opened for a moment, a thin smile forming across her lips. Ros wasn't sure she recognized her.

"Hello, sweetheart," Ros said, leaning down so she could hear. "It's Ros."

"Ros?"

"Yes. I'm here."

"Ros?" Bonnie closed her eyes, drew a deep relaxing breath, then fell back asleep.

Now in her seventies, Bonnie had been widowed years ago and now lived alone. She chose to reclaim her maiden name, Bartholomew, and cling to family roots when her husband passed away. He had been a meticulous man who had made some smart investments. His death, although heartbreaking, left Bonnie financially independent. They had no children. Ros suspected that was Bonnie's choice. She had had several gentlemen suitors over the years but never remarried. "They want my money," she had joked. "It's not a lot, but it's mine and I'm not sharing it with some old coot with happy hands."

"She'll sleep off and on most of the day, poor thing," a nurse said as she checked the IV bag and settings on the pump. "Dr. Smithton is waiting to speak with you."

A doctor in a white lab coat was standing at the nurses' station reading a report when she walked out of Bonnie's room.

"Are you Ms. McClure?" he asked, continuing to read. "I'm Dr. Smithton."

"Yes, hello, Doctor." A short man in his fifties with dark hair, he was wearing cowboy boots with his slacks and white shirt.

"Let's go in here so we can talk." He led the way into a small conference room behind the nurses' station.

He was polite and professional. He wasted no time in explaining what damage Bonnie's fall caused. It wasn't life threatening, but it was extensive and had required multiple surgical repairs.

Ros tried to listen and remember the details as he described them with medical jargon she didn't completely understand, but she kept thinking how difficult this recovery would be for her aunt. Bonnie was an active woman for her age. As far back as Ros could remember, she had done yoga, occasionally walked to town, hiked along the stream at the back of her property, even mowed her own grass, what there was of it, and kept her home, all without assistance. Clearly she had thought climbing a ladder was something still within her ability as well. How was she going to adjust and accept her limitations, however temporary they were?

When Ros said she was prepared to bring up in-patient rehabilitation with Bonnie, Dr. Smithton reported that he had already discussed it with her, although he wasn't sure how well she understood. It was his job to explain the need for rehab to his patient, he explained, and the family's job to support that decision.

"Often patients don't accept this kind of proposal from a family member. It needs to come from me. She's on some pretty strong pain meds and with the residual effects of the anesthesia I'm not sure she understands in-patient care."

"My aunt may understand, but she may not agree."

"That's the feeling I got too. We'll see how she does in a few days. I need to see some improvement before I order the transfer to the nursing home. Maybe by the end of the week. Someone from the social worker's office will be in touch with you about the details, Ms. McClure."

"Thank you, Doctor."

"One last thing. Do you know if your aunt has ever fallen before? I'm curious if she has suffered a concussion in the past few years. Or perhaps a mild stroke. I couldn't find any records on her recent medical history."

"Stroke? No, not that I'm aware of. As you know, I don't live with my aunt. I haven't in many years. If she's had a concussion or a stroke she hasn't admitted it to me. She's a pretty healthy person. At least that's what she tells me."

Dr. Smithton's beeper went off, calling him to the ER. As he left he promised to keep Ros updated on Bonnie's progress and when she'd be ready for transfer.

Ros stopped in Bonnie's room for a few minutes on the chance she might open her eyes again, but she never woke from a sound sleep. Hunger pangs had begun gnawing at Ros's stomach, so she headed to the parking lot and then someplace for a bite to eat

On her way back from the hospital Ros turned down Summit Street. It wasn't the direct route to Bonnie's, but she took it anyway. It was a quiet neighborhood of low- to moderate-income houses, most dating from the mid-century. She drove three blocks and pulled to the curb across from a small white frame house. Two large elm trees flanked the driveway, both needing a good pruning. There was no garage, no fence, and no shutters. The front door had been painted bright red, something she didn't remember from her last visit when she made this pilgrimage down the street.

It was a plain modest home and, like Bonnie's, could use a fresh coat of paint. There was a white mini-blind in the front bedroom window. It was the smaller of the two bedrooms. Large enough for a twin bed and a dresser. The closet was the size of a phone booth. But it was large enough to hide in when Ros heard her parents arguing, usually about money or her father's inability to hold a job. The house wasn't large enough to escape the sound of a slap or a broken dish that often accompanied the arguments. And it wasn't large enough to ignore the front door slamming when one or both of her parents stormed out of the house, leaving a frightened little girl all alone. Ros sat in the car, staring at the house, lost in the bitter memories of her youth. She had seen enough; she heaved a sigh and headed to Bonnie's.

CHAPTER FOUR

It was half past ten when she returned to Bonnie's house. She stood in the middle of the kitchen, hands on her hips, and stared at the clutter. She couldn't stand the thought of her aunt coming home to a sink full of dirty dishes and trash overflowing the wastebasket. The refrigerator wasn't much better. Bonnie's leftovers needed to be cleaned out. Even if she would be home in a couple weeks, she wasn't going to feel like facing this mess.

"Oh, Bonnie. Where do I start?" She pushed back the sleeves of her sweater. A mouse ran across the kitchen floor and disappeared behind the trash. "Oh, we won't start here!" she declared, stepping back from the wastebasket. "We'll do you later." It wasn't the first mouse she had seen in her aunt's house over the years—Bonnie lived at the edge of town on a large lot near the end of the street and that meant rodents occasionally intruded—but that didn't make them any more tolerable.

Ros had just begun washing dishes when she stopped and thought a moment. Something was different. She hadn't noticed it before, but something was definitely different from when she left that morning. Was her sixth sense kicking in? It wasn't an ability she cultivated but, like most people, every now and then she felt a sensation tickling her brain, seeking her attention. What was it this time?

She wiped her hands on a towel and looked around, wandering through the dining room and living room. There was so much stuff sitting around it was hard to tell what had changed. She decided it was nothing. Just one of those feelings stirred by being back in Bonnie's house again.

She was walking back to the kitchen when her eyes were drawn to the middle of the dining room table. A spot had been cleared there in the middle of the odd dishes her aunt collected and other clutter. Bonnie's mail was stacked in the space along with her aunt's wallet and four cans of cat food. None of it had been there that morning. She remembered staring at the table, wondering why the dishes hadn't been put away in the china hutch. And she didn't remember Bonnie having a cat. Someone had been in the house.

She picked up Bonnie's wallet and opened it. Her driver's license, credit cards, ATM cards, and various insurance cards seemed to be all in order. Ros had no way of knowing how much money might have been in the wallet, but there were no bills there now and seventy cents in change. The mail consisted of a water bill, three ads, and a grocery flyer.

"I thought we had your utility bills automatically deducted from your checking account," she muttered as she read it. "Why are you getting this?"

Ros tossed the ads and flyer in the trash, put the cat food in the crowded pantry, and returned to the kitchen duties. She'd check with the bank later. Bonnie used to keep her checkbook in the drawer of the desk in the living room, but it wasn't there. Another detail, along with forwarding her mail, that Ros would have to deal with while in town.

The longer Ros worked in the kitchen, the more she found that needed to be done. Her aunt had a dishwasher, but she didn't use it. She stored her pots and pans in it. The microwave looked like a bowl of tomato soup had exploded in it, then dried.

The refrigerator held six unopened and expired packages of butter, two packages of strange-colored hamburger meat, and over two dozen jars and bottles of condiments. Several take-home boxes were in desperate need of tossing. Ros couldn't tell what some of them had been. Most smelled horrendous.

It took two hours and four trash bags, but Ros finally felt like she had accomplished something. It wasn't perfect and there was still work to be done, but it wasn't unhealthy either. The question of who had let themselves in and deposited Bonnie's mail on the table still nagged at her. Did Bonnie have a neighbor with a key? Could the boorish woman with her phone be the mystery intruder? And who was she anyway?

Mentally making a shopping list so she wouldn't have to eat out at every meal, Ros showered, changed, and headed back to the hospital. When she stepped in Bonnie's room she found that Bonnie had been given a cursory bed bath and a new gown. "We'll change her sheets later," an aide said, carrying the plastic basin of bath water to the sink to empty it. "She preferred we wait. The bath really tired her out."

"Thank you."

"Is that you, Ros?" Bonnie said, squirming to get a better view.

"Yes, Aunt Bonnie. It's me." Ros placed a vase of flowers she had purchased in the gift shop on the bed table and gave her aunt a kiss on the cheek. "How are you feeling this afternoon?"

"Oh, honey, my arm hurts so bad. I don't know what happened, but I can barely move it." A pained expression deepened as Bonnie looked down at the immobilizer on the arm. "They need to take this thing off so I can move it. I can't even sit up in bed without help."

"You fell, Aunt Bonnie. Remember? You fell off the ladder and broke your shoulder. You had surgery yesterday to fix it." Ros held Bonnie's hand as she explained what had happened.

"Oh, my Lord. I fell off a ladder?" She seemed shocked to hear the news.

"Yes, you were painting and fell."

"Yes, yes. I remember. Oh, it hurt so bad. I couldn't get up. Then that nice woman came along and helped me. She called an ambulance."

"And you gave her your phone so she could call me."

"I don't know how long I lay there, but I couldn't even get up."

"When you're feeling better, we're going to discuss house painting. You can't be up on a ladder, Aunt Bonnie. Or even a step stool for that matter. If you want your house painted, we'll find someone to do it for you. You can give the orders and they can do the work. Promise me you won't do this again."

"Ms. Bartholomew, have you decided what you'd like for dinner?" an orderly interrupted. He turned to Ros. "The food service didn't get her menu selection yet. Will she be having dinner? She's not on any diet restriction."

"Aunt Bonnie, what would you like for dinner?"

"I have no idea." She groaned.

Ros scanned the menu card. "Looks like you've got lots of choices. Spaghetti and meatballs. Baked fish. Hamburger. Oh, here's something you like. Chicken fried steak with white gravy. I can cut it for you. You'd be able to eat that. Maybe a little mashed potatoes and they've got green beans tonight. And lemon cake for dessert. That sounds like a decent meal to me. What do you say?"

"Whatever." Bonnie sighed as if she was too tired to decide for herself.

Ros marked the menu card and handed it to the young man.

"Bring her this. She may not eat it all, but she needs something nutritious."

The orderly had no sooner left the room than Bonnie's eyes closed and she drifted off to sleep. Ros didn't wake her. A nap before dinner would probably be good for her. Ros took out her phone and checked her messages and email, content to relax until Bonnie's dinner tray arrived. A knock on the door drew her attention away from an email from Carla.

"Ros McClure?" a woman said with a wide smile. Somewhere in her forties, she was dressed in stylishly fitted jeans, a bright pink sweater, and turquoise cowboy boots. Ros couldn't put her finger on it, but something about the woman's smile was familiar.

"Oh, my. Don't tell me you don't recognize me, Ros." The woman cocked her head and batted her eyelashes.

"Meredith? Meredith Eason?"

"It's so good to see you. I heard you were in town." She gave Ros a warm bear hug, swaying back and forth as if they had been BFFs for eons. "How's your aunt? I heard she had an accident." Meredith took Ros's hand and offered a sympathetic squeeze.

"She'll be all right with time and a little rehab. It's good to see you, Meredith," she said happily.

"I heard Bonnie had a nasty fall off a ladder. Good grief, woman. What in the Sam Hill was she doing on a ladder anyway? She's the reason I'm here. We'd like to run a little blurb in the paper letting people know how's she doing and where they can send their well-wishes. I'm the editor, you know."

"Yes, I heard. Congratulations."

"Your aunt is a very colorful character in this town." Meredith took a small notebook and pen from her purse. "She's lived her whole life in western Kansas and she's got tons of friends who want to know what happened. They'll want to send flowers or a card. I wasn't sure what her full name is." She was poised to write.

"Meredith, isn't printing medical information without the patient's permission a violation of the HIPPA privacy laws?" Ros asked with a raised eyebrow. "I'm not sure my aunt would want the details of her accident printed in the newspaper. I know I wouldn't."

"Ros, she could have a room full of gorgeous flowers by the end of the week. Think how much that would lift her spirits." She nodded as if encouraging her agreement.

"Nice try, Meredith. But I don't think so. Not without Aunt Bonnie's say-so."

"Hey, you can't blame a gal for trying." Meredith slipped the notebook and pen back in her purse and chuckled. "By the way, I haven't received your reunion reservation yet. Are you a plus one for dinner?"

"I may not be able to attend. After this trip I'm not sure I'll have any vacation time left."

"We need at least one of the class officers to be there, Ros."

"I was the class treasurer. That's not very high up in the pecking order. Class president or student council president, that's who you need to be there."

"Ralph isn't coming. He's on sabbatical somewhere in Europe. And no one knows how to get in touch with Denise. Her family moved away after graduation. You weren't here for any of the other reunions, in spite of my repeated email notices. I think you should be here for this one. With the attendance dwindling and no one willing to help with the legwork, this could be the last one we have. Come on, Ros. Where's your Fighting Eagles spirit?"

"Like I said, it's all about vacation time." Ros didn't want to admit she had little interest in stomping old grapes. She hadn't kept in touch with any of her high school classmates in years. Why did she need to come socialize with them now?

"Don't you work at a university? The reunion is in June. Classes will be out by then."

"I work in the auditing department. We work year round. Not just when classes are in session."

"Auditing. I should have guessed you'd have a job like that. You were always so smart in math and accounting. Anything with numbers. Science, not so much," Meredith teased. "Remember the time you screamed bloody murder when that frog squirted you."

"It smelled disgusting," Ros said in her defense, then joined Meredith in a good laugh.

"That reminds me. We're lucky. We've got three teachers still on staff in the high school who were here twenty-five years ago. Sherry Cox in Language Arts, Mr. Garcia, the Spanish teacher, and Ms. Hagen in the Science Department."

"Stacy Hagen?" Ros asked, her interest piqued at the sound of that name. "She's still at the high school?"

"Actually, it's Coach Hagen. She coached the tennis team a few years ago. They went to districts three years in a row. The title stuck for some reason, though I think she's back to just biology now. Didn't you have a problem with biology our senior year? As I remember you did."

"Don't remind me. I still don't know what happened to my lab notebook."

"You flunked biology and I flunked gym class." Meredith shook her head in disgust.

"I didn't flunk the whole class. Just the lab part. But I ended up with a C minus for the semester. It cost me some of my scholarship money."

"They say she'll flunk anyone who crosses her. Last year's football team had three players ineligible for districts because she gave them incompletes. The superintendent stepped in and allowed them to play when they agreed to weekend makeup sessions."

"Some towns put a pretty high priority on their sports teams."

"No kidding. Friday night football games draw crowds like you wouldn't believe. Even more than they used to. It's like a religious event. Coach Hagen should have known that. There was quite a ruckus between her and the head coach. And she doesn't take crap off anyone. Remember those dark piercing eyes that stared right through you if you didn't behave in class? And the dark hair that she wore in a long braid? I saw her several months ago driving a tractor out County Road 20. Her hair has turned completely gray and it's short. Nothing like when we had her in class."

"That does sound like she's changed. At least her looks," said Ros, wrestling with memories of high school that she'd just as soon ignore.

"You haven't changed a smidge, though. You and I were always the same height, five six. But your hair is still the most gorgeous shade of brown with those natural auburn highlights." She swept back a lock of Ros's chin-length hair. "I love the pierced ears. Very delicate. And, damn, girl, where are your pores and gray hair? I bet you're still a size ten, right?" Meredith placed a hand on Ros's hip and turned her slightly to get a better look.

"Ha! I was never a size ten. Maybe a twelve on a good day. And you're looking good, too. I like the hair. Big and brazen."

"My husband said it fit my personality perfectly."

"And what's his name? Anybody I should know?"

"His name is JT Bower. He's from Goodland and it's past tense. He turned out to be an idiot. An idiot mechanic who didn't know one end of a wrench from the other. Or how to treat a lady."

"Oh, honey. I'm sorry."

"That's okay. He had a big truck, but that only lasted so long."

"Big truck, huh?" Ros chuckled at the reference. "I remember that slogan. Guys with big trucks and big other things. Every time Judy had a date with Mark she'd boast how big his truck was."

"No kidding. Our senior year I think she spent more time on her back than the wrestling team." Meredith gave a wicked laugh.

"Shame on you."

"Every farm town has one. The high school couple who can't wait until after graduation and can't keep their hands off each other. I remember rumors about you and me floating around."

"People always need someone or something to gossip about."

"I always wanted to ask if it was true about you having a date with Hagen during spring break our senior year. Someone said you did."

"Who said that?" Ros asked in annoyed disbelief.

"Actually it was Larry."

"Larry, my prom date?"

Meredith nodded. "Was that retaliation?"

"I have no idea, but if you mean was he being vindictive because I wouldn't put out, probably. I wanted a date to prom so I didn't have to go alone. He thought that meant it was open season. I don't worry about rumors and gossip anymore. I do the best I can and let the chips fall where they may."

"Yeah, but sometimes you have to duck. So we can count on you for the reunion? Can I pencil you in at the head table?"

"I can't promise. Like I said, I may not have any vacation time left."

"How can you not know? Most people know exactly how much vacation they have, right down to the minute."

"We've got some personnel changes which may affect things this summer."

"Well, I'm penciling you in anyway, just in case."

"It's your pencil, but don't be surprised if you have to use the eraser," Ros said, walking Meredith out into the hall. "It was great to see you."

"It was great to see you too." Meredith hugged Ros good-bye. "Remember. Reunion. June. Twenty-five years. Be there!" She winked at Ros and headed up the hall.

"Stacy Hagen," Ros muttered to herself as she returned to Bonnie's bedside. "I could have gone this entire trip and not heard that name."

Ros helped Bonnie with her dinner tray, although she wasn't surprised when she didn't eat much of it. She helped her brush her teeth, combed her hair, and did whatever she could do to make her comfortable before heading home to find something for her own dinner.

It was after eight o'clock when she wrapped her jacket around her shoulders and sat down on the porch swing with a cup of herbal tea to unwind. With luck Bonnie would agree to being moved to the nursing home while she recuperated and Ros could return to Cincinnati, knowing her care was in professional hands. She cradled the cup in her hands to warm them against the chilly evening. She wasn't ready to go inside. She took a deep breath and closed her eyes. There was a freshness in the air. A cleanness that reminded her of her Kansas childhood, riding her first bicycle, playing on the tire swing hung from the elm tree, spending a summer afternoon with Aunt Bonnie, eating her homemade cookies. As pleasant as some of the memories remained, some always seem to dissolve back to unhappy moments, overshadowing the happy ones. A jingle on her cell phone brought her back to reality. It was Bonnie's phone.

"Hello?"

"Are you in the hospital somewhere?" a woman asked.

"No. May I help you?"

"I think you should be here. After all, it's your aunt."

"Is this the phone bandit again?" Ros asked.

"Right, the phone bandit. But I seem to be the only one showing concern."

"Now look..." Ros said defensively.

"Are you aware your aunt tried to get out of bed and fell again?"

"What? No, I didn't." Ros stood to go inside, spilling tea on her lap as she did so. "I just left her. When did this happen? No one called me."

"I'm calling you. It happened a few minutes ago."

"Is she all right? Did she break anything?" Ros blotted her pants with a towel, grabbed her purse and keys, and trotted out to her car as the woman explained what had happened and what the hospital was doing.

"They're going to put an alarm on her bed. If she tries to get up, it'll alert the nurses' station."

"I'll be there in ten minutes. Thank you for letting me know."

Ros hung up and sped across town to the hospital, her heart pounding. She stopped at the nurses' station to ask how Bonnie was and why they hadn't called her.

"We were going to do that when she gets back from X-ray. We don't have anything to tell you yet."

"I'll be in my aunt's room if you need me. Please keep me informed."

"Yes, ma'am. We will."

Ros walked into Bonnie's darkened room to find a woman in jeans and a short-sleeved shirt rifling through the drawer in her bedside table.

"Excuse me," she growled, but the woman didn't turn around. "May I help you?"

"I'm making change." She continued to count and sort in spite of Ros walking in on her.

"I don't think so." Ros snatched two twenty-dollar bills from the woman's hand. "You need to leave my aunt's money alone. In fact, you need to leave."

"Do you want the fives and ones as well?" She held out several bills in her other hand.

"Yes." Ros grabbed them as the woman turned around and gave her a scowl.

"Hello, Ms. McClure," she said. "They took your aunt down to X-ray. It shouldn't be long. Should I have called to let you know that too?" She held up what looked like Bonnie's cell phone.

"Ms. Hagen?" Ros gasped, recognizing the piercing gaze if not the short gray, nearly white hair.

"Yes."

Stacy Hagen had changed as Meredith had said, though she still had dark piercing eyes. Her arms and neck were covered with freckles, and she had a rich bronze tan.

"You...You're the one with my aunt's phone?"

"Yes. When I found her, she insisted I take it and call you. I told her I would, although I think she was in too much pain to understand that I was going to wait until the hospital had something definite I could tell you. It was easier to agree with her than argue. And you can keep my money if you need it. Ms. Bonnie was worried she didn't have any cash with her. There wasn't any in her wallet. I assume you saw it on the table with her mail. I left two twenties in this drawer but decided today that smaller bills would be easier for her to use if she needed something."

"Your money?" Ros was still processing Stacy Hagen's appearance. She hadn't seen her in years, and yes, the changes were stunning.

"I don't mind helping out. She's a nice lady."

"You're the one who made all those calls?"

"I thought someone needed to do it."

"Why didn't you tell me who you were when you called?"

"It wouldn't have changed the information, would it? You seemed befuddled enough by my calls without adding ancient history to the conversation."

"I was not befuddled. I just didn't like your accusations. I care deeply about my aunt and wish she hadn't fallen. Now, can we move on?"

"Sure. It's your aunt. Your responsibility on what comes next." She slipped her hands in her back pockets and rocked back on her heels. "That's assuming, of course, she didn't do any more damage when she fell out of bed."

A nurse walked in carrying what looked like a large heating pad. She pulled back the sheets and positioned it in the middle of the mattress then plugged it in the wall outlet.

"The doctor has ordered a bed alarm for your aunt. If she tries to get up again we'll hear it. She said she needed to use the bathroom and couldn't wait." The nurse placed a blue waterproof pad on the bed as well. "We're right across the hall. She needs to press the call button if she needs help. We'll keep the side rails up just in case."

"Have you heard from X-ray?" Ros asked.

"Not yet." The nurse finished straightening and adjusting things before leaving.

"She is not going to like this," Ros mumbled, smoothing her hand down the bed linens.

"I think the proper reply should have been 'Good, I'm glad she won't fall.'"

Ros snapped a look at her.

"Of course I don't want her to fall. But I know how she's going to react. She hates restrictions. If this is your money, here." Ros handed her the bills. "I'll take care of whatever she needs."

"You're sure?" She looked down at the money in Ros's hand, then up at her.

"Yes, Ms. Hagen. I'm sure. Here."

"Ms. Hagen was appropriate twenty-five years ago. Why not just call me Stacy?"

"You're the one who started with the 'Ms. McClure'!" Ros knew, even as she said it, that her retort sounded juvenile. Much like she might have sounded twenty-five years ago. "Here. We don't need your money." She thrust it at her. "I can take care of my aunt's mail also."

"I assumed you could."

"Do you have a key to her house as well as her phone?"

"No. She told me where she hides the key. I put it back."

A pair of orderlies wheeled a gurney carrying Bonnie into the room.

"Aunt Bonnie, it's Ros. I'm here," she said as they prepared to transfer her onto the bed.

"They're making such a fuss," she said, bracing for the move. "I didn't hurt anything. I just fell."

"But they told you not to try to get up by yourself. You've got to press the call button and wait for the nurse."

It took some doing, but the orderlies got her situated and raised the side rails.

"Can you leave these down?" Bonnie asked one of the young men, trying to lower the railings herself.

"No, ma'am. Orders are to put them up. You're a fall risk." He pointed to the sign posted on the wall.

"They don't want you to fall again, Aunt Bonnie. You could rebreak your shoulder and end up back in surgery."

"I don't like being confined."

"I know you don't, but doctor's orders," Ros said, patting Bonnie's hand reassuringly. She got Bonnie comfortable, reminding her repeatedly that she was to press her call button if she needed help. After she was settled, she turned to ask Ms. Hagen to return Bonnie's phone, but she had disappeared without a word. Ros resigned herself to getting it later.

It was after midnight when she returned home, turned out the lights, and crawled into bed. She expected her thoughts to be about her aunt and how she could best help her. She didn't expect them to be about Stacy Hagen, high school teacher and high school fascination. But there they were. Bubbling and churning up memories better long forgotten.

CHAPTER FIVE

Ros spent the next three days running back and forth to the hospital, pre-packing what Bonnie would need for her stay in the nursing home, doing a little light housekeeping, and fielding calls from the doctor and Bonnie's friends—and one call from Steve wondering when she'd be back to work. He seemed very concerned about her ten-day leave of absence in spite of receiving Carla's assurance they could handle things while she was gone.

Ros also received at least one call a day from Ms. Hagen inquiring about how Bonnie was doing. The calls were short, non-confrontational, and polite. She seemed careful not to accuse and Ros was careful not to be defensive. She apologized for being too busy to come see Bonnie in person due to the demands of her teaching schedule. It was just as well. Even though Ros still wanted to retrieve Bonnie's phone from her at some point, she had enough on her plate without running into her.

The house wasn't a large one as farmhouses go, but over the years Bonnie had crammed it full, especially the pantry. While searching for something to fix for lunch, Ros noticed that many, if not all, of the canned goods were expired, some long expired. Would Bonnie notice if she tossed them out, along with the pile of junk mail accumulating in the corner of the dining room? Would she remember what was in the half-dozen expired cans at the back of the shelf without a label?

"Green beans? Peaches? Soup? Who knows?" She dropped them ceremoniously into the wastebasket.

When Dr. Smithton announced Bonnie was being transferred to the nursing home for recovery and rehabilitation the next day, Ros knew it was time to discuss the details with her. Braced for an argument, she entered her hospital room carrying a small pastry box to use as a distraction.

"I brought you a little goodie, Aunt Bonnie," she said cheerily and set the box on her bed table. "It's from the Prairie Bakery, made fresh this morning. One of your favorites, German chocolate cake." She kissed her aunt's cheek and smoothed a stray lock of hair. "How was your lunch?"

"It was okay, I guess." Bonnie giggled. "To tell the truth, I don't remember what it was, so it must have been okay."

"I think you ordered a grilled cheese sandwich and fruit salad."

"Oh, yes." She continued to cackle. "You can't kill a grilled cheese sandwich. It's bread. It's cheese. It's grilled. I remember you liked them as a child. We had them on Saturday night. Remember?"

"I still like them. I can't make them as well as you did, but I'll fix one every now and then when I'm too tired to cook a big meal."

"There's nothing like fixing a grilled cheese sandwich in your own kitchen in your own cast iron skillet. And remember, dear. Never put a cast iron skillet in the dishwasher. You'll ruin the seasoning. I can't wait to get home and make my own sandwich in my own kitchen. It's comfort food, you know."

"Your cast iron skillet weighs a ton. You may have to wait until your shoulder heals before you can wield that thing again."

"You can handle the skillet and I'll supervise." Bonnie grinned. "It'll be like old times when I was teaching you to cook. We need to make a shopping list. I don't think I have any bread or cheese in the house. Do you have a piece of paper and a pencil?"

"We can wait on the shopping list." Ros placed her hand on Bonnie's. "You won't need any groceries until you're discharged from the Health and Rehab Center."

"Oh, honey. Didn't you hear? The doctor said I'm being discharged tomorrow. They're sending me home to do physical therapy. I'll be good as new in no time. You may have to help me with some of it, but you're a smart girl. We can figure it out together. I bet some of my yoga positions will work just as well as any fancy physical therapy."

"They're discharging you from the hospital tomorrow, but you're not going home. They're transferring you to the rehab center." She was careful not to use the term nursing home.

"The rehab center? I thought the doctor said they were sending me home." Bonnie looked confused. "We can clear a place in the living room for any exercises they want me to do."

"Aunt Bonnie, you're not ready to be home on your own. Your shoulder needs to heal and you'll need care while that happens."

"I wouldn't be on my own. Anything I can't do for myself you can do. We'll manage just fine."

Ros shook her head as Bonnie made her case.

"First of all, I'm not a skilled physical therapist or a nurse. You need professional care while you heal. And Aunt Bonnie, I'm not staying in Colby. My job needs me. I'll get you settled in your new room and take care of some things, but then I have to fly back to Cincinnati." Her aunt didn't need to know about what was happening at work or her frustration at being passed over for promotion. Details weren't important.

"You're not staying?"

"I can't. I wish I could, but I can't. This is our busy time of year. I've got to get back. You'll have a room all to yourself in the rehab center. I hear the food is good. And you'll probably discover some people there that you know."

"I can't believe you aren't going to stay. I thought that's why you were here to begin with." Bonnie frowned as if she wasn't going to agree to any of this.

"Sweetheart, I'm sorry, but I can't."

"But she'll be back for the reunion," Meredith said from the doorway. "Won't you, Ros? Hello, Bonnie. Do you remember me? I'm Meredith Eason." She came to the bed. "Ros and I were friends in high school."

"I remember. You had such terrible acne as a teenager."

Ros gasped, then snickered, unable to suppress her reaction. Meredith joined her in a laugh.

"Well, she did," Bonnie insisted.

"But you don't need to bring it up, Aunt Bonnie," Ros admonished, still chuckling.

"Look how attractive she is now. Not a blemish."

"Thank you, Bonnie. A little Cover Girl does wonders. Hey, I hear you're being transferred tomorrow. You're going to like the nursing home."

"Shhhhh," Ros quickly muttered. "Not the n-word, please."

"Oops."

Fortunately Bonnie didn't seem to have noticed.

"How are you feeling, Bonnie? Are you getting better?"

"The answer is still no, Meredith," Ros said softly but with a stern look. "No newspaper. No article."

"Aw heck," she teased. "Okay, but between you and me, how is she doing? Improving? This is a small town. Her friends want to know how she's doing."

"I'd say she's improving, or they wouldn't be transferring her to the rehab facility. If her friends want to know how she's doing, they can come visit her or they can call me."

Ros took Meredith's arm and walked her into the hall. "My aunt's always been a private person. I don't want to embarrass her with her personal information spread all over town in the newspaper. This is going to be difficult enough for her without that. Please, Meredith."

"I understand. It won't come from me. I promise. Scout's honor."

"Thank you. I trust you, hon."

"You were always my confidante, Ros. We told each other everything. Everything," she repeated, leaning in to her. "Being a teenager is hard. I can't imagine what it would have been like without a best friend to confide in." She chuckled. "That must be why teenage girls go to the bathroom in pairs."

"I remember that. Barb and Karen. Esther and Neelie. You and me. We shared more rumors in the ladies' room than I can count." They laughed and bumped shoulders as they relived that time.

"And oh, the things we confided in each other." Meredith smiled at Ros. "You were this pert little thing with silky hair and I was this pudgy flat-chested fifteen-year-old with braces. I was so jealous. We were best friends and we couldn't even share clothes. I so wanted to wear your blue skirt with the stripes on the side."

"You're kidding. I hated that skirt. It looked like racing stripes. My aunt made it. She said it made a statement. But I didn't like the statement it made. Of course, I hated all skirts. You should have said something. I'd have let you borrow it."

"And wear it where? On my right leg?"

"Oh, Meredith, you weren't that big."

Meredith glared at her

"Well, you look wonderful now." Ros squeezed her hand. "I don't know if you remember, but you were the first one I came out to, even before I told my aunt."

"I remember. You were so worried I wouldn't like you anymore. Ros, honey, how are you doing? I mean really. How are things with you in Cincinnati?"

"Great. Things are great, really." Ros felt her face betray her.

"You lie like a rug. I could always tell. If things are great, why didn't your partner come with you to Colby or at least why haven't I heard you mention her?"

"I don't need someone to travel with me when I come to town. I'm a big girl."

Meredith didn't reply but continued to scowl.

"Okay, no, I don't have a partner," Ros added. "Before you ask, there hasn't been one in several years."

"How many years?"

"Still a nosy goat, aren't you?"

"How many?"

"Over ten."

"How many?"

"Okay, I haven't been in a serious relationship in twelve and a half years. Her name was Fran and she turned out to be a little less than faithful. Does that cover all questions?"

"Oh, the witch."

"I consider it a blessing in disguise. We weren't a good fit. I was too busy with my work to notice."

"See what happens when we don't keep in touch. Our lives run off in different directions without us realizing it."

"How about you, Meredith? How are things with you? So, you've got an ex. What else?"

"I've had three exes since high school."

"You've been married three times?"

"No, married once. The other two were more of a trial run but not the marrying kind. The last one was close, but she backed out at the last minute."

Ros's eyes widened. "She?"

Meredith nodded.

"Wow, I didn't know. Why didn't you say something?"

"Like what? 'Hey, your best bud from high school is gay, too'?"

"Something like that."

"I don't think I fully realized it about myself. I think I married my husband because it was expected of me."

"Is there someone on your radar now?" Ros asked.

"No, well, maybe. I'm not sure. And I have no plans to rush things. Not this time. Been there, done that."

"Smart girl."

"Oh geez," Meredith suddenly gasped and turned around. "Don't look now, but there she is."

"Who?"

"The devil incarnate."

"Who?"

"The great and powerful Oz." Meredith nodded over her shoulder.

Ros looked in that direction. Stacy Hagen was at the far end of the hall, walking toward them carrying a vase of flowers.

"That's Coach Hagen, Ros. Remember, I told you she changed. Short gray hair. A little weathered maybe. But that's her. What is she doing here?"

"She's the one who found Aunt Bonnie after her fall and called the ambulance."

"Really? You didn't mention that."

"I didn't know until a couple of days ago. When she called me, she said she was a neighbor who happened to notice that she fell."

"Neighbor? She lives way out on County Road 20. How can that be a neighbor?" she hissed, before greeting the woman coming toward them. "Hello, Coach Hagen."

"Hello, Ms. Eason. Hello, Ms. McClure. How's Miss Bonnie?"

"She's better, I think. They're transferring her tomorrow."

"Good. That'll give her something to look forward to. I thought she'd like some flowers to brighten her room."

"They're lovely. Thank you."

Stacy Hagen walked into Bonnie's room, then stuck her head back out the door. "Three and a half miles out on County Road 20, if you really want to know." She gave Meredith a reprimanding gaze before she resumed heading toward Bonnie. "There's an echo in these halls."

"Double oops," Meredith whispered in Ros's ear. "I better go. Tell Bonnie I'll come visit her in a few days once she gets settled." She headed up the hall.

Ros stood at the foot of the bed while Ms. Hagen visited with Bonnie.

"You're going to like the Health and Rehab Center. I know a couple of the nurses over there," she said, turning the vase so Bonnie had the best view of the blooms she'd brought. "Cheryl gives great neck massages. And Andy brings in homemade cookies on the weekends. I hear his chocolate chip ones are to die for. Of course I prefer peanut butter cookies myself."

She rambled on, very much at home visiting with Bonnie. "Max Zebow lives out there. He was chief of police back in the nineties. MaryEmma Hartley does too. She teaches crocheting. Do you know how to crochet, Miss Bonnie?"

"I prefer knitting," Bonnie replied, hanging on Stacy's every word.

"I can't do either one. Looks way too tedious for me. I'd rather be outside digging a hole or something."

She still has that infectious smile, Ros thought. It was the same smile she had flashed at Ros when she successfully identified all fifteen of the stations set up around the room for a laboratory quiz.

"Do you crochet or knit?"

Ros blinked, realizing the question was directed to her. "No. I never got the hang of it, although Bonnie did try to teach me. You can't say I didn't try." She folded her arms in mock disgust. "I guess I'm not coachable."

"Everyone is coachable to some degree," she said, gently disputing Ros's statement. She turned her attention back to her aunt.

"By the way, Miss Bonnie, don't worry about the ladder and paint. I put them back in the barn. Someday I'd be glad to talk with you about what's the best kind of paint to use on your house." She turned to Ros. "She bought interior flat. That's better for inside walls that don't need to be scrubbed. Not exterior trim."

"You were in my aunt's barn?"

"I assumed that's where she kept her ladder and tools. Leaving it out in the yard is an invitation to having it stolen. There's been a rash of thefts on her side of town."

"Did I make a terrible mess of things?" Bonnie asked, a regretful tone to her question.

"No. Not terrible. When the weather warms up a little it can be fixed."

"But *she's* not going to do it," Ros announced.

Bonnie pressed the call button.

"Do you need something, Aunt Bonnie?"

"Yes, I need to use the bathroom. And I can't do it by myself with these sides in the way."

"That's right. The nurses will help you."

"Miss Bonnie, I'm going to leave and give you some privacy, but I'll come see you when you get moved. Don't worry about anything. You'll be fine."

"Thank you for the flowers, dear. They're beautiful and I love carnations and lilies."

"You're welcome." She patted her hand, then headed for the door. She looked back at Ros and said, "Is that better? Am I forgiven for intruding in your relationship?"

She didn't wait for an answer. She didn't need one, it appeared, and it wouldn't make any difference anyway.

CHAPTER SIX

A gentle afternoon rain had begun to fall when Ros settled into the porch swing with an afghan tossed over her lap. As the rain increased the temperature began to drop. She was ready to go inside when she saw a white crew cab pickup truck turn into the circle drive and stop next to the front porch. Stacy Hagen climbed out of it, her hoodie covering all but the front of her hair.

"Good afternoon," she said, positioning herself out of the rain but not fully onto the porch. "Am I interrupting anything?" She pushed her hood back and raked her hand through her damp hair.

"No. I'm considering another trip in to visit Aunt Bonnie. She'll be transferred to the rehab facility in the morning. I try to go at least a couple times a day, so she knows I'm concerned. I hope it reduces her anxiety when I have to leave in a few days."

"That's why I'm here." She climbed further up the steps. "You seem frustrated by this whole thing. If it's because of my initial phone calls, I'd like to apologize. I didn't mean to upset you. I know you care about your aunt. I've got no right interfering in your business. I was just trying to help." She propped a foot up on the top step. "To tell the truth, Miss Bonnie scared me silly when I found her lying in the yard."

"How long do you think she was lying there?" Ros looked over at the paint-splattered grass next to the porch.

"I'm not sure. It can't have been too long, although the brush was getting a little crusty so it had started to dry. It was about two o'clock. I was on my way home from a tennis lesson at the park."

"Why did you say you were a neighbor? You don't live near my aunt."

"I said I was a concerned neighbor. Miss Bonnie has lots of concerned neighbors. Anyone in Colby who knows her is a concerned neighbor. You grew up here. You know. Small towns are like that, especially for long-time residents like her. People in a big city may not know their next-door neighbor. We do. And their families and their history and their comings and goings. Your private life is pretty much out there. You must remember that."

"I do. I didn't always like it, but I remember it."

"Twenty-five years is a long time, Ms. McClure. People change. People grow and mature. At least some do."

"And some don't." Their eyes met in silent communication.

"You strike me as one who did."

"Okay, here's our baseline. Please stop calling me Ms. McClure. We're both adults now. I call you Stacy. You call me Ros."

"I can do that." Stacy rocked back on her heels and offered a satisfied smile.

"When I was a child I spoke as a child. When I grew up I put away my childish ways," Ros recited reflectively. "Isn't that the way it goes?"

"Something like that. First Corinthians I think. Do you study the Bible?"

"No. My aunt used to recite passages she thought helped her make a point."

"What church does she attend?"

"She doesn't. Never has. She told me she didn't like being told what to believe. She said her faith was between her and her God. And I agree with her. She never forced me to attend church. Said it was my choice."

"So you grew up and put away your childish ways?"

"Gosh, I hope so."

"I suppose you heard about the reunion?"

"Oh, yes. My aunt and Meredith have been hounding me about it."

"There's that face again. I take it you're not sold on the idea."

"Not really. I don't communicate with any of my high school classmates. We have nothing in common."

"Sure you do. You all graduated from the same school at the same time. You did things together."

"Did. Past tense."

"I got persuaded into attending. Seems I'm one of only three current faculty members who were also on staff twenty-five years ago." She shrugged.

"I hope everyone enjoys themselves."

"I have a question for you."

Ros studied Stacy as she pulled herself up straight, readying herself for what looked to be a major declaration.

"You're probably not staying in Colby once Miss Bonnie is settled in the rehab center, right?"

"That's right. I have a job that's calling me home."

"Then with your permission I'd like to keep tabs on Miss Bonnie while she's recuperating. If she needs something… slippers, candy bar, crossword puzzle book, I'd be happy to take care of that for her. I think she trusts me enough to handle that for her. But I want to ask your permission first. She's your aunt. Not mine. I don't want to usurp your duties or take your place."

Ros looked up at her quizzically. "I have a feeling you're going to check on her whether I agree or not."

"Then you don't have a problem with my looking in on her occasionally?"

Ros couldn't think of a good reason to say no. She hated to admit it but knowing that someone, even Stacy Hagen, was checking on Bonnie would relieve some of the guilt she felt at being 1,000 miles away. In spite of the pushy phone calls and any disagreeable history they might have had, Ros was relatively certain she would get accurate and truthful reports from her. She wasn't so sure she'd get that from Bonnie.

"I guess it's okay."

"Can't bring yourself to smile and say 'Thanks, that'll be wonderful'?"

"Okay, yes." She smiled. "Thank you, that'll be wonderful. I appreciate you offering."

"You still haven't forgiven me for that biology grade, have you?"

"Now that you mention it, no." She hesitated. That was ancient history. It served no purpose to dwell on it.

"I do my best to work with my students if they just make an effort. You made no attempt to come see me to rectify your lab grade."

"I'll tell you what. I'll agree to your checking on my aunt from time to time and you'll agree to not discuss my biology grade."

"Fine. The discussion is closed." Stacy held up her hands in surrender.

"Thank you."

"If I'm going to be checking on Miss Bonnie is there anything else I can do to help? Would you like me to take in her mail? Feed the cat?"

"First of all, I don't think my aunt has a cat. I don't remember her mentioning it, and I haven't seen one around the house."

"All I know is she asked me to get a couple cans of cat food, chicken-flavored. I put it on the table with her mail and wallet."

"Yes, I saw it."

They looked at each other with the same stunned, yet curious expression.

"Chicken-flavored cat food? Oh, gosh. She wouldn't." Ros's eyes widened.

"All I know is she asked me to buy cat food. Nothing about a cat."

"My aunt couldn't possibly be eating cat food," she said in disbelief.

"I hope not. I assume she's a senior citizen on a fixed income, but she can't be so hard up that she has to eat cat food." Stacy grimaced at the thought. "Although technically humans could consume pet food. It contains lots of vitamins and minerals as well as rice and wheat. But humans need vitamin C, and pet food doesn't contain any of that."

"Rest assured my aunt is not that hard up. And before you say anything, no, I wouldn't allow that to happen even if she was. It's disgusting to even consider."

"Hey, you wouldn't starve if that's all there was to eat in an emergency."

"I hope I'm never in an emergency where cat food is my only option." Ros shuddered at the thought.

Before Stacy could reply, the phone in Ros's pocket chimed. "I need to take this," she said, frowning when she recognized the university exchange on the screen.

Stacy nodded, returned to her truck, and drove away without a backward glance. If there was anything else she had wanted to discuss, Ros thought, it must not have been very important.

"Hello," Ros said, answering the phone on its fourth ring.

"Ms. McClure, this is Dean Thorpe. I understand you're out of town. Is that correct?"

"Yes. I'm in Kansas. My aunt had an accident and is in the hospital."

"That's what Carla Sweeney said."

"She okayed my trip since she'll be in the office for a couple more weeks helping Steve Hansinger get his feet on the ground."

"Unfortunately Carla had to take an immediate departure. She is officially retired and off campus."

"What? Why, for heaven's sake?"

"Her husband had triple bypass surgery yesterday, and she needs to be with him."

"Is he going to be all right?" Ros gasped.

"According to her sister, it's been touch and go. That's all I know. And I'm afraid that leaves us in kind of a bind. The department is severely shorthanded."

"And you're asking me to cut my trip short, is that it?"

"I'm sorry, Ms. McClure, but yes. It would be greatly appreciated if you could be here to resolve some problems before the end of the month. The university will be happy to cover the cost of changing your ticket. Bring me a receipt and I'll take care of it personally."

"I can't get there tomorrow, Dean Thorpe. My aunt is being moved to a rehabilitation facility in the morning and I have to be there."

"The day after tomorrow will be fine. We'll handle things until you get here." Ros could hear muffled conversation in the background. "I have to go. We'll see you Friday." She didn't wait for a reply.

"I guess you will," Ros muttered disgustedly. She dashed out a concerned and caring message to Carla, then contacted the airline to change her ticket.

"Three hundred dollar change fee and yes, Dean Thorpe, I'll gladly let the university pay for that." She bounded up the stairs, changed her clothes, and headed to the hospital to look in on Bonnie, then find someplace to get a sandwich she could call dinner.

"Hi, Aunt Bonnie. How's your dinner?" Ros looked under the plastic dome covering her dinner plate. Bonnie had barely touched her fish sticks and mashed potatoes. She had eaten all the bread and butter and the dish of rice pudding so Ros assumed she wouldn't starve. "Would you like me to cut up your fish sticks?" she asked, hoping to coax her into a few bites.

"No, I'm full. You may have them."

"Thanks, but I'm not hungry yet." Ros wasn't a fish stick fan. "They're moving you to your new room in the rehab center tomorrow. I think you're going to like it there."

"Don't be patronizing, honey. It isn't a flattering trait," Bonnie sneered. "I know exactly where they're moving me. It's the nursing home."

"It's also a Health and Rehabilitation Center for people who need care while they recover from surgery, like you."

"Maybe so, but it's still a nursing home."

"I'd hope so. You need nursing assistance while you heal." Ros took Bonnie's hand then continued. "After we get you all settled in your new room I have to fly back to Cincinnati. I'm sorry, Aunt Bonnie, but my work called and they need me back there on Friday."

"You're not going to stay a little longer?" Bonnie pleaded.

"I can't."

Ros stayed for an hour, visiting and reassuring Bonnie about the move to a new building. It was dark when she returned home to finish her packing. When she returned, something again seemed different. She had left the suitcase propped open on her bed when she left to visit Bonnie. She would swear she left a pair of underwear and a bra next to the suitcase to wear in the morning. But they weren't there.

"Okay, I'm not losing my mind. I know I left them right here," she said. She opened the suitcase, thinking maybe she only thought she left them out. When she flipped the lid open, she jumped back and screamed. A pair of fluorescent green eyes were looking up at her. A cat, long-haired and pure white, was curled up in a nest of her clothes, including the underwear and bra she thought she had left out. She had dragged them into the suitcase, it seemed,

"Where did you come from?" Ros gasped, her heart racing.

The cat meowed and blinked lazily, as if that was enough information.

"Oh, my God. Bonnie does have a cat. What am I going to do with you?"

She couldn't take the cat with her. And she couldn't leave it without adequate food and water. She went downstairs in search of food dishes and a litter box. The cat followed at a safe distance, occasionally meowing.

"Is this yours?" Ros pointed to a small flap door to the outside, partially blocked by a wicker basket, in the back corner of the laundry room. Behind the laundry room door she found a nearly dry bowl of water and a bowl with food crumbs in it. A half-full bag of dry cat food was on the top shelf. The cat rubbed against Ros's leg, meowing vehemently.

"Am I supposed to fill these? Is that the idea?"

She filled the bowls, large enough that she assumed they could last at least two days. She leaned back against the doorframe and crossed her arms as the cat crouched over the food bowl, crunching and purring, as if in a race to the bottom of the dish. Just what she needed. Another detail to handle. Surely, though, there was someone in town, a veterinary clinic perhaps, where she could take the cat in the morning to be boarded. She had just enough time to arrange that on her way out of town. She hesitated a moment, then pressed the button to call Bonnie's cell phone. Stacy answered after only one ring.

"Yes, I know. I still have Miss Bonnie's phone."

"I assumed you did. That's why I called. I've answered the question regarding the cat food."

"Oh? Did you have chicken bits with gravy for dinner?"

"No. But Fluffy would probably like some."

"Fluffy?"

"My aunt has a cat after all. At least I assume it's her cat."

"That's a relief."

"Not really. I have to head back to work tomorrow, and I can't leave without making arrangements to have the food and water bowls filled occasionally."

"And you called to ask if I'd do that?"

"No. I called to ask if you knew where I can take the cat to be boarded. There has to be some place in town."

"Depending on how long, that could get pricey."

"I'm not a barbarian. I can't just leave it. That wouldn't be right."

"The right thing to do would be to ask me to feed and water the cat since I'm going to check on her house anyway."

"I didn't want to impose."

Stacy laughed. "I'll take care of Miss Bonnie's cat. Eventually she's going to ask about it. When she mentions the cat, I can tell her it's being taken care of."

"The food and water bowls are in the laundry room. The bag of cat food is on the shelf."

"Where's the litter box?"

"I didn't find one. There's a flap door in the back corner of the laundry room so the litter box must be the great outdoors. Are you sure about this?"

"I think I can handle one cat while Miss Bonnie recuperates. I am a little surprised it took you this long to notice it."

"I noticed it because it was napping in my suitcase. And from what I've observed, it's a lazy feline. The first day I was here I saw a mouse scurry across the kitchen and disappear behind the wastebasket. The cat must not like rodents any more than I do."

"There's thirty-eight species of mice, but you're probably talking about the common house mouse or *Mus musculus*."

"I don't care what it's called. It's a dirty little rodent."

"Cats are born with natural hunting instincts although this one may not have chosen to demonstrate those qualities as of yet. You may have to set a trap for the mice. There are a couple types that are pet friendly so the cat won't get snapped."

"I'll think about it. Right now the cat is my only concern. I'll make sure there's no trash left in the house."

"The mouse isn't after the trash necessarily. It probably knows exactly where the cat food bowl is and when it's filled."

"Oh, I hadn't thought of that. I'll leave some money on the dining room table for additional cat food when it's needed. I guess I'm feeding two."

"Don't bother. I'll take care of it. Cat food is cheap."

"I'll leave money for my aunt's cat's food," Ros repeated firmly.

Stacy was silent a moment then said, "Okay."

"Her utility bills will be paid through her checking account. Her mail is being forwarded. Any expenses she incurs as part of her stay in the rehab center will be covered. They know how to get in touch with me."

"Sounds like you've got everything taken care of. Very efficient. Don't worry about the cat."

"Thank you."

"You're welcome, Ros. By the way, has anyone ever called you stubborn?"

"All the time. When you work with figures and data all day, accuracy is paramount. I can't afford to be complaisant."

"Detail-oriented then."

"Extremely. And yes, the problem with my biology grade grated on my compulsion to detail, even back then."

"Which is why I expected more from you. You were an A student."

"You promised," Ros said adamantly, even though it had been she who raised the subject.

"They're right."

"Who? Who's right?"

"All those who call you stubborn."

CHAPTER SEVEN

Ros was back in her office Friday morning as promised and once again consumed with work. Some of what fell across her desk used to be Carla's responsibility. It should now be Steve's, but he was still struggling to understand the software on his computer. She didn't have time to give him a point-by-point tutorial. That didn't stop him from asking questions throughout the day. She used to think it was convenient to have her boss's office right across the hall from hers, but his repeated interruptions with trivial questions had her rethinking that idea. She kept reminding herself he was her boss, the one she answered to. She tried several times to find a spare moment to call the rehab center to see how Bonnie was doing, but each time Steve appeared at her door with a confused look on his face. She'd call later.

Ros worked late on Friday and came in on Saturday to not only work on the quarterly report but to rectify some of what Steve had tried to do unsuccessfully. Saturday also provided several hours of uninterrupted solitude at the office.

Sunday was going to be her day to catch up on things at home, but when Steve called with concern over whether they'd be ready for the upcoming meeting of the Board of Regents she suspected the day would not be her own.

"We'll be ready," she reassured him.

"I can meet you at the office in an hour. I think we need to iron out a few little glitches I found. With you out of town like that we got behind. Transition periods aren't the best time to schedule vacations."

Ros's first thought was "glitches?" How was it possible he found glitches when he didn't completely understand the format? And her time away was a family emergency cleared by her boss. Not a frivolous vacation. She was tempted to tell Steve to stay out of the program, but she didn't want to start her relationship with him on the wrong foot.

"I'm sure we can finish things up tomorrow," she said with as much reassurance as she could muster.

"I'd be happier if we could take a quick look this afternoon. It shouldn't take long."

"Okay, I'll meet you at the office." She resigned herself to working with him on Sunday, although she had a feeling she'd accomplish more working by herself.

She was ready to walk out the door when a text message chimed on her phone. It was Bonnie's phone, so it had to be Stacy. It was a thumbs-up emoji. Nothing more. It was a cryptic message, but it said volumes. Bonnie was doing okay. The house was fine. The cat was surviving. She didn't need to call or worry.

As year-round employees of the university, the chief internal auditor and his or her assistant were allowed keys to the administration building in order to deal with just such situations. Ros wished they didn't have that luxury, at least not today. She let herself in with a friendly nod to the security guard.

"Hello, Ms. McClure," he said from his desk in the lobby. "Did you forget something?"

"Yes. I forgot to stay home. How are you, Tom?"

"Same ol', same ol'."

Ros had no sooner sat down at her desk and booted her computer when Steve called.

"I'm here," she said, scanning down through the report draft.

"Good. Good. I'm running a little late. You go ahead and see what you find. Check page six. There seems to be some discrepancy there."

"You mean the investment compliance chart? I'll check it over. What time will you be here?"

"I'm not sure. Give things the once-over and if I'm not there by six you can call it a day."

"It's two fifteen."

"That should give you enough time, shouldn't it? If you need a little longer that's fine with me. I want us to be sure and have all the T's crossed and the I's dotted for this report. I've got to go. This has been a hell of a busy day. If I don't see you this afternoon, I'll see you bright and early tomorrow morning." She could hear what sounded like children's voices in the background as he said good-bye and hung up.

"I think I got suckered into working my day off," she muttered. "He's not coming. He had no intention of coming. I should have told him it was my day off and I was busy. But noooooo. I was a good girl," she continued as she opened the pages he mentioned. She heaved an exasperated sigh and went to work. She might as well. She'd driven all the way across town and didn't want to waste time being angry. There would be time for that later.

It was well past six when another text message chimed from Bonnie's phone.

Did you get my message?

Oh, yes. I did. Thank you. I'm sorry I didn't reply. I was busy.

No problem. I want to let you know Miss Bonnie is doing fine. It's not her favorite place to be, naturally. But the staff is taking good care of her.

"Ms. McClure, are you going to be much longer?" Tom asked from her doorway. "I was going to take my dinner break if that's okay with you."

"You go ahead, Tom. I'll be finished in a few minutes. I need to print off these last pages, then I'm out of here." She pressed the print key and leaned back in her chair. "I need a dinner break too."

"You're sure dedicated, Ms. McClure. There aren't many on staff who put in the hours you do. Mrs. Sweeney used to be like that. The university is lucky to have people like you. You take care of yourself."

"You too, Tom," she called after him.

She shut down her computer and headed down the hall. She pressed the elevator button and stood waiting for what seemed like an unusually long time.

"Oh, no you don't. You're not trapping me again. Not today." She took the stairs instead. She wasn't in the mood to be stuck in a temperamental elevator.

She was nearly home when she realized she hadn't replied to Stacy's last text. Maybe no reply was needed. She hadn't sent anything additional. As she sat at a traffic light she reread the last message, then sent a quick reply, acknowledging Stacy's effort. Ros sent the same thumbs-up emoji. Almost immediately she received a text reply.

No problem.

That was fast, Ros thought with a smile. What were you doing? Sitting on the phone?

* * *

In spite of Steve's lack of familiarity with department procedures, the quarterly report was finished and submitted on time, thanks to Ros's usual efficiency. And as expected, he was congratulated on reaching his first successful milestone as chief internal auditor. Ros had given up on receiving even a thank-you for her long hours and dedication to getting the report done on time when Steve paused as he passed her office door, looked in, and gave her a thumbs-up. She nodded her acceptance and returned the gesture. Stacy's thumbs-up emoji message seemed more genuine somehow, but at least Steve acknowledged her efforts. Carla was always generous with her praise for her staff. That may not be Steve's style and Ros was okay with that. She'd take the gratitude where she found it.

CHAPTER EIGHT

Stacy finished up at school, did a few chores around the house, then headed into town with a small loaf of banana nut bread she had made for Bonnie. It wasn't much, but she wanted to bring Bonnie something to show she wasn't forgotten. It had been five days since her last visit. She stopped at the nurses' station to check in and see if Bonnie needed anything the center didn't provide.

"Hello, Coach Hagen," one of the young nurse's aides said proudly. "Remember me?" She was a stout young woman in her twenties with a long ponytail and wearing pink scrubs.

"Sure, Tiffany. Four years ago and you spilled a pail of pond water all over the floor in the lab."

"You don't have to remind me." She blushed and hid her face.

She patted her on the shoulder and said, "That's okay, Tiffany. You cleaned it up. You're forgiven. You were a good student. I'm glad to see you chose a career in the sciences. You'll be an asset to your patients."

"My mom thinks I should go back to school and become an RN."

"Do you want to be an RN?"

"Maybe. That's a lot of classes though," Tiffany said with a disparaging groan.

"Nothing is accomplished unless you put forth the effort. You know that, Tiff. And I think you'd make a terrific RN."

"You think so?"

"Yes, I do. You wouldn't have mentioned it if you weren't seriously considering it. You care about your patients."

"They're such nice people. They deserve respect and good care, whatever their age."

"Speaking of, how's Miss Bonnie doing?"

"She's fine. She's eating well and doing her physical therapy. But I think she's counting the days until she can go home."

"Has her doctor said when that might be?"

"No, but she's able to get up on her own and can do a sponge bath with only minor supervision. She's been teaching some of the residents chair yoga. It's really just simple exercises, but she calls it yoga. It gives the patients something to look forward to. I think she looks forward to it too. She says it helps her battle cabin fever."

"So she's up and doing things, not sitting in bed?"

"Oh, no. She's very active for someone her age and in her condition. The doctor encourages her to do things she likes. Although sometimes she's a little too active. They worry she'll fall again. You can't tie them down. That would be cruel. Everyone needs to be as active as they can."

"Does she need anything? Toothpaste? Socks?"

"I don't think so. Most of our patients' needs are simple."

"I brought her banana nut bread. Is that okay? No allergies?"

"Yum. She'll love that. She says she has a terrible sweet tooth. She keeps talking about her niece. She says she taught her to cook when she was a teenager and lived with her. She talks about her as if she was a daughter instead of a niece. Says she was a better mother to that girl than her sister. You know how elderly people get."

"Does her sister ever come visit Miss Bonnie?"

"Not that I've ever seen. I don't think her niece has been here either. She calls and asks how her aunt is doing, but she hasn't been here."

"She was here when Miss Bonnie was admitted, but she lives and works out of state."

"Oh, there's Mr. Wilson again," Tiffany said as a call light lit the panel behind the desk. "He probably can't find his razor. He shaves three times a day. I better go see what he needs."

Stacy walked to the end of the hall and tapped on Bonnie's open door before entering. She was sitting next to an open dresser drawer, folding the contents.

"Good evening, Miss Bonnie."

"Hello, dear," she said with a worried look. "I simply cannot find that new bra Ros got me. It fits so much better than these old things." She continued to sort and refold.

"Could it be in the dirty laundry?"

"No, I looked."

"Could you have it on?" Stacy teased.

"Oh, good question." Bonnie cupped her hands over her breasts and gave a shake. "Nope, not wearing one."

"Where did you last see it?" Stacy resigned herself to help search, but Bonnie closed the drawer, seemingly giving up on finding the missing bra.

"I'm so glad I'll be home in a few days. I can finally get back to normal."

"Did the doctor say your shoulder was healing and you were being discharged?"

"Oh, yes. It doesn't hurt near as much as it did. I have my exercises to keep it loose, but I can do those at home. They're sending a visiting nurse to help me bathe and wash my hair for a week or so, but at least I'll be doing it in my own home. My own bathroom."

"That's good news." Stacy was skeptical. Ros hadn't mentioned her aunt being discharged, and surely the staff would have alerted her as well. "Speaking of home," she said, deciding to change the subject. "I've been feeding your cat, but I thought I should ask if it has any special needs. Flea medicine? Special food?"

"Piano eats about anything. I buy whatever sounds good and is cheap."

"Piano? That's the cat's name?"

"The first time that cat ran in my back door it hid behind the piano then ran across the keys, tinkling out a little tune." Bonnie laughed. "So I named it Piano. She's been hanging around ever since. I had her fixed. I didn't want a bunch of little kittens running through my house."

"She seems well fed and healthy. And friendly enough." Stacy took Bonnie's cell phone out of her pocket and set it on the bedside table. "Maybe it's time for you to have your phone back so you can keep in touch with Ros."

"No, no. You keep it for now," Bonnie insisted, putting the phone back in Stacy's hand. "I don't want it here. Someone will walk off with it when I'm sleeping. I've seen people in other people's rooms, going through their things. You keep it for me until I get home. It'll be a couple days." Bonnie was quite adamant.

"All right, I'll hold on to it, but if you change your mind you let me know."

Stacy finished her visit with Bonnie and headed home, although she felt a strong urge to ask aides if discharge plans were truly in her immediate future. Maybe Ros was keeping the information to herself. Maybe she had been in touch with the doctor and they had discussed it amongst themselves. She'd put it out of her mind. She'd continue to visit Bonnie as long as she was in the rehab center, and when she was dismissed, that would be the end of her obligation. She'd keep her nose out of their family business.

Stacy wondered how long she could hold herself to that promise.

* * *

How much truth is there in Miss Bonnie's expectation she's going home soon? She sounds like it's a done deal, but you didn't mention it so I thought I'd ask, not that it's any of my business, of course.

Ros hadn't heard from Stacy in a few days and had assumed no news was good news. This text was curious news, however.

I'm not aware she's being released in the foreseeable future. Probably just optimistic thinking. But thanks for the heads-up. If she mentions anything, I'll check with the staff.

Ros sent the text on its way. There wasn't an immediate reply. An hour later, when she was preoccupied with a detailed section of an email, a text appeared on her phone.

Sorry. Biology quiz. Organelles in the cell.

Ros did a quick reference check online before replying.

Organelles are those specialized parts of the cell, right? Like nucleus and nucleolus and mitochondria?

Correct. Give Google a gold star for that answer.

Stacy added a smiley face.

Knowing she'd been caught, Ros sent a thumbs-up emoji in response.

Half an hour later she got another text.

By the way, I've tried to give back Miss Bonnie's cell phone, but she said not until she goes home. She's afraid it'll disappear.

I can understand that. Since she has a telephone in her room, I've been able to talk with her so we can keep in touch. By the way, I asked her and the cat's name is Piano. Something about a walk down the keyboard. Thanks for looking in on Bonnie, but I've got to get back to work and you've got quizzes to grade.

It was several minutes before the next text arrived.

Yes, I heard the story about the piano-playing cat. Interesting.

CHAPTER NINE

It had been less than three weeks since Bonnie's accident. Although deeply concerned about her aunt's recovery, Ros was consumed with work. Steve's constant questions and concerns about timetables and accuracy only added to the stress level. Carla was right. This new work environment was going to test her patience and her dedication.

She had returned from a meeting when a message chimed on her phone. It was from Stacy.

Can I call? Need to talk.

Ros had a lot to do before lunch and not a lot of time to do it, but the request was worrying. Up to that point, their communication had been confined to text messages.

Sure.

It was a few minutes before the call came through.

"Hello." Something in Stacy's voice was different, apprehensive. "I hate to bother you at work, but are you aware the doctor is discharging Miss Bonnie today?"

"No, I hadn't been told anything. She hasn't had time to heal. I think it's her wishful thinking."

"It's more than wishful thinking. She's packed and dressed. They called me at school and asked me to come ASAP. I thought there was some kind of emergency. When I got here she was sitting on her bed, her jacket on and her suitcase by the door. The nurse was waiting with her discharge papers."

"You're there now?" This conversation now had Ros's full and complete attention.

"Yes. I told her I had to see about her paperwork so I could come out in the lobby and call you. She's ready to leave. She's not taking no for an answer. I asked if she was capable of being home alone and they seem to think so. They ordered twice a week visiting nurses and three times a week visiting aides. Miss Bonnie is convinced she can do this. She's expecting me to take her home. I don't mind giving her a ride, but I thought I better clear this with you first."

"Let me call you right back," Ros said and ended the call. She called Dr. Smithton's office and demanded to speak with him.

"Ros, can I see you in my office?" Steve said from the doorway. "I think we've got a problem with the library funding request."

"I'll be with you shortly," she replied. It wasn't like her to put off work-related issues, but this was more important and he'd have to wait. "I won't be long."

He frowned and returned to his office. She closed her office door and waited for the doctor to pick up.

"Dr. Smithton here. Can I help you, Ms. McClure?"

"Yes. I understand you're discharging my aunt from the rehabilitation center today. Is that correct? And if so, why wasn't I informed?"

"I assumed you had been informed. Yes, your aunt is ready to go home."

"It's barely been three weeks. How can she be fully healed and ready to take care of herself? I can't be there to be her caregiver. I have a job and I'm a thousand miles away. What if she falls again?"

"Ms. McClure, there is no guarantee she'll not fall tomorrow or next year, but in this situation I believe it's in Bonnie's best interest to be home in her own environment. She needs her familiar surroundings. Psychologically it's better for our older patients to be home as soon as it's safely possible. A home environment can improve her health as much as sitting in a nursing home in a strange atmosphere."

"People like your aunt are often subject to what we call sundowning. Late in the day strange or unfamiliar environments can contribute to confusion and agitation. Being in their own home with their own familiar possessions around them can be very reassuring. So we like to get them back home as soon as safely possible. And I'm convinced your aunt is ready. Visiting nurses and aides will help with continued physical therapy and any personal needs she has."

"What do you mean people like my aunt, Doctor? The fact that she's over seventy?"

"Partly her age, yes, but also with her dementia."

"Dementia?" Ros released a desperate gasp, taken aback by the word. "My aunt doesn't have dementia."

"Early signs, yes, she does. Some family members don't notice because the changes are so gradual. Memory loss. Difficulty doing familiar tasks. Misplacing things. The changes can be so slight you don't realize them until they become significant."

"You honestly believe my aunt has dementia?" Ros asked, almost afraid of the answer. But this could explain some of the things she noticed when she was in Colby a few weeks ago.

"Yes, she has shown signs of being disoriented and forgetful. Occasionally her decision-making has shown poor judgment. These are early symptoms and shouldn't interfere with her resuming her independence. I discussed it with her and I think she's aware of her situation. She asked me not to say anything to anyone, but you have a right to know. You are her next of kin. She didn't want to worry you, Ms. McClure."

"My aunt is perfectly ready and able to be home alone?" Ros asked cautiously.

"Yes, as ready as we can make her. As I said, I think being at home will improve her state of mind. I can have the visiting nurses keep in touch with you so you're aware of how she's doing. With a few more weeks of physical therapy to increase range of motion and to strengthen that shoulder she'll be almost good as new, assuming she'll stay off ladders." He gave a slight groan. "She'll have follow-up appointments in my office regularly. At any time she needs to be back in the hospital, we'll let you know, but I think she knows her limitations. I went over the strict dos and don'ts with her."

"And she agreed?"

"Yes. We printed them off and asked her to post the list on her refrigerator as a reminder. The visiting nurses will remind her as well and keep track of how she's doing. Your aunt is an otherwise healthy woman. Give her credit for taking good care of herself over the years. Let's assume she can do this. Try not to worry and try not to create undue stress for her."

"Thank you, Doctor. I'll try."

Bonnie was going home. The doctor could justify it, although his news was startling. Ros had noticed a few odd things at her aunt's house but, like Meredith said, Aunt Bonnie was a colorful character. This was just how she'd always been. During her teen years Ros had assumed her antics were Bonnie's way of easing any feelings of abandonment that Ros felt over being left to live with her while her mother took up over-the-road trucking with her husband, an out-of-work machinist, in an attempt to save their troubled marriage and make enough to live on.

"Ros, you can't live in a semi like a gypsy," her mother had explained. "You have to finish your schooling. You may want to go to college someday. All your friends are here in Colby. Your Aunt Bonnie has lots of room, and you've always loved being with her. We'll come see you often."

That was her sophomore year in high school. It took months before she fully accepted and understood her mother's reasoning for leaving her behind. And it took even more months to become resigned to the diminishing number of visits. There was more money in the coast-to-coast routes and those up the Alaskan Highway, she had heard her mother tell Bonnie. "Ice road trucking. That's where the real money is."

Ros received cards and gifts from all over the country, mostly souvenirs from truck stops. A Christmas visit was promised the first year, but a Montana blizzard made it impossible. A truck breakdown in upstate New York canceled the second Christmas and the third. But Bonnie was there with a shoulder to cry on and an understanding heart. Aunt Bonnie became her rock.

"Oh, Bonnie," Ros muttered to herself with a heavy sigh. "I don't like this. I don't like it at all." She felt guilty for not noticing any of the changes the doctor mentioned. Perhaps he was right. Perhaps they were only early symptoms. Very early. Perhaps it would be years before dementia interrupted Bonnie's life to any substantial degree. That's what she would cling to. Years.

"Ros?" Steve said, again standing in her doorway.

"I'll be right with you. I have to return this call. It'll only take a minute to leave instructions," she said, pressing the speed dial for her aunt's phone.

"Is it work-related?" he asked.

"No, it's family-related and unavoidable." He left her to her call. "Hello, Stacy. This is Ros. I just spoke with the doctor."

"And?"

"And Aunt Bonnie *is* going home. I can make arrangements for a taxi to take her if you need to get back to school. I'm sorry they called you in on this."

"That's not the problem. Miss Bonnie's safety was my concern."

"Thank you. I'll explain the details to you another time, but I understand the doctor's reasoning."

"Then I'll be glad to get her home and settled in, if that's okay with you."

"Yes, if you don't mind. That would be greatly appreciated. If she needs anything I'll be glad to send you a check. Groceries. Anything."

"I got it covered," Stacy said confidently. "I'll let you know when she's home. I think it's time for her to have her phone back so she can communicate with you directly."

"Yes, that'll be fine. I'm sorry this has taken so much of your time. We appreciate it immensely."

"That has nothing to do with it. I think she'll feel better if she can reach out to you if she needs someone to talk to. I don't think she has a land line."

"You're right. She doesn't. She didn't like the automated spam calls so she had it taken out."

"And don't worry about taking up so much of my time. The school has lots of qualified substitute teachers who love to give quizzes. I always keep a couple extra in my desk drawer." She chuckled. "Quizzes for the unsuspecting."

"I remember that. Draw parts of a plant."

"That's one of them."

"Thank you again for taking my aunt home and for keeping me informed."

"No problem. I'll text you later."

"Ros, are you coming?" Steve called from his office.

She ended the call and went into his office to defuse whatever problem he thought he'd found. But Bonnie would be on her mind the rest of the day and so would Stacy's kind assistance, a surprising turnaround.

* * *

Stacy carried Bonnie's suitcase, tote bag, and several vases of flowers into the house while Bonnie sat in the porch swing. She lazily swung back and forth as if reacquainting herself with her own surroundings, smiling off into space with a satisfied look on her face.

"It's a glorious day, isn't it?" Bonnie said as Stacy descended the front steps for another load. "You know, being away from home, cooped up in that nursing home, you forget even what day it is." The cat sauntered up on the porch and jumped onto the swing. She curled up next to Bonnie and looked up at her expectantly. "Hello, baby. Sweet kitty. Did you miss your mama?" Bonnie obliged, stroking her softly.

"Friday, Miss Bonnie. It's Friday, the sixteenth."

Bonnie looked at her quizzically.

"April sixteenth," Stacy added as she went back to the truck for the last load.

"April sixteenth," Bonnie said reflectively. "My mother's

birthday. She'd be a hundred and three. Can you believe it?"

"What was her name?"

"Sophie Maria."

"Then happy birthday, Sophie Maria." Stacy caught the screen door with her hip so it wouldn't bang.

"Yes. Happy birthday, Mama," Bonnie said as her eyes rolled upward. She was still gazing to the heavens when Stacy returned.

"That would be Ros's grandmother, right?" she asked.

"Yes. She never met her. She's been gone for years and years."

"Okay, you're all moved back in. I put your suitcase in your room on the bed so you can empty it." Stacy sat down next to Bonnie on the swing. Piano moved a little closer to Bonnie's leg. "How about you tell me what you need at the grocery store and I'll run in to Dillon's."

"I haven't given it a lick of thought. Whatever it is, it can wait. You run along now. You've done enough."

"Are you sure? Even a gallon of milk? I promised Ros I'd get you in and settled. There's probably nothing in your refrigerator to eat."

"I've got cans of soup in the pantry. I'll be fine. I'll tell you what. I'll make a list. We'll talk about it tomorrow."

Stacy hadn't planned on devoting Saturday to Bonnie's shopping needs, but she'd find the time somewhere.

"Miss Bonnie, tomorrow the high school athletic department is having a barbecue fund raiser to send the boys' baseball team to the state championship in Kansas City. How about I bring you a barbecue sandwich and we'll see about that grocery list?"

"Barbecue, huh? That sounds good. I always try to support the school."

"Hank Poole donated half a cow. Prime Angus. That'll be some good eatin'. My treat."

"I'll make us some sun tea and we can sit out here and have lunch together. You come by around noon."

"Deal. Now, Miss Bonnie, I'm going to give you back your phone." Stacy placed the cell phone in Bonnie's hand. "You're home and you need it. I have added my name and phone number to your contact list. Stacy Hagen. It's under the H's." She showed her. "If you need anything, you call me. If you can't get a hold of your niece and you need assistance, call me. Okay?"

"Thank you, dear. You've been so sweet to help an old lady like me." She kissed Stacy on the cheek. "I can't thank you enough. I'll be sure and tell Ros how wonderful you've been."

"My pleasure, Miss Bonnie." Stacy patted Bonnie's knee, petted the cat, then stood and stared down at her. "And you stay *off* the ladder, you hear me. Leave that sort of thing to us younger folks. I'll see you tomorrow around noon."

As Stacy drove away, she placed a call to Ros. Since it was the first time she had called her from her own phone, she suspected it would show up as Potential Spam. Sure enough, Ros didn't answer and the call went to voice mail.

"Ros, this is Stacy Hagen. I thought I'd let you know Miss Bonnie is happy to be home. She has her phone now, so you can talk with her. I'm sure she'll be glad to hear from you. And did you know today would be your grandmother Sophie's birthday? She'd be a hundred and three. Anyway, I thought I'd tell you she was home. I'm off to watch the girls' softball game. Colby versus Goodland. Big rivalry game tonight. Too bad you're not here to see it. Bye-bye."

CHAPTER TEN

Stacy was first in line Saturday morning when they started serving the barbecue. She purchased three sandwiches, one for her and two for Bonnie, one she could save for later. She hated to do it, but she canceled a tennis lesson at the park. She had a feeling she wouldn't be finished at Bonnie's by three. Her grocery list might require more than a quick run into the store and out again.

She knocked on the front door, rang the doorbell, and waited, expecting it to take a little time for Bonnie to answer if she was upstairs. Several minutes passed and still no answer. She knocked again, this time harder, and rang the bell twice.

"It's Stacy Hagen, Miss Bonnie," she called through the door. "I've got your lunch."

Still no answer. She knew Bonnie was home. She had talked to her less than an hour ago and she was expecting her.

"I brought you a piece of pie, too. The bakery donated ten pies. It was a tough decision, but I brought you peach," she added even louder and pounded her fist on the door. "Miss Bonnie?"

She retrieved the hidden key from behind the porch light and unlocked the door. "Miss Bonnie, it's Stacy. I've got your lunch," she called from the hallway. "Are you napping?"

"I'm up here," Bonnie called faintly. "In the attic. I need your help."

"Oh, good Lord." Stacy quickly set the food containers on the dining room table and vaulted up the stairs toward the distress call. "Okay. I'm coming. Hang on."

Whatever Bonnie was doing in the attic, Stacy strongly suspected she shouldn't be doing it, at least not yet. The stairs to the third-floor attic were narrow and steep and turned halfway up, a bend that was not conducive to Stacy's normal two steps at a time climb. "Did you fall?" Stacy expected to find Bonnie sprawled on the floor, writhing in agony.

Bonnie was sitting on a storage tub and examining the contents of a cardboard box. The attic was a jumble of boxes, odd unused household items, and an old wooden piano stool. True to her name, Piano was curled up on top of the stool, watching Bonnie with a jaundiced eye.

"Hello, dear."

"Are you all right?" Stacy was breathless from the climb and from the fear of what she'd find.

"Do you need rags for anything?" Bonnie asked without answering the question.

"What?"

"Rags. I'm going to throw this whole box out if you can't use them. It's such a mess up here. I've got to clean it out before it becomes a fire hazard." She sounded exasperated.

"Rags? Is that all you wanted? Good God, woman. I thought you fell and broke your neck," Stacy said as she dropped her hands to her knees in relief.

A dozen or so cardboard boxes sat on the floor, divided and grouped by the markings on the end of the boxes. Most were dusty and aged with torn or missing tops that revealed what looked like old clothes and linens.

"Could you carry this box downstairs? I need them out of here and I'm afraid to try carrying anything down those steep steps." She pushed a box toward the stairs. "It's all junk, just junk. Anything you don't want either donate it to the thrift store or toss it out. I don't want it back. None of it. These three also." Bonnie waved her hands dismissively. "There might be a sweater or something in there. It's just junk. I've got to get this clutter hauled out of here. It's got to go. It makes me so nervous to know this is up here."

"You want these four boxes hauled away?" Stacy asked as she hoisted the first box. It seemed like a lot of fuss for what probably needed to go straight to the trash.

"We'll start with those." Bonnie pointed. "I need to go through the rest of them. I don't want to give away my mother's wedding dress. It's up here somewhere. It was handmade. My grandmother spent weeks sewing the beads and lace." She seemed lost in thought, staring off into space as Stacy carried the box down the stairs. When she returned Bonnie was rummaging in a trash bag. "This was Ros's old bedspread. Pink chenille. She never liked it."

"This one next?" Stacy asked as she picked up another box.

"Yes, and take this bag, too." Bonnie set the bag on top of the box in Stacy's arms, making it hard to see over the top.

"Are you sure? If it's Ros's, shouldn't you ask her first?"

"Of course, I'm sure. It's been up here for years," she snapped. "I've got to get this out of here. She doesn't want it."

Stacy obliged, wondering what brought on Bonnie's sudden urge to purge her attic of excesses.

"Why don't you come down and have your lunch, then we'll see about your grocery list. We can finish this another time," Stacy said as she carried what she hoped was the last load.

"Are you throwing those in the trash?" Bonnie followed her down the stairs.

"I'm putting them in my truck. I'll take care of them later." She wasn't sure she should trash anything without at least looking in the boxes first. She didn't mind carrying it down, but she didn't want to throw out anything important. She also suspected if she didn't haul them away Bonnie might try to carry the boxes down the narrow stairs herself. When she returned from the truck, Bonnie was plating their sandwiches and preparing a glass of iced tea.

"Remember you're not to bring any of that junk back. I can't deal with it."

"I promise. I'll take care of it, Miss Bonnie."

Bonnie sat in the porch swing to eat her lunch. Stacy sat down on the top step and leaned back against the post.

"Have you talked to Ros about coming to the reunion?" Stacy asked between bites, trying to find a topic of conversation other than Bonnie's trash.

"She's busy. I tried to talk her into coming, but she doesn't have the time. She gets so wrapped up in her work. She works at the university, you know. She's some kind of accountant or auditor. That girl can add six columns of figures down or across in her head without using a pencil or her fingers." Bonnie grinned. "She's so smart. She can't cook worth a dang, but she can balance a checkbook like nobody's business."

"That's a good quality. You can always defrost a pizza."

"You know she doesn't have a husband," she said as if it was a secret. "Never will." She shook her head. "Nope. Ros is a lesbian. Has been since I can't remember when. She confided that in me years ago. I told her that's okay. So long as she's happy, I'm happy. I support her anyway. Always have."

"Where are her parents? Do they live around here?"

"Her father died ten, fifteen years ago. Heart attack. Dropped dead walking out of a hardware store in Topeka. He was a good-for-nothing part-time mechanic. Out of work most of the time. He tried truck driving a while. She went with him. Rumor around town was he cheated on my sister every chance he got. She finally divorced him. She lives in Montana somewhere. I don't hear from her except at Christmas. She's mad at me. She's my sister and she hates my guts." Bonnie cackled. "I told her she was a terrible mother, walking out on her daughter like that, leaving her during her important teenage years to be raised by an aunt. God knows I love my niece like she was my own, but her mother should have been there. She remarried, I think. Couple times from what I heard. I don't want to know.

She wanted to come live with me after the first divorce. She said I was family and I owed it to her."

"Did you let her?"

"No." Bonnie turned a venomous stare on Stacy. "Absolutely not. And I told her she better not ask to live with Ros or I'd wallop her behind until hell won't have no more."

"That sounds rather final."

"Sylvie remarried about two months later."

"Sylvie? Her name was Sylvia?"

"Nope, just Sylvie. Some family name from way back when."

Stacy felt a tug at her emotions at hearing what heartbreak Ros had had to endure. High school must have been torturous for her. She had long assumed Ros was gay and was glad to have it confirmed, but she knew from her own experience how tumultuous those teen years can be. Coming to grips with her sexual orientation must have been difficult without a mother's love and support.

"I'm sorry to hear Ros lost her father, but what about her mother? Doesn't she want to know where she is and how she's doing?"

"I don't know. If she does, she doesn't tell me. She knows how I feel about the whole thing."

Stacy was tempted to say family is still family, at least that's what she always believed, but she decided not to interfere.

Bonnie's gaze turned toward the splotch of beige paint on the porch wall as if she wanted a new topic of conversation.

"Since Ros insists I don't climb on a ladder I promised I'd find someone to paint my house. She is very adamant about it. She said she'd paint it herself before she'd allow me to do it." Bonnie laughed. "Love the girl to death, but that'll be the day when she can paint a house, unless you can do it with a calculator and a computer."

"She's right. You shouldn't. I'd think you'd have learned your lesson."

"I'll call around and see who I can find that won't charge me an arm and a leg. You know I've always done things like that for myself. I built my backyard gazebo with my own two hands. I wanted someplace to do my yoga. It's not perfect, but I made it."

"I do some painting every now and then. I can't promise, but I might be able to suggest someone," Stacy said nonchalantly.

"You give me an estimate in writing and we'll see."

"I didn't mean me. I wasn't trying to drum up business, Miss Bonnie. I was just making conversation."

"Do you paint houses or not?"

"Well, yes. I do. Not usually during the school year, but summertime I occasionally do. I like being outdoors. It depends on the job, of course. I'm not afraid to turn down a job if I can't do it safely. Depends on the customer, too. I won't work for a jerk trying to take advantage of me."

"I don't blame you. You can't be too careful these days. So, are you going to submit an estimate or not? This has to be strictly business."

Stacy stepped off the porch and scanned the two-story house, examining the siding, trim, and shutters. Bonnie was right. It needed painting.

"What color?"

"Yellow siding. White trim and shutters," Bonnie declared. "I changed my mind on what I thought I wanted."

"So, no beige?" She smiled at the small section Bonnie had painted before her fall.

"No. I don't like it after all. Yellow and white. Daffodils and summer clouds. I'll get a couple gallons to start."

"First of all, for the siding you need about three five-gallon buckets of paint to start. It all needs to be boxed, mixed together, so you have a uniform color. And it needs to be exterior eggshell finish. Not too shiny. Not too dull. The trim needs to be exterior too, but semi-gloss."

"Isn't that what I bought?"

"No. You have interior paint. Exterior paint is formulated to combat fading and fight mildew. Each kind is meant to do specific things. They're not interchangeable. The mildicides in exterior paint shouldn't be used indoors."

"I did not know that. Learn something new every day." Bonnie beamed. "You sound like you know what you're doing."

"I've painted a few houses in my time. I painted the Hollingsworths' house up the street." She nodded in that direction.

"You did? I wouldn't have picked that color, but it looks all neat and tidy."

"The customer chooses the color. They have to live with it."

"When you fill out your estimate, put down how much and what kind of paint I should get."

"I'd pick up the paint, Miss Bonnie. I get a contractor's discount."

Bonnie watched expectantly as Stacy surveyed the house one more time.

"Okay, I'll give you a good price, Miss Bonnie. I can't start for five weeks or so, not until the end of the school year. And we need warm temperatures to help dry out the moisture in the siding. I don't want the new paint to bubble and peel."

"Good. I'll tell Ros I've found a painter. She'll be glad to hear it won't be me up on a ladder."

Stacy wasn't so sure Ros would be all that pleased with who Bonnie had hired.

Bonnie finished her sandwich and carried her dishes inside. Stacy followed, mentally calculating just how much paint she'd need.

It was after six when Stacy returned home after shopping for Bonnie's few grocery needs and stopping for some prices at the hardware store. She had dropped her clothes in the hamper and was ready to step in the shower when her phone rang. It was Ros.

"Good evening, Ros," Stacy said, standing naked in the bedroom.

"I hear my aunt hired a housepainter. Is that right?"

"Well, perhaps. She wants to see an estimate in writing. Said she wants it strictly business."

"Have you painted houses before?"

"Yes, I have. Several. Do you need references?"

"No, I don't. But I have to watch out for my aunt's interests. You understand."

"Sure. I understand. I can feed the cat, visit her in the nursing home, shop for her and offer occasional reports on how she's doing, but I'm not qualified to paint her house. Is that it?"

"That's not what I meant. It just came as a surprise that you paint houses for a living. I thought you were a full-time teacher."

"I am. Biology one and two. AP biology. And environmental science. And I'm occasionally the assistant tennis team coach when they need an extra warm body on the court. House painting is a part-time job. Something I sometimes do in the summer."

"So you're qualified?"

"Picasso, I'm not. But I think I can get a coat of yellow paint on your aunt's green house."

"Yellow? She changed her mind again, didn't she?"

"Well, let's just say beige is out. Yellow and white trim are in. But I'm not buying even one gallon until we discuss it again and I have her decision in writing."

"When are you starting? After school is out?"

"Correct. She probably wouldn't like it if I did a little at a time on weekends. And I'd worry she'd change her mind again."

"Agreed. You should wait until it can be done all at once."

"Then I have your permission to submit an estimate to Miss Bonnie?" Stacy asked, as if it was Ros's decision to make.

"Yes." She seemed pleased with the prospect of getting it done and knowing the person doing it.

"Okay then. If you'll excuse me, I'm naked and ready to step in the shower. I think I'll go do that."

"Oh, well. Good night then." Sounding flustered, Ros hung up.

Stacy chuckled to herself as she walked down the hall to the bathroom. Ros had challenged her qualifications, so she couldn't help but try to embarrass her. It seemed to have worked.

CHAPTER ELEVEN

It had been three days since Stacy loaded Bonnie's boxes of attic clutter into the backseat of her pickup truck. It was time to clean it out and either throw it away or donate it somewhere. She carried the boxes into the house, prepared to make at least a cursory search through the contents.

The first box contained old sheets and towels, most threadbare and holey. Bonnie was right. Stacy could use them as rags, especially since she had a house to paint. The next box was filled with newspaper-wrapped dishes, nothing matching and some with chips. A heavy platter was on the bottom of the box. She pulled it out and examined it. It was a vintage china piece with sunflowers around the rim. Stacy assumed it was a Kansas state flower souvenir from one of Bonnie's adventures.

"I think I'll keep this," she said, rubbing her thumb across a smudge. "Miss Bonnie won't mind."

She set the platter aside and rewrapped the rest of the dishes to be donated to the thrift store. The pink chenille bedspread Bonnie was certain Ros didn't want was speckled with tiny holes and mouse droppings. It was destined for the trash, nothing more. Another box contained sweaters and jeans, all well-worn and stained plus a dozen or so pairs of socks with holes in the toes. There was also a disgustingly dirty bed pillow in the box. More trash, she thought, pushing the box aside.

She was tempted to cut short her inspection of the last box, assuming it held nothing more than additional rummage, but she'd give it two minutes. She opened the lid and took out a plastic bag full of bottles of dried-out craft paints and well-worn colored pencils. Under the bag were several craft magazines with missing and ripped pages and three unused canvas boards. This must have been Bonnie's craft supplies, she thought. Everyone has the urge to be creative sometime. The box also contained a pair of wooden drumsticks, several empty diploma-size picture frames, a black bowtie, and a worn brown leather diary with a lock but no key.

"This looks interesting." Stacy fumbled with the lock, trying to open it without damaging the strap, but it was no use. It was locked tight. She wondered if Bonnie really wanted to trash her diary. It looked like it hadn't been opened in years. The metal lock was scuffed and rusted. Stacy suspected it contained secret confessions from Bonnie's past and shouldn't be for public dissemination, but she couldn't bring herself to put it in the trash, not yet. And she certainly wasn't going to give it to the thrift store. She set the diary aside; she would decide later what to do with it. Maybe Bonnie would rethink getting rid of it and wish she had it back.

Stacy headed into town to drop off the items for the thrift store and do an errand or two. She parked on the street and walked two blocks to the flower shop on the corner. The Green Thumb had been in business for many years with only marginal success but when the new owner added kitchen décor and accessories plus one of a kind gift items, it began to thrive. That and the fact the new owner was a wonderfully charismatic woman in her sixties. Meade Carvarian was a fastidious woman with long graying hair that she wore in a bun. She was also known for her outlandish earrings and pale lavender lipstick.

Originally a French-speaking Canadian, she enjoyed the quiet rural life Kansas provided. And she was one of Stacy's closest friends. They shared a love of growing things.

A bell jingled over the door when she opened it. "It's me," Stacy called, assuming Meade was in the back room.

"Good. Make yourself useful. Pick six carnations from the bucket in the cooler. Pink ones."

Stacy opened the walk-in cooler and retrieved the flowers, picking the freshest-looking blooms.

"And three fern sprigs."

Stacy reopened the cooler. "Leather leaf or tree fern?"

"Leather leaf," Meade said, striding into the front of the store as she dried a glass vase with a towel.

"I thought you said flower arrangements should always have odd numbers of blooms." Stacy held the flowers in one hand and the ferns in the other, waiting for Meade to take them.

"When the customer specifically asks for half dozen, I give them six. And what you're talking about is the three bloom rule for bud vases." She arranged the flowers and ferns in the vase, adjusting them just so. She added a satin ribbon and a small card that had already been signed. "There. Now Mr. Gonzales can impress his wife on their anniversary and stay out of the doghouse." She gave the arrangement another tweak.

"And how are you?" Meade turned a smile to Stacy. "I haven't seen you in weeks. Not since you bought those flowers for Miss Bonnie. How is she doing, by the way?"

"She's better. She's home."

"Wow. Already?"

"She thought she was ready, and I guess she talked the doctor into dismissing her."

"Good for her. There's nothing like being in your own home when you're recuperating."

"I guess."

"What's wrong, honey?" Meade gave her a sideways glance.

"Nothing."

"Stacy? What is it? Are you ill?"

"No, I'm fine." Stacy ruffled her fingers across the top of a stack of gift cards.

"Okay. Let's try it this way. Who is it?"

"I have no idea what you mean." Her gaze drifted out the store window.

"The last time you had this faraway lost look you were moonstruck over that woman who wouldn't give you the time of day. McCoy something or other."

"McClure?"

"Yes. McClure. Ros McClure. I remember you were looking at an old yearbook and you said she had a cute smile."

"That's not moonstruck. That's just noticing a pleasant smile."

"It's moonstruck when you keep turning back to that same page over and over and over," Meade said. "I remember you telling me you were pretty sure she was gay." Meade drew a quick breath. "Ros McClure. She's Miss Bonnie's niece, isn't she?"

"Uh-huh," Stacy said, trying to sound nonchalant.

"Does she know you're interested?" Meade asked.

"What? I'm not interested. What makes you think I'm interested?"

"Because your eyes sparkle when you talk about her. That's why."

"They do not." Stacy turned around and stormed out of the door, the bell jingling as she left. Less than a minute later she marched back through the door with the same disgusted look on her face. "I am not interested. I promised to keep an eye on how her aunt's doing. That's all. My contacts with her are merely to inform her how things are going. Nothing more."

"Contacts, huh? So she doesn't know you're interested." Meade pulled a mischievous grin.

"Will you stop saying that? I am not interested. Besides, she doesn't like me nor little hick towns like this. She has no intention of moving back to Colby. She was here because of her aunt's accident. That's all."

"When are you going to tell her you're interested?" Meade had a devilish look in her eyes as she continued to needle her.

"You are a mean, vindictive woman you know," Stacy grumbled. "Why do I bother coming in here anyway?"

"Because you want to confess your feelings to someone and have them agree with you."

"When have I ever needed someone to agree with me about relationships?" Stacy offered.

"You haven't been in a relationship in forever. And you don't want to screw this one up. Before you say anything, ours doesn't count. It was ten years ago and only lasted a few months. It wasn't a real relationship. We were both lonely, that's all. Not that I minded," Meade said, bumping Stacy playfully. "You need a real relationship. And if you like this woman, tell her. What are you waiting for? You're fifty-four."

"Fifty-three."

"Okay, fifty-three. It's time."

"She doesn't like me."

"Has she ever told you that?" Meade asked.

"She told me to stay out of her family business."

"But she's corresponding with you regarding her aunt. She could have done that herself through the nursing home."

"There's probably going to be a lot more correspondence now. I agreed to paint her aunt's house."

"When in the world are you going to find the time to do that?"

"After school's out this summer."

"Uh-huh, uh-huh. You took the painting job so you could have contact with Miss Bonnie's niece. Very clever."

"I didn't do it for that reason. I was afraid Miss Bonnie would try painting it again herself, and we know what kind of disaster that caused."

"You are not the only brush-toting house painter in Thomas County. You may not realize it, but subconsciously you took the job so you could keep in touch with Ms. McClure. And you came in here so I could encourage you to do that."

"I came in here to ask if you'd be my date to the class reunion in June. I understand you're doing the flower arrangements and centerpieces so the superintendent thought it would be nice for you to be one of the guests."

"That's nice of him. Yes, I'd love to go."

"No more needling or I take back my invitation."

"Agreed. I saw the picture in the newspaper of the high school class twenty–five years ago. Nice looking bunch of kids. And I noticed Ms. McClure was in that picture. So she'll be there?"

"I don't think so. She said she was too busy to attend."

"Maybe she'll change her mind. You come see me if you want to give her a sweet little bouquet of flowers when she comes to town. I'll make something special."

"No special bouquet and no coming to town."

"You never know. Twenty-five years is a significant milestone for a small-town group of kids."

"I'm ignoring you. Do you want chicken, pasta, or catfish at the dinner?"

"Is it Arnold Reading's catfish?"

"I have no idea. All I know is I'm supposed to get your menu choice before the end of the month."

"What are you having?"

"Chicken," Stacy said without hesitation.

"What the heck. I'll chance it. Catfish. Who would want pasta when you could have chicken or catfish?"

"I'm guessing vegetarians."

"In farm and pond country?" Meade rolled her eyes. "What do you think Ms. McClure would choose?"

"Heck if I know. She's not coming anyway."

"Don't be so negative. I have a feeling things might change for you. You never know."

Stacy left Meade's shop muttering to herself, wondering how the conversation got so skewed away from a dinner invitation and toward Ros McClure. Not that she minded, but it was frustrating how Meade had drawn a bead on the topic so perfectly. Of course, she was interested. How could she not be? She had been since the gorgeous teenager first walked into her classroom over twenty-six years ago. Even though Ros had been eighteen at the time, it was unthinkable for a teacher to acknowledge an interest in a high school student, even to herself. It was a secret Stacy would take to her grave.

CHAPTER TWELVE

"How's your aunt?" a woman asked from the doorway to Ros's office. An attractive fifty-something blonde in a well-fitting bright red suit, she stood in four-inch black patent high heels with rhinestone buckles on the toes. Her makeup was tasteful and flawless.

"Much better, Sue. She's home and behaving herself, I hope."

"Good. Glad to hear it. Second question. How many weeks has it been?" she asked with a smile that suggested she knew Ros more than just professionally.

"Let's see." Ros gave a quick reflective thought. "Six weeks and four days. And the last time you asked me that same question was three weeks and two days before that."

"Right. Six weeks and four days and that's long enough, don't you think?"

"Depends on the situation. Six weeks and four days between colds isn't nearly long enough."

"How about between dinner dates? And remember, I'm known for making reservations before inviting you out."

"A reservation, eh? I assume it's not at Skyline Chili for a three-way and fries."

"Does Skyline take reservations?" the woman teased. "Talk about your cheap date."

"No, Sue. Skyline does not take reservations unless you're having a birthday party for a raft of six-year-olds." Ros folded her hands across her desk and looked up with a smile. "So where are we going to dinner and when?"

"I'm taking you to The Melting Pot on Montgomery Road."

"Wow, The Melting Pot. Fancy."

"I decided I owed it to myself. It's my birthday."

"It's not your birthday. Your birthday is in November. I happen to know because last year we went to the zoo to see the baby gorilla and it snowed."

"My other birthday. Fifteen years sober," she said proudly. "And with God's help there'll be fifteen more. Actually it was last Wednesday, but I had meetings all week and today is my first free evening."

"Does the university know how lucky they are to have a dean of student services as dedicated as you?"

"They will after tonight. I'm billing this dinner to my expense account. We can talk shop for three minutes and call it work-related." Sue winked.

"How about I pay for my dinner? You write off yours?" Sue was already shaking her head before she finished.

"Absolutely not. Now, I have a meeting. I'll meet you at seven at the restaurant? How does that sound?"

"Sounds good to me."

Sue started to leave, then looked back.

"How about I pick you up at your place at seven?" There was a glint in her eye.

"Okay." Ros had a pretty good idea what that look meant. She and Sue were good friends. A few times over the years their friendship had been more than platonic. Neither had a partner or the time for a fulltime commitment. They knew their relationship wasn't destined to be a permanent partnership either. But occasional intimacy wasn't out of the question.

Ros returned to work, but with a dinner date looming in her evening plans she couldn't help but smile. Sue was right. It had been over six weeks since she had a date with anyone. It was before Carla's retirement and before her emergency trip to Colby. A little social life couldn't hurt. She had started an email when she burst out laughing. Colby, Kansas, didn't have any restaurant that was even close to The Melting Pot. A steak and barbecue place out by the interstate was about as high class as it got. The food was good and the service was friendly, but it wasn't The Melting Pot. She couldn't help visualize Sue walking into JoJo's in her bright red suit and stabbing a peanut shell off the floor with her stiletto heels. And she couldn't help wonder what kind of looks Sue would attract from Stacy Hagen.

Sue was a few minutes late, but that was normal.

"Wow oh wow," she said as Ros climbed in the car. "You look good. I like that sweater. Blue is definitely your color. Although you look good in every color." She allowed her hand to fall onto Ros's knee. "Except green. I don't like women in green. Detracts from their gorgeous looks."

"Thank you. I'll remember not to wear my forest green pantssuit to work if we're scheduled to have a meeting."

"Are you ready for The Melting Pot? I looked over the menu online and they've got some choices I haven't tried before. Are you game?"

"Hey, you order it. I'll eat it, probably."

They talked and laughed all the way to the restaurant. Sue was a good conversationalist. She knew how to keep Ros engaged and interested in whatever the topic was. Dinner took almost two hours to work through the cheese, meat, and dessert fondues with lots of time for catching up on each other's private lives.

"We've talked about everything else under the sun tonight. Can I ask you a personal question since you don't seem to want to offer an explanation?" Sue asked as she sipped her after-dinner coffee.

"Sure. And yes, we always gossip like a couple of seventh graders at these dinners."

"What's wrong? I sense it has something to do with your aunt since you've avoided that subject like the plague."

"My aunt? No, there's nothing wrong. She's out of the rehab center and home. She didn't want to go there, but what choice did I have? I can't be there as her full-time caregiver. Visiting nurses will help her for a few weeks. She'll be good as new before you know it."

Sue cocked her head as if she didn't believe her.

"She will," Ros insisted. "The doctor said other than the broken shoulder she's in surprisingly good health."

"Then why do I feel like you're concealing something?"

Ros released a long slow breath.

"Dementia, Sue. The doctor said he strongly suspects my aunt has the early symptoms of dementia. Nothing dramatic, yet, but still. That word is about as disturbing as the word cancer. Maybe worse. Some cancers are curable these days. Dementia is not."

"Oh, honey." Sue reached across the table and squeezed Ros's hand.

Ros couldn't help it. Tears pooled in her eyes. She discreetly dabbed at them with her napkin, but that only brought on more.

"Honey," Sue cooed. She slipped out of her seat and into the booth next to Ros, wrapping an arm around her. "It'll be okay. If the doctor said early symptoms it could be years and years before you notice any drastic changes. Maybe you never will."

"That's the problem. I think I already have. Nothing major but little things. Little hints that things are changing."

"She still knows you, doesn't she?"

"Yes. But that's a more advanced symptom."

Sue noticed they had attracted attention from nearby customers.

"Come on. Let's go. We'll talk about this at home."

The ride to Ros's house was eerily quiet. Both women seemed to be mulling over what they would say and how they would discuss Bonnie's dementia. Sue followed Ros inside and excused herself to use the restroom. When she returned to the living room, she had a concerned look on her face.

"Are you worried you'll need to bring Bonnie here to live with you?"

"It's crossed my mind."

"Not now, of course."

"No, but perhaps someday. Who knows how long it will be before she can't live on her own."

"You mentioned something about a high school reunion. I think you should seriously consider going. I know, I know, you don't want to go but it could give you a baseline for her condition now. When did you say it was? June? I think you need to go and see how she is doing. That way you'll be able to recognize any changes that occur in the future. See how she has changed since you lived with her all those years ago. Maybe you won't notice anything different. But aren't you at least curious if she can still do all the things she's always done for herself? Go shopping. Go out to eat with her friends and still find her way home? My father couldn't," Sue confessed.

"Your father has dementia? I didn't know that."

"Had. He's been gone a long time. It was a blessing. He didn't remember his grandkids or his own address. In the end he couldn't remember how to tie his shoes."

"You never mentioned it. I'm so sorry, Sue."

She shrugged and added, "He got to be more of my child than my father. His was diagnosed as Alzheimer's, the specific type of dementia. I wish I had known more in the beginning. Known what to expect. I think you should go. Reassure yourself, Ros. You have vacation time. Don't tell me you don't. You never take more than a few days each summer, and that's so you can attend conferences. How long were you gone when your aunt was in the hospital last month? Three days? Four days? With all the commotion going on in your department, I think a vacation is a great idea. Let things settle. You never know. The university may realize what they did when Carla retired was wrong." Sue sat down on the couch next to Ros. "Aren't you curious about your aunt?"

"Of course. But she'll suspect something is wrong if I just show up."

"Reunion, kiddo. You're going to your high school class reunion. No one needs to know differently."

"Do you think I'd get much static from the university if I took my vacation in June? I'm not sure Steve is ready to handle things on his own."

"You are entitled to your vacation. If Steve can't handle things, the university needs to know that. You've got six coworkers who can step up and do their fair share. You don't need to be burdened with the whole enchilada. What do you say, Ros? Do you see a vacation in your future?" she said with a confident smile.

Ros thought a minute.

"Yes. I think I do. I appreciate your support and understanding, Sue."

"My pleasure, sweetheart." Sue kissed Ros gently on the cheek then stood and crossed to the door. "I'm going to go home now and let you contemplate your vacation plans. I have a feeling anything else we thought might happen this evening, your heart wouldn't be in it." She blew Ros a kiss before leaving.

Ros followed her out onto the porch and watched as she drove away. Sue was right. Her heart wouldn't have been in it and for several reasons she didn't fully understand herself.

She spent the next thirty minutes getting ready for bed and contemplating attending the reunion. She could list several reasons not to go. Surprisingly there was more than one compelling reason supporting the venture. Bonnie wasn't the only person beckoning her back to Colby. Though she had no idea why Stacy Hagen had anything to do with it.

Is my name still on the list for the reunion dinner?

Ros tapped out the text and sent it on its way, then snuggled down in bed expecting to receive a reply in the morning but her phone rang almost immediately.

"You're coming?!" Meredith squealed. "No, it's not too late and even if it was, I'd make room for you. And you've contacted the right person. Somehow the reservation list has fallen to me. That'll teach me to open my big mouth and make suggestions. But I'm excited that you've decided to come. What made you change your mind? Actually, I don't care. I'm just excited you'll be here. It'll be like old times. First things first. You'll be at the head table as a class officer so are you a plus one? And do you want chicken breast, fried catfish, or pasta primavera?" Meredith asked, chattering away.

"I need to decide that now?"

"Yes. Let's get the details out of the way then we can talk."

"Okay, no, I'm not a plus one. And how about the pasta primavera. That sounds good."

"I took you for a catfish person. Are you a vegetarian now?"

"No, I'm not a vegetarian, but primavera sounds like a nice colorful alternative to a heavy meal, especially in the hot summertime. The last time I had catfish it was what I caught in my aunt's pond. I don't care for the muddy taste."

"The Cooper Barn is air-conditioned. A cavernous venue but air-conditioned."

"That's where they're having the dinner?"

"The committee decided they wanted a dance floor and it's the only place big enough to accommodate classmates and their spouses at a sit-down dinner plus a band and dancing. And so you know, Larry is on the list of attendees, he and his wife."

"Larry Collins?" Ros asked without much interest.

"Yes."

"Good for him. I hold no grudges."

"Don't say I didn't warn you."

"Not a problem."

"You'll be at the head table with Coach Hagen and her date. That won't be a problem either, will it?"

"Nope. Why would you think it might be a problem?" Ros wondered who Stacy Hagen was dating. She hadn't noticed Stacy wearing a wedding band and she hadn't mentioned a spouse, but for all Ros knew she could have a partner. It might be interesting to know who she considered an acceptable companion. Femme? Possibly. Whoever it was, Ros had no reason not to be polite.

"I wanted to let you know. That's all."

"We discussed it and came to an agreement. She promised not to mention my high school biology grade and I promised not to be frustrated about it so I see no issue. She helped with my aunt when I wasn't available and I appreciated that. End of story. How about changing the subject? Who is your plus one for the reunion? Anyone I know?"

"I'm not a plus one either," Meredith replied after a moment for contemplation. "We can be each other's plus one. How's that? We need an even number at the head table."

"That's fine, although I still don't know why I'm head table material."

"Not only were you class treasurer, you will be the only class officer in attendance. Even Mikala isn't coming. She said she'll be with her grandkids in Disney World that week. Counting classmates, spouses, teachers, and administrators, we're down to about sixty people. That's pretty bad. Oh, damn. I gotta go, hon. My dog dumped over the trash and is digging in it. Talk with you again soon. I'm so glad you're coming. Bye."

Meredith hung up, leaving Ros with things to think about, not the least of which was Stacy Hagen and her date. She wondered why she felt the need to dwell on it. She had two and a half weeks to put it out of her mind before she arrived in Colby.

CHAPTER THIRTEEN

Ros spent the last week before her trip catching up on details at work, making sure everything was ready to hand off to whomever Steve assigned to take her place. He'd grumbled at the news she'd be out of town for two weeks but seemed relieved to know she would have her laptop and cell phone handy in case an emergency arose, something Ros prayed wouldn't happen but was prepared to handle if it did.

"I'm leaving early in the morning, Aunt Bonnie. I may drive through some dead zones so don't worry if you can't reach me," Ros said as she dropped a few last things in her suitcase.

She'd resigned herself to the thousand-mile road trip to Colby. It would take two days and a night in a hotel, but it was cheaper than flying into Denver and renting a car. She didn't mind the drive. She'd pop an audio book in the CD player and be there before she knew it.

"Drive carefully, dear. Don't be going over the speed limit, you hear me? Wear your seat belt and don't pick up any hitchhikers."

"Yes, Aunt Bonnie." It wouldn't be a road trip without Bonnie's warnings. There was no need to complain about them. She knew it was her way of saying "I love you and want to keep you safe."

"I've got your room all ready for you. Clean sheets and I've kept Piano out of there. She likes to sleep on your bed, but she leaves it covered with cat fur."

"I don't mind. I packed a lint roller." Ros knew any house with a long-haired cat was a house with cat fur stuck to everything. She packed her blacks slacks anyway.

Ros was on the road by six o'clock, rolling toward Indianapolis before she stopped for breakfast. The overcast skies and moderate temperatures made for perfect midweek driving conditions. She made periodic stops for food, gas, and to stretch her legs. It was after seven when she pulled off the interstate in Columbia, Missouri, and checked into her hotel. She ate dinner in the hotel restaurant, showered, and sent Bonnie a text before crawling into bed. In spite of the long day of car motion she fell asleep almost immediately, surprising herself.

The next day started even earlier. Ros wanted to be at Bonnie's as early in the afternoon as possible, knowing her aunt would be pacing and wringing her hands in anticipation. She hoped to be in the driveway and waving hello by four o'clock.

A midday rainstorm decreed differently, slowing her progress. Wind whipped across the Kansas prairie at the car, and driving rain made the windshield wipers work overtime. The smart decision would have been to pull off at a rest stop, call Bonnie to let her know, and wait out the rain. But she wanted to get to Colby; there were only fifty miles to go. This wasn't the first summer rainstorm she had driven through, and it probably wouldn't be the last. Leisurely cruising the interstate next to golden wheat fields, this was not. She turned the wipers on high, slowed to twenty-five miles an hour, and kept a firm hand on the steering wheel. Slow and steady, she told herself as a trucker determined to get where he was going in a hurry blew past, throwing up a curtain of rain.

"A-hole," she muttered.

It was still raining lightly when she turned into Bonnie's driveway and circled up to the porch. As she suspected, Bonnie was standing at the door. She rushed out to greet her as soon as she pulled to a stop.

"Hello, dear," she said, hurrying down the front steps, her arms wide for a hug. "It's so good to have you home." She could hardly wait for Ros to climb out and stretch her legs before wrapping her in a bear hug.

"Hello, Aunt Bonnie. It's good to be back."

"I was worried. We had a terrible storm earlier. Wind and hail. It didn't last long, but it sure was noisy. I'm glad you're finally home safe." She didn't seem to notice or didn't mind that they were standing in the rain.

"Let's go inside. I'll unload the car later."

"I've got everything ready to make us a grilled cheese sandwich for dinner," Bonnie said, locking her arm through Ros's as they walked up the steps. "You've got to be starving. I made chocolate pudding for dessert. Your favorite."

Just like old times, Ros thought. Bonnie hadn't forgotten. Her memory was still intact and functioning.

"You go wash your hands and I'll get things started." She kissed Ros on the cheek and headed for the kitchen. A few minutes to relax and get her bearings would have been nice, but it was dinnertime. She would relax later.

Bonnie chattered away all through dinner, which they ate on TV trays in the living room with the Weather Channel on mute. She explained how wonderful it was to be out of the nursing home and how well her physical therapy was going but how her shoulder occasionally ached so—all things she had relayed in numerous phone conversations over the past few weeks. Ros helped wash the dishes, including the heavy cast iron skillet Bonnie proudly kept on the back burner of the stove.

Ros was finally able to unload the car between rain showers. She was exhausted from her long day of driving and would have loved to be excused to go to bed, but Bonnie insisted they sit in the porch swing to enjoy their dishes of chocolate pudding and the fresh smell after the rain. She couldn't say no. Bonnie seemed to have been anticipating her arrival for days and was happy and relieved to have her back in Colby.

"Are you going to the reunion, dear?"

"Yes, Aunt Bonnie. Remember, I told you that's why I'm here. It's this coming Saturday."

"Oh, yes. I remember. Are they having it at the school?"

"No, at the Cooper Barn."

"That's a nice place for a party. Lots of folks have their weddings out there. When is it again? Friday?"

"Saturday." Ros wasn't prepared for that. But they had talked about so many things she could understand how that detail had slipped Bonnie's mind.

"Did I tell you I hired someone to paint the house?" Bonnie offered as if she needed to change the subject.

"Yes. You mentioned it. Stacy Hagen, right?"

Bonnie gazed off into space a moment, then nodded and headed inside with her dish. Ros followed, ready to call it a day and hoping Bonnie was too.

"I think I'll go on upstairs, Aunt Bonnie. I'm tired. It's been a long day."

"Don't you want some more pudding? It's homemade."

"No, I'm stuffed. It was delicious, though."

"Okay, you go on up. I'll be along shortly."

Ros kissed Bonnie good night and went up the stairs. She heard Bonnie rattling around in the kitchen for over an hour before she turned out the lights and came up. She could tell when Bonnie was climbing the stairs. She smiled when the third step from the top squeaked when she stepped on it. It had always been a comforting sound to her, telling her she wasn't alone in the house.

"How did you sleep?" Bonnie asked as Ros came into the kitchen the next morning.

"Wonderfully. I don't remember that bed being so comfortable." Ros poured herself a cup of coffee.

"That's because it's new. I got you a new mattress last week."

"You didn't have to do that. I could have slept on the old one. I slept on it when I was here two months ago and it was fine."

"I got myself a new one too," she said with a kind smile. "Abraham's Furniture Store was having a bedding sale. I'd been meaning to replace mine for years. When you can save fifty percent, it's time to buy, buy, buy."

"I guess. It's very comfortable."

"Do you have any plans for today?" Bonnie handed her a piece of freshly buttered toast.

"Unpack." She stirred extra milk into her coffee, something Bonnie always made on the strong side. "Is there anything I can do for you?"

"Yes," she said immediately as if she had been waiting for the opportunity to bring it up. "If I show you where, could you plant those for me?" She pointed to two vigorously blooming pink plants sitting on the kitchen table. "Those azaleas need to go in the garden. They're getting pot-bound. The Women's Auxiliary sent me one and Judith sent the other. Aren't they beautiful?" Bonnie read the little cards. "Elizabeth sent this one. Not the Auxiliary."

"They're lovely. Yes, I'd be happy to plant them for you. How hard can it be? Grab a shovel, dig a hole, drop them in," Ros teased. She knew her aunt was very fussy about her garden and what she put in it.

"I've got some organic fertilizer I want to mix in with the soil. Don't overwater them. We had enough rain to keep the soil moist for now."

"I'll plant them. You can water them. Where's the shovel? In the barn?"

Bonnie showed Ros where she wanted them planted, how deep, and how much fertilizer to add before going into town for her hair appointment.

"I'll be back," Bonnie called as she headed out the back door. Piano followed as far as the back porch.

Ros went upstairs to change into gardening clothes, a pair of older jeans that she didn't care if she got dirty. When she stepped out onto the porch, ready to retrieve a shovel from the barn, she noticed Stacy's truck pulling into the drive. She had a surprised look on her face as she climbed out.

"Ros, what are you doing here?" she asked, seemingly frozen in place.

"Visiting my aunt. And going to the reunion."

"Really? You didn't mention you were coming." Stacy was wearing faded jeans, worn cowboy boots, and a paint-splattered gray T-shirt as well as dark sunglasses.

"I decided it was something I wanted to do. You only have one twenty-five-year class reunion."

"True."

"What are you doing here? My aunt isn't home. She had an appointment to have her hair cut."

"I told her I was coming by today to check on what I'd need to bring over to start painting tomorrow. She said she has a couple of ladders. I want to see how tall they are. I'll need a stepladder for the porch ceiling. That's where Miss Bonnie got into trouble. She tried to use her extension ladder instead of a stepladder on the porch trim. She got her center of gravity off balance."

"I assume they're in the barn. Everything else like that is. All her tools and equipment are. At least I hope that's where I'll find a shovel."

Stacy lifted the first of three buckets of paint out of the back of the truck. "I'm going to leave these here. If it warms up enough and doesn't rain anymore today, I'll start first thing in the morning. I'll start on the porch. It'll be dry."

Stacy carried one of the heavy buckets of paint toward the barn while Ros went inside to fetch the azaleas to be planted.

"Don't go in the barn," Stacy said as she hurried past on her way to her truck. "And don't open the door."

"Why?"

Stacy opened a toolbox and began rummaging inside, first on one side then the other.

"If the door's off the hinges again I can go in the side door." Ros started for the far side of the barn.

"Don't go in there!" Stacy said adamantly. "For once, just listen and do as you're told."

"I beg your pardon?"

Stacy pulled a small revolver from the toolbox. She removed the trigger lock, checked the cylinder, then headed for the barn.

"What are you going to do with that?" Ros demanded. "I really don't approve of guns."

"I don't either in most circumstances, but I approve of snakes even less."

"Where?" Ros took several quick steps backward. "There's a snake in my aunt's barn?"

"Snakes." Stacy unlatched the barn door and opened it a crack, the gun at her side. "Why don't you go wait on the porch?"

"What kind of snakes?" Ros had no idea why she asked. It didn't matter. She hated them all.

"*Crotalus atrox*," she said as she peered around the edge of the door.

"A *Crotalus* what?"

"*Crotalus atrox*. A western diamond-backed rattlesnake."

"Are they poisonous?"

"Very."

"You're really going to shoot them? Maybe they're passing through and will be gone in a few days."

"You wanna shoot them?"

"Well, no." Ros backed up a little more.

"They only consume warm-blooded prey. Mice and rats. Small rodents, like the ones living in Miss Bonnie's barn and feasting on the dozen bags of birdseed she has stored in here. I'm surprised this particular species is this far north instead of where they belong in Oklahoma, but they are in no hurry to leave. Now go stand over there and stop asking questions."

"Will you please stop treating me like a child?"

"Just move over there and let me handle this." Stacy opened the door wide enough to quietly slip inside.

"Be careful," Ros called, not sure what else she could offer. A moment later she heard a bang, then another and two more. She flinched. She assumed the gunfire was finished when she heard another muffled blast.

"Are you okay?" There was no reply. "Stacy?" Still nothing. "Oh, my God. She tripped over a hay bale and shot herself," she muttered nervously. "Stacy!" she shouted. "Stacy, can you hear me? Are you all right? Do I need to call for assistance?" Ros stepped closer, her fear throttled by her concern Stacy hadn't replied. "Should I call 911?"

As Ros reached for the latch, the door flew open and Stacy stepped out carrying two snakes by the tail, one in each hand. Both were nearly four feet long. And both had bloody holes in their heads. The pistol was stuffed in the waist of her jeans.

"I don't think 911 can do anything for these guys. Even CPR wouldn't help." Stacy held up the grizzled-looking snakes. Drops of blood puddled in the dirt.

"Oh, gross." Ros curled her lip.

"From that look I'm assuming you don't want these."

"No, thank you."

"Rattlesnake makes for good eatin'!" Stacy thrust them toward Ros, obviously teasing her.

"Please, help yourself. Enjoy." Ros turned her head and swallowed hard at the thought.

"You're sure?"

"Do I strike you as a snake eater?"

"You grew up in western Kansas. I assumed you might have tried some of our more exotic delicacies. Rabbit. Squirrel. Pheasant. Prairie oysters."

"No. No. No and definitely no. The most wild and exotic thing I remember eating was lamb chops."

"Lamb chops aren't wild or exotic. Just the opposite." Stacy headed for her truck with her trophies.

"Are you really going to eat those?"

Stacy chuckled and said, "No. I don't care for rattlesnake. It's tough and has lots of little bones. But barbecued frog legs. Now there's a treat."

"Well, you can have mine."

"That's what they're serving at the reunion dinner."

"They are not," Ros argued. "It's pasta, catfish, or chicken. Meredith already asked me my choice."

"I bet you picked chicken, right?"

"As a matter of fact, I chose the pasta primavera."

"No exotic meat in that," Stacy said as she reattached the lock to the trigger and returned the revolver to the toolbox.

"I think it's possible to live in Kansas without eating exotic food."

"Sure, it is. You can live in the big city and not eat that stuff either." Stacy went back to the job of carrying another bucket of paint into the barn. She returned with a shovel and handed it to Ros since she hadn't made a move to retrieve one herself.

"Thank you."

"I'd suggest your aunt store those bags of bird seed in a sealed container. Something that discourages rodents and the snakes that eat them."

"I'll get something to put them in. I'd rather she doesn't know about the gun and the snakes."

"Why? It's her barn," Stacy said, lifting the last bucket out of the truck.

"Let's just say she doesn't need that on her plate right now. Please don't mention it."

"If that's what you want, consider it a done deal."

When Stacy returned from the barn, she had a concerned look on her face. "Is there something else going on with Miss Bonnie? I know I shouldn't be asking, but you said there was something you'd explain later. Something about when she was discharged from the nursing home. Is she ill?"

"No. She's not ill exactly."

Stacy stared at her curiously.

"Okay, what I'm going to tell you I do because you have been very kind to my aunt and for that reason you have a right to know. But it has to go no further than this conversation. Promise?"

"I'm listening."

"When you called to tell me my aunt was being discharged, I immediately called her doctor and asked if he really thought she was ready to go home and be on her own. I explained I couldn't be here to take care of her. He said in her condition, being in her own home, in her own surroundings, was the best thing for her."

"'Her condition'?" Stacy asked.

"That's what I said. He assumed I was aware of my aunt's dementia. He said seniors in the early stages of dementia are more confused and agitated when they aren't in their own environment. That's why they try to get patients home as soon as safely possible."

"Dementia?" Stacy scowled in disbelief.

"Dr. Smithton said she is demonstrating some symptoms. She has shown poor judgment at times. She's occasionally disoriented and forgetful, especially in the evening. They call it sundowning. The problem seems to be exacerbated more so late in the day."

"Wow. I noticed a couple little things in her behavior, but I assumed that's Miss Bonnie's way."

"My aunt isn't to know this, but that's why I'm here. I want to see how she is doing. I want to know what she can and can't do for herself. I told her I was coming to the reunion so she wouldn't suspect anything unusual. She is very perceptive. She may occasionally be forgetful but she is still very perceptive. Dr. Smithton said she understands her diagnosis. I wanted to be here and see for myself. Establish a baseline, so to speak."

"I can understand that. See how she is now so you have a comparison for the future. Disease progression assessment."

"Yes. Exactly. But she can't know. I don't want to worry her. She may only be my aunt but she is my family. If she has to come live with me, so be it."

"I can't imagine Miss Bonnie would give up her independence kindly."

"I agree. Hopefully it won't come to that. The early symptoms could go on for years without interfering with her ability to live on her own. She's lived in this house in this town for decades. She's used to it. It's familiar surroundings."

"I appreciate you telling me. I want you to know I'm here for Miss Bonnie. And for you." Stacy placed a soothing hand on Ros's shoulder. "If you need anything, I want you to know you can call, day or night."

"Thank you. Given all you've done for her, I thought you needed to know what's going on."

"Thank you for including me. Remember I told you about being a concerned neighbor for Miss Bonnie. It goes for you, too. Neighbors supporting neighbors."

"Good. Now, I'm going to plant my aunt's azaleas and hope I don't kill them."

"I'll be here in the morning to start painting, if that's okay with you?"

"Absolutely. My aunt hired you to paint the house, so paint it. She'd really suspect something was askew if those plans got changed."

Stacy climbed in the truck, slammed the door, and put the window down. "And so you know, I'm not taking Miss Bonnie's money. I haven't told her, but this job is, as they say, on the house."

Ros laughed out loud.

"That will never fly. My aunt won't let you do that. She'll insist on paying you. You don't need to worry about her being able to afford it. She can, many times over."

"We'll see," Stacy added as she started the engine and pulled out of the drive.

CHAPTER FOURTEEN

Stacy was standing in the yard, washing out her paintbrushes and roller when Ros returned from errands and the grocery store.

"Looking good," she said as she carried the first armload of sacks in the house. "Is that two coats?"

"Nope. Just one. Good quality paint doesn't require two coats."

Bonnie was watching from the swing. Piano was at her side, purring contentedly.

"I don't remember that color looking like that," Bonnie said as she cocked her head slightly.

"It's always a little darker when it's wet. I think you'll like it once it's finished and dry," Stacy replied, tossing an exasperated look at Ros.

Bonnie followed Ros inside to help unpack the groceries. When Ros returned for the second load, Stacy whispered in her direction, "If she changes her mind on what color she wants, I'm going to scream."

"Ignore her and carry on. I think it looks nice."

"I tried to explain I needed to do the caulking first, but she wanted to have at least some of the exterior painted. I'll finish the caulking in the morning before the reunion. I need it to dry completely."

"You're the paint pro. You do what you think is best. She'll understand. She has always accepted advice from those in the know."

"Normally I don't paint on Sunday. I allow folks to go to church or have a quiet day without a lot of mess and fuss. But I think Miss Bonnie might be more comfortable with me working so she can see progress."

"Whatever you think is best. If you need a day off, I'll explain it to her." Ros headed in the house with the last of the groceries.

"Did you get butter?" Bonnie asked as she unloaded the last sack.

"You already have two pounds of butter. I didn't think you needed any more just yet."

"Are you sure?" Bonnie opened the refrigerator and scanned the contents.

Stacy came into the kitchen, drying her hands on a rag.

"Miss Bonnie, I'll be back in the morning to finish caulking the windows on the back of the house."

"Do you want to come for breakfast?" Bonnie asked. "I'm making biscuits and gravy."

"Thank you but no. I usually have an apple or a handful of berries. I can't work on a heavy breakfast."

"Me either," Ros mumbled to herself.

"Did you get berries, Ros?" Bonnie asked.

"You didn't have them on the list, so no, I didn't."

"Stacy likes berries for breakfast."

"Miss Bonnie, don't worry about it. I have some in my fridge. I'll have breakfast at home."

"If you change your mind, Ros can run to the store for you."

Ros stared blankly at Stacy as if to say "please don't."

"If you're not coming to breakfast, how about dinner tonight? I'm making tuna casserole, one of Ros's favorites. Right?"

"Comfort food," Ros said as she stacked the canned goods in the pantry.

"It's Agnes Castro's recipe. Potato chips and parmesan cheese on top."

"Sounds wonderful, but I'm giving a tennis lesson in an hour. I better get home and shower. I'll see you in the morning." Stacy nodded for Ros to follow her outside, leaving Bonnie to sort the groceries.

"How's it going?" Stacy asked once they were safely outside.

"Fine. No problems." Ros wasn't sure what she was expecting. It had only been a few days.

"Here I go again sticking my nose in your business, but while you were gone today Miss Bonnie said something about getting lost."

"Lost? Where? Here in town?"

"Evidently she was trying to find some church her great-grandfather built. She drove around backcountry roads for hours but couldn't find it. She was almost in tears about it. First she couldn't find the old church, then she couldn't find her way home. I wondered if she said anything to you about it."

"No, she didn't. When was this?"

"A couple days before you got here. She wanted to be able to show you."

"I've heard the stories about it, but I've never seen it. He was some kind of Civil War hero and was a minister. He built this church outside some teeny-tiny farm town in northern Kansas back in the late 1800s."

"Well, just so you know, she's going to try again to find it. She didn't say when, but it's on her mind."

"Oh, good grief." Ros heaved a sigh.

"Sorry to bring it up. I thought you should know. I sound like a tattletale."

"I'm glad you did. I won't mention your name, but I'll see what she says."

"Do you know the name of the church or the town?" Stacy asked.

"I'm not sure. If she remembers I can look it up online."

"There's one over in Rook County. It's small and made of white stone. It's right across the road from a cemetery. I don't think the church is used much anymore, but the cemetery is."

"It could be. She mentioned a cemetery where some of her distant relatives are buried."

"The one I'm talking about is the Ash Rock Church outside Woodston, Kansas," Stacy said. "Definitely off the beaten track. I can see how she got lost."

"Woodston?" Ros asked, trying to remember if she knew where that was. "Maybe I should take her to find it so she doesn't go alone."

"Probably a good idea."

"It might be interesting to see a piece of family history."

Stacy headed home and Ros went back inside, deciding when would be a good time to mention an excursion to find the church. Not today. And not tomorrow. Saturday was reunion day and she didn't want to worry about Bonnie roaming the countryside on a quest while she was having dinner at a party. Next week maybe.

* * *

Ros's phone was ringing when she stepped out of the shower the following morning. She wrapped a towel around herself and hurried into the bedroom to answer it. It was Meredith.

"Good morning, Ros. Did I wake you?"

"No, I was up."

"It's going to be a gorgeous day for the reunion. I'm so excited."

"Yes, I've got the windows open and there's a pleasant breeze." Ros patted herself dry and ruffled her hands through her wet hair as she balanced her phone under her chin.

"Ros, I'm sorry to ask at the last minute, but I desperately need your help."

"What can I do?"

"The decoration committee, namely Meg Wilson, didn't get the table favors put out and she can't be there until right before the dinner starts. She's going to some family thing over in Goodland. I hate to ask, but is there any chance you could help me get these things out? We spent the money on them. We might as well use them."

"What are they, if I may ask?"

"Typical stuff. Pens, coasters, travel cup, earbuds, hand sanitizer, lip balm, shot glass, luggage tag, key ring. Everything with our twenty-five year class reunion logo on it."

"Wow, that's a lot of stuff."

"Which is why I need help, hon. Please," Meredith whined childishly. "It should only take us an hour or so."

"Sure. Why not? What time do you want me to meet you?"

"When can you be ready?"

"Can I have thirty minutes?"

"Why don't I come pick you up? It's the least I can do since you're helping."

"Okay. I'll be ready."

"Thirty minutes," Meredith said, then ended the call.

Ros dressed in her underwear and bra, then went into the bathroom to blow dry her hair and shave her legs. That way she'd be ready for tonight even if she had to come home and change. She hadn't decided which outfit to wear anyway. How dressy was this event supposed to be? Slacks and top? Dressy suit? She had a feeling there would be a wide range of what people thought was appropriate.

"Aunt Bonnie?" Ros called from the top of the stairs when she realized she had forgotten to pack a razor.

"Yes, dear?" Bonnie replied from somewhere downstairs.

"Do you happen to have an extra razor? I forgot to pack one."

"Sure. Under the sink, blue plastic tub. Help yourself. There's toothbrushes and toothpaste in there too if you need them."

"Just a razor. Thanks."

Sure enough, like always, Bonnie had a stockpile of surplus toiletries. Ros sat down on the edge of the tub and applied a thin layer of lotion. This was a ritual she had endured since junior high school. Bonnie had jokingly said when she was older the dark stubble on her legs would magically disappear and reappear on her chin, something to look forward to.

"Are you finished in there, Ros?" Bonnie called from the bottom of the stairs. "Did you find what you needed?"

"Yes. Almost done," she replied, shifting to the other leg. Glancing in the mirror over the sink as she turned, Ros saw Stacy's reflection. She was standing on the ladder outside the window, a caulking gun in her hand, but her eyes were on Ros.

Ros quickly diverted her gaze but continued to shave, knowing she had an audience. *I'm certainly not doing my bikini area today*, she thought, smiling to herself. Ros considered herself modest, far from an exhibitionist, but somehow it didn't seem all that tragic that Stacy had seen her in her underwear.

She finished dressing and went downstairs to wait for Meredith. Stacy was cleaning the caulking gun and putting away her tools when Meredith pulled in the driveway and Ros came out to greet her. Ros could feel Stacy's eyes on them as they drove away.

"I appreciate you helping me do this, Ros," Meredith said as they headed across town with the boxes of table favors. "Was that Coach Hagen's truck?"

"Yes, my aunt hired her to paint the house. She's caulking around the windows. It's not something I can do. I'm not a ladder person."

"Oh, me either. I can't stand heights."

Ros grabbed several boxes and followed Meredith inside the reunion venue. The Cooper Barn, on the historical register as the largest barn in Kansas, had been moved from its former location to the Prairie Museum in Colby some years ago. A huge white wooden structure over a hundred feet long. it could accommodate seven hundred people for weddings and parties.

Inside, round dining tables were set with white tablecloths, service for dinner, and floral centerpieces. Streamers, strands of twinkle lights, and flower arrangements in school colors dotted the posts and beams. As Ros expected, the decor was country-western-themed, with lariats, cowboy hats, and bales of hay strategically placed around the room. The raised stage was set up with musical equipment, instruments, amplifiers, and cables running across the floor in every direction. The caterer was at work preparing for the dinner crowd, and a woman in dress slacks, white shirt, and a burgundy vest was setting up the bar area.

"Looks nice, huh?" Meredith said, setting the boxes on a nearby bale. "Aren't you glad you decided to come?"

"Yes, it looks great. I like the flowers. Did Meg do that?"

"No, the flower shop in town did them. She's coming this evening. She gave the committee a nice price on the arrangements so the superintendent invited her. Of course she'll get some free advertising."

"I thought you said about sixty people were coming. This looks like way more than sixty."

"Yes. There were a number of late replies. We're at over a hundred. Isn't that great? Okay, how shall we do this? We each take an item and go around, putting one at each place, then do another one?"

"Works for me," Ros said, pulling the first bag from the box. "Key rings and corkscrews," she said, examining the contents.

"I've got coasters with eagles on them and Chapstick," Meredith said and headed off around the room in the opposite direction.

"Why did they get so many things? One or two might have been sufficient."

"Somebody's husband is a promo supplier so they kind of went overboard. Don't forget to put those up here at the head table. You and I are at the far end. I got us the best seats. We can see the whole room without having an amplifier blaring in our ear."

Meredith winked at Ros. "I put the principal down at the other end. He drives me crazy. Or rather his wife does. She always gets into people's business, acting like she knows what's best. And I'm not the only one who thinks so. She was trying to tell the reunion committee how to run things and she's not even one of the classmates."

"Then why did the committee invite them?"

Meredith stopped and stared at Ros's question.

"Oh, yeah. I forgot. The high school principal gets invited to everything that has anything to do with the high school, right?" Ros said.

"You got it." Meredith started passing out the next item, then stopped and smiled over at Ros.

"Wouldn't it make matters more tolerable if you just avoid the principal's wife as much as possible?"

"I wish."

Ros stopped the at the head table and stared down at the name cards.

"Stacy Hagen and Meade Carvarian?" she said, studying the names. "Who's Meade Carvarian? One of the teachers?"

"She owns the Green Thumb Flower Shop. She's the one who did the floral arrangements. She's Coach Hagen's plus one. Nice lady the few times I've met her. Neat as a pin."

"Stacy Hagen's date then."

"Yep. I guess. She has the most lyrical French accent. She's from somewhere in Canada. Montreal I think. I can see why she's Coach's plus one."

"I guess I haven't met her." Ros felt a sudden and strange pang of jealousy. She had no idea where it came from, but it was unmistakable. She had never met Meade Carvarian, but she found herself instantly making a judgment about her, something she tried not to do usually until someone proved themselves unworthy.

"Hey, what are you doing? Everybody gets one, just one," Meredith said when she noticed Ros had absentmindedly placed two of each table favor at Stacy's place and none at Meade's.

"Oops, sorry. I dropped them." She quickly corrected the oversight.

Meredith was right. It took over an hour to distribute the goodies, including all the chatting and laughing they did to catch up on each other's lives.

"What time shall I pick you up this evening?" Meredith asked as she dropped Ros off back at Bonnie's house. She checked her watch. "You've only got a couple hours, but I sure appreciate your help." She picked up Ros's hand and kissed her palm before she climbed out. "Five thirty?"

"Why don't I meet you there? I can drive myself. I'm not sure how long it will take me to get ready and I need to stop and gas my car."

"Nope, you're my plus one. Says so on the reservation list. Social hour is at six. Dinner at seven. Dancing at eight 'til the cows come home." She laughed. "I'll pick you up and we can walk in together. We're going to have a great time. Everyone I've talked to is excited about this evening. Come on, let me pick you up. We haven't finished yakking about old times."

"Are you sure?"

"I'm sure. I'll be here at five thirty. Put on your dancing shoes. It's party time."

CHAPTER FIFTEEN

Meredith was early. A full thirty minutes early and Ros wasn't ready.

"I'm coming up," Meredith called after Bonnie announced she had arrived.

"Okay, but I need a few minutes," Ros replied as she stood at the bathroom mirror brushing her hair.

"Is this what you're wearing?" she asked from the bedroom. "The outfit on the bed?"

"The one hanging over the door. The gray slacks and yellow blouse."

"Oh, I like that. I love the metallic thread in the slacks. Is that top see-through? Very sexy, Ros."

"That's the top layer. It has a matching shell underneath." Ros came into the bedroom wearing underwear and a pale yellow camisole as she worked lotion into her hands and arms.

"Which shoes?" Meredith asked as her gaze roamed down Ros's body, hesitating at her pink lace panties.

"Black ankle boots." Ros stepped into the slacks and buttoned the blouse. "I like your outfit. Turquoise is a good color on you."

"I thought it went well with the reunion cowboy theme."

"Very stylish, theme or not." Ros stepped into the boots, aware that Meredith was watching her every move. It might not have been so obvious in high school, but with Meredith's recent admission she was gay, there was a new and different feeling to having her eyes on her body. It wasn't the same as changing in front of classmates after gym class.

Ros decided she was being silly. Meredith was a good friend. They had seen each other in their underwear many times, even seen each other naked when they used to go skinny-dipping in the creek during Kansas summer heat waves.

She slipped a necklace over her head and hooked a bracelet around her wrist, then grabbed her purse. "Okay, I'm ready," she said, dropping her cell phone in her purse. "Shall we go?"

"Absolutely," Meredith declared with an admiring smile. "You look stunning, by the way."

"Thank you."

Ros could feel Meredith's eyes on her as she followed her down the stairs. *Yep, she's definitely practicing being a lesbian*, Ros thought. *She's got her eyes on my butt.*

"Aunt Bonnie, we're leaving," Ros said from the hall. "Aunt Bonnie?"

"Out here, dear." Bonnie was sitting in the porch swing with the cat, thumbing through her recipe box. "Oh, don't you two look nice," she said, beaming up at them.

"You have a nice evening, Aunt Bonnie," Ros said as she leaned down and gave her a kiss on the cheek. "Don't wait up. This thing could run late."

They were twenty minutes early, but many of the attendees had already arrived and were visiting, drinks in hand. Meredith seemed to know and remember everyone, even spouses, and joined right in the conversations. Ros hadn't seen most of these people since graduation and didn't recognize many of them. *Thank goodness for name badges*, she thought.

"Ros McClure," a woman said as she extended her hand to Ros. She was a tall, striking woman in a geometric print sundress and heeled sandals. "How have you been?" She offered a half-hug and a kind smile.

"Meg?" Ros said, quickly reading her name badge. "Meggie," she repeated gleefully. "I'm great. It's so good to see you."

"I wanted to thank you for helping Meredith with the table favors. I feel so stupid for forgetting to put them out. Thank you, thank you, thank you." She squeezed Ros's arm. "We had a birthday reception for my grandmother and I couldn't miss it. You know how family things are."

"No problem, Meggie. I was glad to help."

"Meredith said she could talk you into helping," she said with a chuckle. "That woman can talk anybody into anything. She said since you were her date for the evening you wouldn't mind."

Ros hadn't considered herself Meredith's date, but helping out in a pinch wasn't a problem.

"There's Eva," Meg said, waving at the couple coming through the door. "Doesn't she look good? I haven't seen her since the last reunion. I better go see what she's been up to." She hurried off in that direction.

Ros ordered a cranberry juice and vodka from the cash bar. "Go light on the vodka," she told the woman mixing drinks.

"You've waited twenty-five years to come to one of these," Meredith said, striding up to the bar. "Why not jump in with both feet? Give her a full shot of vodka, barkeep. And I'll have a Bacardi and Coke."

"No, please. Just a little."

"Okay, but you're going to be sorry. The first half hour is open bar. It was part of the cost of the dinner. You paid for it." Meredith took a sip of her drink. "Oh yum. I can tell this is going to be a fantastic evening." She took another sip and grinned.

It was well past six thirty, but Stacy and her date hadn't arrived. Ros visited with several classmates, some she had nearly forgotten. The football and volleyball teams, the band, and the National Honor Society were all well represented along with 4-H, Thespians and the Saddle Club.

"Which one is the flower shop owner who did the arrangements?" Ros asked Meredith as she drifted past.

"You mean Coach Hagen's date?"

"Yes. I want to tell her how creative they are. Flower arranging is not part of my skill set."

"Mine either." Meredith finished her drink and set the glass on a nearby tray. "Oh, there she is. The one coming in the door. And speak of the devil." Meredith nodded in that direction before heading back to the bar for another drink.

Ros watched as Stacy and a silver-haired woman stopped at the check-in table. The woman was dressed in a floral peasant dress and had an amicable smile directed at Stacy as they checked in and received their name badges. Stacy wore black western-cut slacks with polished black cowboy boots. Her deep purple shirt was also western style with pearl snaps and tucked in the pants with a silver concho belt at the waist. They, or at least Stacy, had captured Ros's attention completely, enough so she caught her toe on a table leg and stumbled, dropping to her knees. The contents of her purse spilled across the floor, including her cell phone, wallet, tissues, Tic Tacs, and a tampon.

"Oh good grief," she muttered, more embarrassed than hurt. She scrambled to collect the strewn items, hoping no one had noticed.

"Are you all right?" a man said as he hooked a strong hand under her arm and hoisted her to her feet.

"Yes, thank you," she said, brushing barn dust off the knees of her slacks.

"Are these yours?" Stacy said, coming up behind her, holding out the Tic Tacs and tampon.

"Yes. Thanks." She quickly retrieved the items from her hand and dropped them in her purse as a blush raced up her face. It was just a tampon, one of those emergency items she always carried, but she was still embarrassed Stacy had seen it.

"You never know when you'll need a Tic Tac," Stacy said with a wry smile.

"True." Ros couldn't help but notice Stacy's cologne. Vanilla musk, she thought. Nice. Very nice.

"You spilled your drink. Can I get you another one?" Stacy put the empty glass on the tray and dropped a couple of paper napkins on the spill to soak it up.

"That's okay. I don't need another one," Ros replied.

"Are you sure?" Stacy seemed to be struggling with where to allow her eyes to wander. Ros knew her layered blouse wasn't see-through, but Stacy's stare and reserved smile made her wonder.

"Yes, I'm sure."

"You look very nice this evening," Stacy said, bringing her gaze up to meet Ros's.

"Thank you. So do you. I like the silver belt."

"It was my mother's. She wore it when she went square dancing. Of course she wore it over a western skirt with a dozen petticoats so it stood out like an umbrella." Stacy smiled at the memory.

"And she gave up square dancing or just gave up the belt?"

"Both. My mother passed many years ago."

"I'm so sorry, Stacy."

Stacy gave a resolved sigh, then said, "Hey, I didn't come to this shindig to be melodramatic. I came to enjoy myself." She turned to the woman visiting with a group of people behind her. "Meade, I'd like you to meet Ros McClure. Ros, this is Meade Carvarian, proprietor of the Green Thumb Flower Shop."

"Hello, Meade," Ros said, extending her hand. "I'm very impressed with your talents. The arrangements are lovely."

"Thank you. I've heard a lot about you or at least I've heard a lot about your aunt. How is she doing?"

"Much better. Thank you for asking." Ros wondered how much Stacy had confided in her about Aunt Bonnie's condition. When Ros rolled her eyes up to meet Stacy's, Stacy gave a slight shake of her head as if to say she hadn't divulged any private information about Bonnie.

"What would you like to drink, Meade?" Stacy asked.

"White wine, I think. Something dry."

"And you, Ros? Are you sure you don't need another something or other with a little umbrella in it?"

"Well, how about a cranberry juice, no umbrella and no booze?"

"Done," Stacy said and headed to the bar, leaving Ros and Meade to visit.

"Stacy said you weren't going to come to the reunion. She said it was a last-minute decision to attend. I bet your aunt is glad you did. She is such a dear woman. I delivered a plant to her right after she returned home from being in the nursing home. She invited me in for tea. I was sorry I didn't have time to accept her hospitality. She said she was hoping you'd change your mind and come."

"Things have been busy at work so I wasn't sure I could get away. I'm glad I did."

"I think Stacy was glad you did as well. She said she has had some pleasant conversations with you about your aunt. She worried so about how she was doing. Stacy doesn't have any family, you know."

"I didn't know that. She mentioned that her mother had passed. Doesn't she have siblings or cousins or someone?"

"Nope, not a soul. At least no one I've ever heard her mention. She's one of those people who keeps her personal feelings all bottled up inside. Independent woman, that one is."

"Here we are, ladies," Stacy said, carrying three glasses. "Meade, white wine, dry. Ros, vodka and cranberry juice minus the vodka, no umbrella. And for the biology teacher, seven and seven. Cheers, ladies." They all clinked glasses and sipped.

"What do I owe you?" Ros asked, fumbling with her purse to find her wallet.

"A simple thank-you," she said with a smile. "And maybe a dance later. How's that?"

"Then, thank you," Ros said, enjoying Stacy's smile.

"Ros?" A man in a cowboy hat wrapped an arm around her shoulders and grinned broadly. Stacy was greeted by some of her former students at the same moment and stepped away with Meade, leaving Ros to visit with him.

"Larry?" she said. "Larry Collins." Like many of her classmates, he had changed. Not a lot but the graying goatee, wrinkled suntan, and extra twenty pounds around the middle were significant enough differences that she had to rely on his name badge for confirmation.

"You got it, cutie. I heard you were going to be here. I had to say hello and see if you'd changed. And you have." He leaned back and scanned her up and down. "Looking good, Ros. Looking really good." He gave her shoulders a tight squeeze, almost to the point of being crushing.

"Thank you, Larry." His overly aggressive hug and roving eyes made her uncomfortable, as uncomfortable as his roving hands had after prom when they parked on Sappa Creek Road. Ros raised her drink to her lips, as much to break his hold on her arms as to take a sip. "Have I met your wife?" she asked.

"Bridget? Oh, she's around here somewhere." He didn't seem interested in locating her for an introduction. "But man oh man, I can't get over how good you look. Twenty-five years have been good to you. Where are you now? Chicago, is it?"

"Cincinnati," she offered.

"Cincinnati, eh? Big city."

"Yes, big city." Ros looked over at Meredith, standing a few feet away and grinning at her.

"Well, big city or not, I expect a dance, for old time sakes. Right, Ros?" He gave another squeeze, his hand lingering on her rib cage.

"Ladies and gentlemen," Meredith said, going to the microphone on the stage. "Grab your drink and find your table. If you don't like where you're sitting, blame the seating committee," she said, raising soft laughter.

"Isn't that you, Meredith?" someone shouted, which brought on more laughter.

"Shut up and sit down, JJ. Your wife helped me put out the place cards. As soon as you all are seated we'll get this meal under way."

"Come on, Larry," a woman called, waving at him.

It took several minutes for the groups of visitors to wrap up their conversations and move to their tables. Stacy, Meade, Meredith, and Ros found their places at the head table along with the other former teachers and school administrators. To the surprise of neither Ros or Meredith, the principal and his wife had moved their place cards to the optimum seats at the far end of the table. The repositioning of the cards meant Ros and Meredith were no longer seated next to Stacy and Meade but were several chairs apart. Ros nonchalantly glanced down the table as Stacy was doing the same in her direction. Stacy shrugged as their eyes met.

Salads were served along with baskets of rolls followed by the entrees. "Pasta primavera, ma'am?" a server asked, setting the plate in front of Ros.

"Doesn't that look good?" Meredith leaned into Ros, admiring her dinner. "Asparagus and carrots and peppers." She picked a cherry tomato from the plate. "I love bow tie pasta. I should have ordered this." She took a piece of pasta as well.

"Do you want to trade?" Ros asked, wishing Meredith would keep her hands out of her meal.

"No, no. You ordered it. You eat it."

A message from Stacy chimed on her phone.

Yours looks good. I bet Miss Bonnie would enjoy that. And you can stop worrying about her. She's fine. And BTW, you look very nice this evening.

Ros returned a thumbs-up emoji, then muted her phone and set it aside.

Dinner took over an hour with occasional announcements and raffle drawings from the stage. Stacy and the other teachers were given desk clocks in appreciation for their years of dedication to their students. Ros won a leather-bound day planner. Meade won a gift certificate to JoJo's Restaurant. Stacy won a pair of leather work gloves, something she decreed to be very handy in spite of those who thought they were a gag gift. Meade's gorgeous centerpieces were even raffled.

Dessert was still being enjoyed when the band began to play, offering a few tunes to get people in the mood for dancing. By the time the tables were cleared, couples were two-stepping around the dance floor. Most people were on their second, third, and fourth drinks. And most of the men in cowboy hats and boots were drinking bottles of beer.

Stacy and Meade danced a two-step, agile and graceful as they moved around the floor. Ros watched, tapping her foot in time with the music. Meredith was busy being the ringleader to whatever came next. She finally came to the table, pulled Ros out of her chair, and headed toward the dance floor. She wasn't an expert dancer, but Ros didn't mind. They shuffled their way around the floor, both gleefully having a good time. They were well into their third dance when Larry made his way through the crowded dance floor and tapped Meredith on the shoulder.

"Do you mind, Meredith? I want to dance with Ros," he said. He didn't wait for her answer. He took Ros in his arms and began dancing, twirling, and swinging her round and round, grinning broadly.

"Hey!" Meredith perched her hands on hips and groaned her displeasure.

"Sorry," he said and continued dancing.

Ros didn't say anything. She knew this dance was inevitable. And as she had told Meredith, she held no grudges. She wasn't going to make a scene. She and Larry dated briefly in high school and they attended prom together. She could allow him a dance. Twenty-five years ago she learned to keep up with his rather athletic style of dance and keep her toes out of the way. It was still necessary.

"You're still a good dancer, Ros. Like always."

"You're what I'd call an energetic dancer, Larry," she said, feeling sweat through the sleeves of his shirt. "Reminds me of prom."

"I was a clumsy kid back then. But hey, weren't we all?" He laughed.

The music changed to a slow dance. With one final twirl he pulled her into his arms and began to sway.

"This is a good song," he said, cupping his hand in the small of her back, just below her waist. "'Could I have this dance for the rest of my life,'" he sang.

"Anne Murray song, isn't it?" she said, as his embrace grew more and more constricting. The more they danced and the more he sang, the more he bent her backward. And the more she struggled to find a comfortable position.

As they turned Ros could see Stacy dancing with Meade, but her eyes were on Ros, a curious look on her face. Ros looked back at Stacy with a plea to be rescued, then smiled as if she was only kidding. She must have read something in her expression. She whispered something in Meade's ear, then released her and crossed to Larry, tapping him on the shoulder.

"My turn, big boy," she said, jokingly. "The teacher gets a turn."

Stacy didn't wait for him to say anything. She wrapped her arms around Ros and gracefully moved them away as they continued the dance, leaving him alone in the middle of the dance floor.

"Thank you," Ros said with a relieved sigh.

"No problem." Stacy loosened her grip but kept Ros in her arms. "You looked like you needed a little help back there."

"I thought I owed him a dance. After all he was my prom date."

"From the rumors I heard around school back then, you don't owe him anything."

"I was trying to be nice."

"Stubborn but congenial." Stacy gave her a twirl, then drew her back into her arms. "Are you enjoying the reunion?"

"Yes, actually."

"I know what you're thinking." She twirled her again. "You're thinking you agreed to come as an excuse to be here in Colby to visit you aunt."

"That's part of it. Maybe most of it. But I'm glad I came."

Yes, Ros came to Colby and the reunion so she could see how Aunt Bonnie was doing. But there was more. She hadn't planned on it or anticipated it, but now something was smoldering below the surface. And swaying in Stacy's arms only compounded it. Those feelings from years ago hadn't died. They were still as vibrant and fresh as when she first walked into Ms. Hagen's classroom and felt her heart skip a beat. It wasn't Stacy's help with Bonnie. It wasn't checking in on her or the shopping or the painting. It was far more.

But she didn't have time for those kinds of feelings. She had a job waiting her return. She had a boss still learning the ropes and in need of her guidance. And she had her beloved aunt battling a gradually debilitating disease. She didn't need a beguiling interest in Stacy Hagen vying for her attention. She hadn't been in a serious relationship in years. *That has to be the reason for the fascination*, she thought. *Blame it on being lonely*. Besides, Stacy seemed to have her own attachment and to an endearing and personable woman. She and Meade Carvarian made a lovely couple.

As the strains of the song indicated it was about to end Stacy drew Ros close and spun them around and around, their bodies tight against each other. The feel of Stacy's firm round breasts against her own was enough to take her breath away. Enough that she released a soft guttural moan.

"Too much?" Stacy whispered.

"No," Ros said breathlessly. "That was fun."

Stacy did it again even though the music had stopped. Ros closed her eyes as they spun. When they came to a stop, Stacy turned and led her off the dance floor without a backward glance.

"Okay, ladies and gentlemen, we're going to do a little square dancing now," a man announced from the stage. "I need couples right down here in front. Four couples to each square. Come on now. Don't be shy. Get your husbands up here, ladies."

Most of the couples left the dance floor, but a few made their way to the front. Some were husbands and wives, but several women who couldn't talk their husbands into joining in paired up and headed to the floor.

"Don't look at me," Meredith said as she returned to her seat. She unbuttoned another button and fanned herself. "I need to sit a while and cool off. I can't square dance anyway. And I don't want to learn."

"You're the event director. You should participate," Ros teased, taking her seat as well.

"Yes, you should," Meade said as she and Stacy passed behind them to take their seats.

"I don't see you out there," Meredith replied in their direction.

"Me? Heavens no. I can't do that." Meade gave a deliberate shudder. "Never learned. But it's fun to watch others do it. And I like the music."

"We need one more couple. Come on. Somebody needs to join this middle square," the announcer said. "Larry, how about you and Bridget? Get on down here."

"Not me," he shouted, dismissing the idea with a wave.

"We've got to have one more. Who's it gonna be? How about the head table? One of you teachers? Somebody's gotta be brave."

There was a round of applause as if encouraging one of them to join the group.

"Ms. Hagen. Best biology teacher in western Kansas. Grab a partner and come on out here, Ms. Hagen."

There was an even louder round of applause when Stacy stood up, grabbed Ros by the hand, and headed for the group of dancers waiting for a final couple to fill the square.

"Are you confident I know how to do this?" Ros said, following along behind.

"We're about to find out."

Everyone hooted and cheered as they took their place. Stacy bowed and waved, going along with the fun. She moved to Ros's other side and said, "The lady is on my right hand."

"Whatever you say, Coach," Ros curtsied politely and grinned, knowing they were the center of attention for the moment.

"Vern is going to be our caller, folks. Yep, he's been driving school buses for thirty years, but he's a damn good square dance caller too. So here we go." The announcer handed the microphone to a tall, imposing man with white hair and a handlebar moustache.

"Look at all the glamorous ladies we've got down here," Vern said, standing at the edge of the stage and smiling out at the dancers. "You gents still sitting on your backsides, shame on you. You're missing a golden opportunity to wrap your arms around a pretty gal."

A man standing at the bar waved his hat and yelled, "I'll pay someone ten bucks to hug my wife. Valerie's the one in the blue dress with the angry look on her face."

The crowd erupted in laughter.

Valerie yelled back, "Only ten bucks? You think this is angry, wait 'til we get home tonight, Frank."

The crowd laughed even louder, the sound echoing through the rafters of the barn.

Ros leaned over to Stacy and said, "We're a bawdy group, that's for sure."

"I feel sorry for Frank," she replied with a nod and a smile.

Vern turned to the band and signaled them to begin.

"Okay, partners," he said, tapping in time to the music. "Here we go. Let's all circle to the left."

Stacy held out her hand and Ros placed hers across her palm. The couples all joined hands and began moving around in a circle, Ros's hand firmly in Stacy's.

"Now swing your partner and promenade home. Couples, now right and left grand then swing your partner. Now promenade home."

It had been years since she square danced, but the steps and moves came flying back. Every time Stacy wrapped her arm around her or took her hand she eagerly accepted, grinning and enjoying the fun. When the two dances were over the couples drifted away, applauding and hooting raucously.

"Thank you, Ros. I enjoyed that," Stacy said, placing her hand on her back as they made their way back to the table.

"Me too."

Ros was ready to ask her for the next dance, a two-step, when Stacy pointed at Meade, sitting quietly at the table all alone.

"I think I should dance with the one I brought," Stacy said with a smile.

"Absolutely. She's a charming woman."

"Yes, she is, isn't she?"

Ros, Meredith, Meade, and Stacy danced with various partners for the rest of the evening, socializing and returning to the bar once or twice. Ros toyed with idea of asking Stacy to dance, but there always seemed to be someone or something that got in the way.

"Classmates," Meredith said from the stage. "Our evening together is almost over. Before anyone leaves or passes out," she teased, which brought a round of laughter, "I want everyone who walked across the stage and received their diploma from Colby High School twenty-five years ago to come down front. We're going to take a group picture. So leave your drinks on the table and mosey on down here."

It took some doing but the classmates were finally lined up and arranged on the risers for the photographer.

"Damn, we're a good-looking group," Meredith said from the stage before coming to take her place in the front row.

The photographer was patient and took several shots, encouraging people to smile, hold still, look at the camera, and behave. Somehow, Larry had wormed his way into a spot next to Ros. She could feel his hand on her back as everyone moved closer together.

"Keep your hands to yourself, Larry," she said, hoping her good-natured teasing would be heeded. It wasn't.

"One more, folks," the photographer said. "Smile and look like you're glad you graduated."

Two or three more were snapped before the group was dismissed, signaling that the evening was officially over. The last of the drinks were consumed, hugs were shared, and a few tears were shed for those members of the class lost over the years. Kisses were also shared by a few.

"How about a kiss for old times sake?" Larry said, smiling confidently at Ros as he slipped his arm around her waist and pulled her close.

"No thank you," she said, pushing back.

"Ah, come on," he insisted and leaned down.

"Larry, twenty-five years ago you couldn't keep your hands to yourself and you still can't. You've never been good at accepting no for an answer. And when it comes to kissing, I'd rather kiss your wife. Now go home. You're drunk."

She gave him a shove and stepped away. He glared back at her, a wicked glint in his eye.

"One little kiss. What's the freaking big deal?"

"The big deal is, the lady said no," Stacy said, stepping between them. "I don't think you need more of an answer than that." She was closer to his size than Ros was but still several inches shorter and much thinner. That didn't seem to intimidate her.

"Oh for God's sake, Larry," Bridget said, striding up to them and grabbing him by the arm. "Stop acting like a jerk and get in the car. I'm driving." She pushed him toward the door, then looked back. "I'm sorry. He can't handle his liquor." She followed him out the door. Her yelling at him to shut up and get in the car could be heard inside.

"Thank you," Ros said. "I could have handled it, but thank you."

"I know you could have. I was just practicing being a tough teacher." Stacy patted Ros on the arm and turned to Meade. "Shall we go? It's getting late."

Ros shared a few last goodbyes before following Meredith to her car.

"Boy, am I glad I'm not on the cleanup committee." Meredith climbed in the car, raked her hands through her hair, and groaned. "I don't know about you, but I had a great time. That was so much fun. It was like we were all teenagers again."

"Some more than others," Ros said with a chuckle. "But yes. I had fun. I almost wish I had attended our other reunions. I'm taking away lots of memories."

"Only almost?"

"Okay, yes. I wish I had."

Meredith turned to Ros and placed her hand on Ros's.

"Ros, I know I need to apologize. I'm sorry, hon. Really."

"For what?" Ros had no idea what she was talking about, but whatever it was Meredith seemed genuinely ashamed.

"I know. I know. I spent way too much time making announcements and doing things. But it was my job. I agreed to do it. I should have spent more time with you. You were, after all, my date. We didn't dance nearly enough. I'm so sorry. Can you forgive me?"

"There's nothing to forgive." Ros patted her hand. "We danced and visited and had a great time. The meal was wonderful and all the joking and prizes and, wow, the square dancing. I didn't think I remembered how to do that. You were a wonderful event director. You did a great job. Don't worry about it."

"Are you sure?"

"I'm sure."

"Meade and Stacy seemed to have fun too."

"Yes, I think they did," Ros agreed.

"And yes, you were great at square dancing. You'll have to teach me how to do that someday. Stacy was good too. Not as good as you, but good."

Stacy was the square dance expert, but Ros saw no need to contradict her. The evening was a great success and it was over. Meredith started the car and followed the line of cars out of the parking lot.

CHAPTER SIXTEEN

Ros didn't awaken until after seven Sunday morning. It had been a long reunion, but she could happily say she enjoyed herself. She hadn't danced or laughed that much in years. By the time she dressed and headed downstairs, she could hear Bonnie talking to someone outside.

"Good morning, Aunt Bonnie," Ros said, coming out onto the front porch with a cup of coffee. "And good morning, Stacy. You started early." Stacy was on the extension ladder, putting a coat of white paint on the second story gable peak on the front of the house.

"Looks very nice. I'm obviously no house painter," she continued, squinting up through the morning sun at what Stacy was doing. "I would have done everything that needed to be painted yellow first, then gone back and done the white trim color."

Stacy continued to paint with long determined brush strokes. She rolled her eyes down to Ros, her jaw tight.

"I thought it would look better to have one side of the house complete," Bonnie said proudly. "I want people to know what it will look like when we're all finished."

"Oh, so that's why." Ros sipped her coffee, holding her cup to her lips to hide a smile. "Aunt Bonnie is supervising?"

"Yes," Stacy said dryly and continued to paint.

"Ros, sweetheart," Bonnie said, patting the swing and encouraging her to sit with her, in spite of the fact that Piano was sprawled across the vacant space. "Let me know what you'd like me to make for your dinner. I'll leave it in the fridge and you can heat it up in the microwave."

"Why? Where will you be?"

"I'm going to Rona's for potluck and cards this afternoon. She's having a bunch of us old ladies over to celebrate her sister's birthday."

"That sounds like fun. What are you taking?"

"She asked me to make some of my barbecued baked beans and I think I'll take some ambrosia salad. It'll taste nice and fresh on a hot day like this."

"That sounds good."

"I can leave you a little container of salad and some beans, but you'll want something else to go with it."

"No, I won't. The salad will be plenty."

"Don't be silly. I can defrost a pork chop. How do you like yours cooked? Breaded?"

"Aunt Bonnie, I don't need a pork chop. I'm still full from last night."

"I'll leave you a banana to have with your dinner. You need to eat a banana every now and then for the fiber, dear. You know we all need fiber in our diet to help our system work properly. You shouldn't neglect your fiber especially as you get older. Take it from me. A well-balanced diet with plenty of fiber will help everything come out all right." Bonnie gave Ros a mothering nod. "You don't want to get all bound up."

"Yes, Aunt Bonnie. I eat plenty of fruit and vegetables. My system is working just fine." Ros wanted the discussion of her bodily functions to be over and quickly.

"Sometimes even coffee doesn't do the trick," Bonnie added with a frown.

Ros could hear Stacy chuckle from her perch on the ladder.

"Do you need me to leave out two bananas, dear?"

Stacy laughed a little louder.

"No, I don't need any bananas, thank you very much."

"Just one then. Better safe than sorry, I always say."

"Aunt Bonnie…"

"She's right, you know. Bananas are high in fiber, but low in fat and unfortunately low in protein," Stacy offered, obviously eavesdropping.

"You, too?" Ros glared up at her. "Can we please stop talking about my *system?*"

"Ros, dear, have you…" Bonnie started to ask, but Ros stopped her.

"Aunt Bonnie, please. I'm doing fine. Can we please change the subject?"

"I'd like your recipe for that ambrosia salad, Miss Bonnie," Stacy called down from the ladder.

"Who's got a recipe? It's mandarin oranges, pineapple, coconut flakes, unsweetened if you can find it, and mini marshmallows." Bonnie seemed happy she was asked.

"What holds it together?"

"I use equal parts plain yogurt and whipped cream. And whatever you do, don't use that frozen stuff."

"You mean Cool Whip?"

"Don't use it. It's nasty. It'll ruin a perfectly good recipe."

"Should I write that down for you?" Ros offered.

"No, I got it. If I forget I can ask again. Thank you, Miss Bonnie."

"My mother called it five-cup salad. A cup of each," Bonnie added. "If you want a little color, add a few cherries but rinse them off first. They'll bleed red all over the salad."

Bonnie was in her element. She loved to give recipe guidance. More than a few women in town had called to ask her advice over the years. She was an expert on everything from what weather was best to make a pie crust to how long to cook a Christmas goose. If she didn't like what someone was serving, she wasn't afraid to tell them. Ros had always been proud of Bonnie's straightforward honesty although she sometimes wished she could temper it a little for those with thin skin.

Stacy climbed down and repositioned the ladder. Sweat was already dipping from her brow and it wasn't yet nine o'clock.

"Where does Rona live, Aunt Bonnie?" Ros didn't recognize the name. She wanted to satisfy herself it was someplace Bonnie could easily find.

"Rona? She's up the street." She pointed toward town. "She's lived in that brick house for fifty years. It's not big but she's got it nicely decorated. She's got good taste."

"Rhonda Howard?" Ros suggested.

"Sure. Rhonda."

Ros noticed Stacy's gaze had rolled down to meet hers.

"Do you want to come with me? I'm sure she won't mind. What's one more?"

"Thank you but no. You ladies have a nice evening. I've got a report to look over and I'm going to be in a conference call."

"I thought you were on vacation," Bonnie said with a worried look on her face. "Why are you working and on a Sunday? It is Sunday, isn't it?"

"Yes, it's Sunday and sometimes things come up that can't wait." Ros finished her coffee rather than explain why she had to work on Sunday. Bonnie didn't need to worry about the problems she was having with Steve.

"Well, I'm going to do a little yoga, then I'm going to the store. I need onions, bananas, and yogurt." Bonnie stood, slung the cat over her shoulder, and went inside.

Ros stepped out into the yard to get a better view of the front of the house. Daffodil was what Bonnie called the color and she was right. It was definitely yellow but if she was happy, that's what mattered.

"It'll fade some," Stacy said, seeming to notice Ros's squint at the color.

"Hey, it's her choice." Ros thought a moment, then looked up at the house and recited, "'I wandered lonely as a cloud that floats on high o'er vales and hills, when all at once I saw a crowd, a host of golden daffodils.'"

Stacy smiled and added, "'Beside the lake, beneath the trees, fluttering and dancing in the breeze.' Very good, Ros. William Wordsworth would be proud of you for remembering."

"I haven't thought of that poem since college," Ros said reflectively and added. "'Then my heart with pleasure fills, and dances with the daffodils.'"

"That's it." Stacy looked over at Ros with a satisfied smile. "One of my favorite poems." Their eyes met for a brief moment before Stacy stepped off the ladder. "I'm going to clean my brush and get back to painting yellow," she said, touching a dot of white paint onto the back of Ros's hand. "It's time for more daffodils."

"You paint daffodils. I'm going to get my conference call started," she said, stepping up on the porch. "After I wash off the paint." She tossed a disciplinary though comical glare at Stacy.

What Ros had hoped would be an hour or so conference call ended up lasting well into the afternoon. Stacy spent the day painting, following the shade around the house.

"Ros, dear, I'm leaving," Bonnie called from the kitchen. "I should be back by ten."

Ros heard the back door slam followed by the sound of Bonnie's car starting and pulling away. "Have fun," she said although no one was home to hear; Stacy had finished her painting for the day and left over an hour ago. She sighed. *Just another day at the office—like so many other weekends of late.* She made a few notes on her laptop, then went downstairs to enjoy her ambrosia salad.

It was a warm summer afternoon and ceiling fans stirred the air throughout the house. Ros collected her salad, a few crackers, and a strawberry wine cooler, then went out to enjoy her dinner in the porch swing. Piano meandered onto the porch and looked up at her with a curious meow.

"Sorry. She's not here. You'll have to settle for sitting next to me, McFluff." Ros patted the swing beside her.

The cat seemed to understand and accept the terms. She hopped up on the swing and curled up next to her. Ros quickly realized the furry kitty was sitting too close for comfort and nudged her over a ways. "I don't need your body heat, thank you very much."

Ros finished the salad and crackers and was sipping the last of her wine cooler when she noticed the evening sun glinting off something shiny in the yard. A cell phone was lying in the grass. She first assumed Bonnie had dropped it, but the closer she got, the more it looked like Stacy's phone.

She brushed off the dirt and pressed the home button. Sure enough, it was Stacy's. There were three text messages and two unanswered calls on the screen. Ros refrained from opening any of them, respecting Stacy's privacy, although one of the calls was clearly from Meade.

"I bet you're looking for this," she said as she looked up the road.

She went inside to wash her dishes and decide what to do with the phone. The less aggressive approach would be leave it on the table and return it to her tomorrow when she came to paint.

Then there was the other option, the one Ros was inclined to follow. Return it this evening. After all, it was early and she knew if it were her phone she'd want it back as soon as convenient. What was it Stacy had said? Three and a half miles out County Road 20? Surely she could find it. She'd drive out that way and look for a white pickup truck in the yard. Returning the phone was a perfectly justifiable excuse to stop by for a visit. Unless she already had company. She didn't know what kind of car Meade drove, but if there was more than one vehicle in the drive she wouldn't stop.

Ros changed shirts to one without pit stains, combed her hair, and started down the stairs. Halfway down she stopped and twirled her key ring around her finger. She thought a moment, then turned and bolted back upstairs. She pulled out a pair of khaki shorts, a blue shirt, and clean underwear, then headed into the bathroom for a quick shower. Fifteen minutes later she bounded down the stairs, smiling contentedly. She may not stay as fresh as a daffodil in this Kansas heat, but at least she would start out that way.

It was surprisingly easy to find Stacy's house. The name Hagen on the handcrafted Conestoga wagon mailbox took the guesswork out of it. Ros turned in and followed the gravel drive toward a shingled roof that seemed to be mounted on the ground. Once she rounded the drive she could see the front of the house. It was a red brick berm house nestled into the hillside overlooking a lush green pasture. It was a neat and tidy home with white window trim and shutters. A fan-shaped patio with wrought iron table and chairs was home to several vigorously blooming plants in large pots. Shade trees flanked the patio and cast long evening shadows over the house.

"Hello," she called, knocking on the door. She assumed it was safe to knock. No other car was present other than Stacy's pickup. "Hello, Stacy." She called again. "I'm returning your phone. You left it at Aunt Bonnie's." But no one answered the door.

Before she could knock again she heard an engine start. Her Kansas country girl upbringing told her it was a tractor, and it was coming from the barn on the far side of the driveway. She headed for the barn, but an orange tractor with a bucket scoop on the front came through the doors before she got there. Stacy stomped on the brake and slid to a stop when she noticed Ros standing near the entrance.

"Hey, I know you," she said, throttling down the engine.

"And I have your cell phone," Ros replied, holding it up.

"Dang, no wonder I couldn't find it. I figured it just fell under the seat of the truck. I was going to look for it later."

"Nope. It was in the yard, in the grass, next to a clump of mud." Ros handed it up to her and stepped back.

"That was nice of you to bring it out. Thank you, but you didn't have to do that. I could have gotten it tomorrow."

"I know, but there are some things flashing on your screen I thought might be important."

"Oh, yeah." She gave the screen a quick look, then slipped the phone in her jeans pocket.

"I just know I'm lost without my phone so I thought I'd return yours in case you were as fanatical about it as I am."

"Probably not as much as you, but it's nice to have it back. Thanks again. I was on my way to check on a section of fence I think is down. I've got a cow who doesn't like being fenced in. If she doesn't stop it she's going to be freezer beef."

"You go ahead then. I didn't mean to bother you." Ros took another step back.

"You weren't bothering me. Want to go for a ride?"

"I don't think there's room for a passenger on that thing." Ros laughed as if it was a real offer.

"Maybe not, but there is in my ATV," Stacy said and started the engine. "Be right back." She backed the tractor into the barn and a minute later came driving out in a two-seat ATV. It looked like a small pickup truck with knobby tires and a large toolbox mounted in the bed behind the seats. "Come on, hop in."

"I didn't mean you had to do that."

"Sure. I'll show you around." Stacy waved her in.

"I've never seen one like this." Ros maneuvered over the side bar and climbed in the passenger seat. "It's like a golf cart on steroids."

"And it's fun to drive. Want to try it?"

"No," Ros said instantly. "I don't think so."

"Another time," she said with a chuckle and started down the path toward the tree line.

"I like your house, by the way. You can't tell it's a berm home from the road."

"I did that on purpose. And I needed it to face south to take advantage of the solar energy for heat and light. There was no existing slope there, so it's backfilled to create the illusion of a hillside."

"You designed it?"

"Yes. There was a little farmhouse on the property, but it wasn't energy efficient and had a leaky roof. Berm living took some getting used to, but I like the privacy since it looks out into nature, not a dusty dirt road."

"You mean like my aunt's house?"

"I didn't mean her house isn't nice. I just wanted something a little different from the normal Kansas farmhouse. I'll show it to you after I deal with this. Let you see what a berm house looks like inside," Stacy offered.

"Yep, there it is," Stacy said angrily, pointing to a section of barbed wire fence hidden by the trees. "Stomped flatter than a fritter. All five strands." She pulled to a stop next to the fencerow and climbed out. She retrieved a pair of work gloves and a few tools from the toolbox and went to work reattaching the strands of wire to the metal posts.

"Need some help?" Ros asked, watching intently.

"No, I got it. Shouldn't take long."

"Good, 'cause I have no idea how to do that stuff."

"You're a Kansas girl. What do you mean you don't know how to string fence?" Stacy groaned and grimaced as she pulled the first one tight.

"If you can do it with a calculator, I'm your girl. If it requires hand tools and muscle, don't look at me. Fortunately, I don't need farm girl skills in Cincinnati. I seldom mend a fence, other than arguments between my coworkers. And the only hand tool I use is a stapler."

"It's never too late to learn a new skill set." Stacy pulled the next strand of wire into place and attached the clip, but the wire slipped and one of the barbs scraped her wrist just above the glove cuff, immediately generating a trickle of blood.

"Ouch," she grimaced but kept a firm grip on the wire until it was secured.

"Oh, my God. You cut yourself, Stacy. You need a bandage on that. Come on. Let's get up to the house, so we can wash it off. You'll need a tetanus shot too."

"I'm okay. It's not that bad." Stacy gave the cut a quick glance, wiped it across the leg of her jeans, and began attaching the next wire.

"You should get that tetanus shot right away. It could be dangerous to wait."

"I got my booster shot six months ago. I'm good to go."

"You're sure?"

"Living on a farm, even a small one, periodic tetanus boosters are routine events. Have you had one recently?"

"Um, I don't remember. But I didn't get a puncture wound from a rusty wire."

"Neither did I. This is galvanized wire. Not rusty." Stacy tugged the last wire into place and attached the clip. "There, all finished." Stacy returned the tools and gloves to the toolbox and climbed in.

"Let me see your arm," Ros said, reaching for it.

"It's nothing. Little scrape is all." It was still bleeding slightly, so she wiped it on her jeans again.

"Now, that's real clean and sanitary," Ros scoffed.

Stacy reached under the seat, pulled out a container of wet wipes, and went about cleaning it.

"There, how's that? Happy?"

"No. Give me that." Ros took another wipe and carefully but methodically cleaned the cut. "Now it's clean. And stop wiping it on your jeans. They aren't."

"Still a stubborn little cuss, ain't ya?"

"When it comes to cleanliness, yes, I am. Now, where are the cows?"

"Probably down by the pond."

Stacy started across the field, following the well-worn path that meandered toward a gate.

"I'll get it," Ros said and hopped out.

"Lift up, then release the latch."

She did as she was told and the gate swung open. Once Stacy drove through, Ros closed the gate and latched it. Twenty or so head of cows, some with a calf at their side, were grazing near the slope of the pond.

"Aw, aren't the little ones cute?" Ros said with an adoring smile.

"If you say so. Yes, they're cute."

"Is this all you have?"

"For now, yes. I sold some steers last fall. The new spring crop will fill out the herd as much as I need."

"Angus, right?"

"Yep. Black Angus or Aberdeen Angus. Originally from Scotland. Naturally polled and best beef you can buy," Stacy said proudly, propping her foot up on the side.

"Wait a minute," Ros said with a gasp as she scanned the area. "I remember this place. I remember that clump of trees and there should be a little peninsula that extends into the pond right over there."

"Yep."

"This is where you brought the biology class to collect pond water so we could look at it under the microscope."

"Yep," Stacy agreed, seeming pleased Ros recognized it.

"We came in from over there and walked down the hill."

"And half the class stepped in meadow muffins even though I warned them to watch where they walked."

"I didn't know you owned this farm. I don't remember you mentioning it."

"I didn't twenty-five years ago. Harvey Atkins owned it. He was always very kind to let us access the pond for our lab work. I bought it or at least eighty acres of it from him ten years ago when his wife died. He kept the other two hundred acres on the other side of the road to lease. That was more land than I needed or could afford."

"That sounds similar to the choices I made. There were two apartments available in my building when I moved in. A two-bedroom and a three-bedroom. The three-bedroom was very nice. It had a fireplace and a good-size pantry, but I didn't need three bedrooms. I need two for when Aunt Bonnie comes to visit, but three seems unnecessarily extravagant."

"So there's just you?"

"Yes."

"I guess three bedrooms would be unnecessary," Stacy said with a strange twinkle in her eye.

"How many bedrooms do you have?"

"Three. One's a guest room and one is my office." Stacy steered the ATV around the pond and up the hill, then headed back toward the gate. Ros climbed out and opened it again, gesturing like a bullfighter at a charging bull as Stacy drove through it.

They were nearly back to the house when Stacy's cell phone chimed an incoming call in her pocket. She hesitated as if she might not answer it, but Ros insisted it was okay.

"Hello, Meade. What's cooking?"

Ros couldn't hear the other side of the conversation, but it sounded like Stacy had agreed to bring her something and she was amending the quantity.

"No problem. How about tomorrow afternoon? I'll bring them by the shop. I'll bring three dozen. That'll give you extras just in case. Enough?"

Stacy had a disappointed look on her face when she ended the call.

"I'm sorry, Ros. Would it be okay if I show you the house another day? Meade is doing the flowers for a wedding and I promised to cut some tree branches for centerpieces. She wants white bark birch, and I've got one down by the stream I can use. I'll need to drive the tractor down there with my chainsaw."

"There's another tool that isn't part of my skill set," Ros said and climbed out. "You go ahead. It's getting late and you're running out of daylight."

"Thanks. I'll see you tomorrow. I'll be finished with the house trim in another day or two, that's if it doesn't rain. I heard there's a chance of showers in the morning. I can't paint wet siding."

"I'm sure Aunt Bonnie will love it whenever you get it finished. The house looks a thousand times better than it did. I'm anxious to see the finished project before I head back to Cincinnati."

"You're going back already?" Stacy seemed surprised.

"Yes, I only took two weeks of my vacation. I plan to leave on Saturday."

"Miss Bonnie will hate to see you go."

Ros searched Stacy's expression, looking for a clue whether she'd hate to see her go as well.

"I can't stay forever. My work is calling."

Stacy didn't reply. Whatever she was thinking, Ros couldn't read it.

"I'll see you tomorrow," Ros said and headed for her car. She felt Stacy watching her as she crossed the driveway. She expected her to drive the ATV back in the barn and bring out the tractor, but she sat waiting until Ros pulled away.

CHAPTER SEVENTEEN

As Stacy had expected, rain began just before dawn and according to the weather forecast it would continue off and on throughout the day. She suspected Bonnie would be fretting and stewing that nothing was being accomplished during lulls in the rain, so she called her to let her know she wouldn't be over to paint, but she shouldn't worry. She'd make up for lost time.

The day off from painting gave Stacy a chance to catch up at home. Do a load or two of laundry. Run the vacuum. And tend to some chores around the house.

While carrying trash out to the barrel she reached in the box of rags Bonnie had given her to replenish the supply in the truck. When she drew out a handful something dropped on the floor. It was Bonnie's diary. She had forgotten she had tossed it in the box to be disposed of later. It was still locked and she still didn't have the key. Why she hadn't discarded it already was a mystery.

She placed the diary on the kitchen table and went to finish her chores in the barn. She told herself she would just toss it the next trip out to the trash barrel. It wasn't worth the worry. And it wasn't her property. She shouldn't snoop.

But something about the little book with the brass lock attracted her attention. As much as she tried to resist, her curiosity eventually got the better of her. Something as a scientist, she had tons of.

She wanted to know what was inside. She could use scissors and cut the leather strap securing the lock. But she didn't want to do that. She told herself she would only look if she could open it without damaging it. Returning from the barn with a tiny screwdriver, one she had used to repair her fishing reel, she sat down at the kitchen table and set the diary in front of her, like a surgeon examining her patient before making the first cut.

"Sorry, Miss Bonnie. I'm going to open it." She carefully inserted the screwdriver into the lock and wiggled it. As if it had been waiting patiently to be liberated, the tiny latch clicked and released without resistance.

Stacy took a deep breath and opened the cover. And closed it almost immediately. "Oh crap," she gasped, pushing it back on the table. This wasn't Bonnie's diary. The name on the first page, handwritten in bright red ink below the words *This Belongs To*, read Ros McClure.

Stacy pressed the latch back into the lock until it clicked. She felt like she had been caught spying. This was more invasive than watching Ros shave her legs through the bathroom window. That, after all, wasn't her fault. She had been standing on the ladder, caulking the window. It was an innocent observation. And it wasn't as if she saw her naked.

But this was Ros's private thoughts and memories. Did she know Bonnie had given it away? Stacy comforted herself in the assumption that if Ros thought it was important she would have it in her possession and it would not be boxed with junk in Miss Bonnie's attic. Still, Stacy was snooping.

She laced her fingers through her hair nervously as she stared down at the diary. Her curiosity had not been quenched. She inserted the screwdriver and popped the latch again. She slowly opened the cover and read the first entry.

Mother says I have to stay. I hate her. I hate her. I hate her. I hate her. I hate her. I hate her. I hate her. I hate her.

It was written in bold letters, underlined and repeated down the page. Stacy continued to read. The first dozen or so pages were brief but heartbreaking confessions of feeling abandoned and unloved in spite of calls from her mother from various truck stops across the country and periodic presents arriving in the mail. She didn't make entries every day and occasionally made only a few doodlings or sketches on a page. It wasn't until near the end of her sophomore year in high school that Ros included bits of happiness and normality.

Aunt Bonnie and I went mushroom hunting. I filled a paper sack full of morels. They don't look like mushrooms but Aunt Bonnie said they are. She cooked some for dinner. They're pretty good. She's going to teach me how to do it. Flour and salt and pepper and you flop them around in the sack then fry them. She's a good cook. Better than Mom.

At the bottom of the page was a pencil drawing of a honeycombed-shaped mushroom.

"Very good, Ros. That's exactly what a *Morchella* looks like. And you're right. They are delicious." Stacy turned the page.

I saw the grossest thing. We took a picnic to the river and there was a dead cow in the woods. It was just bones. Aunt Bonnie said it was nature's way. It was still gross.

Stacy chuckled at the face drawn at the bottom with its tongue out.

Saturday Aunt Bonnie took me out in the country on a dirt road and I GOT TO DRIVE. She said it's time for me to learn but I just can't tell anyone. I'm not legal. It was fun. I went a whole thirty miles an hour. There was dust flying everywhere. It was awesome. Aunt Bonnie said you have to feel for the friction point on a stick shift. I don't like cars with a clutch.

"Me either, Ros. Me either." Stacy slipped a napkin in the page to mark the spot and went to change the laundry load.

The next few pages were ramblings about clothes and homework that failed to challenge her and which hairstyle she liked best on her friends. Sometime in the fall of her junior year she drew a heart on the page with the letters BT inside, nothing more. Stacy wondered who BT was. She couldn't remember anyone with those initials, but she had taught hundreds of students over the years. Surely Ros would eventually mention who BT was. She read on.

Aunt Bonnie and I rode the bus to Goodland yesterday for her eye doctor appointment. She got her eyes dilated so she couldn't drive and she said I'm not ready to drive that far yet. I could do it. I saw BT at the grocery store buying milk and cookies. I love Oreos.

"Me too." Stacy replaced the bookmark and went to load the birch branches in the back of the truck. It was time to deliver them to Meade. Her phone rang before she pulled out of the drive.

"Hello, Meade. I'm just leaving and heading your way with the branches. Three dozen, maybe four."

"Thank you, hon, but I'm not going to be at the store. I have to run over to Oakley with a delivery to the funeral home. Then a home delivery near Brewster. I'm afraid I won't be back until late. Would it be terrible if we make it tomorrow?"

"No, that's fine. Any particular time?"

"I'll be in the shop all day, so whatever works for you is okay with me."

"See you tomorrow then. Drive safely."

Stacy started the ATV and drove across the pasture to check on the fence she had mended and get a little fresh air. She had spent several hours reading Ros's diary and needed a break. She needed a break from feeling like she was prying into someone's private life. But she knew she'd read more. She couldn't resist. She had to solve the mystery of who BT was. Which one of Ros's classmates could it be? Does Ros ever confess her attraction for BT? Like reading a mystery romance novel, she had to know.

The fence was still intact and the cows were still grazing peacefully. Stacy returned the ATV to the barn and went inside for a little more reading. Although the next thing she read was disappointing.

Meredith and I made friendship bracelets but I'm not sure I'm going to wear mine all the time. She thinks I should. I got an A on the math test. No one else did. It wasn't that hard. Why do people make fun of you just because you're smart? Mrs. Stanley said I have a knack for numbers, whatever that means. Mom forgot my birthday.

"How can you forget your kid's birthday?" Stacy stuck the napkin in the page and went to make a sandwich for dinner.

OMG, I went skinny-dipping in the Mr. Waltonburg's pond. I snuck in without him seeing me. Barb and Karen dared us but I'm the only one who did it. Meredith and Neelie chickened out. They don't believe I did it. But I did. The water was cold and the bottom is all slimy and muddy. And I know I felt a fish bite my ankle. Ewwww!!!

Stacy chuckled and continued eating her sandwich as she turned the page.

I have a cold. I didn't tell Aunt Bonnie I went skinny-dipping. She'd say I caught cold from that icky old pond water. I didn't. I caught it from BT. She had one at school. I know that's where I caught it. But I don't care. It was hers and now it's mine. She gave it to me.

There was a series of little hearts drawn with a red pencil across the bottom of the page.

"Who the heck is BT?" Stacy muttered. "At least I know it's a girl, like I'm surprised."

The biology lab smells. So does the girls' locker room. Which smells worse? I probably can't use that as my debate topic in class. I bet the boys' locker room smells worse. Why do boys stink? Girls smell better, as a rule anyway. Not after gym class though. I wish I was more athletic. BT is probably the most athletic person I know. Well, not counting the boys football team. Gracefully athletic. That's it. BT is gracefully athletic.

"Interesting observation," Stacy said and turned the page.

Mrs. Stanley thinks I should enter the accounting competition. She thinks Colby could win districts and maybe go on to state if I'd join the team. Aunt Bonnie thinks I should do it. I wonder what Mom would say. I wonder if she even knows how I'm doing in school. I'm on the honor roll again. Straight A's. She hardly ever calls anymore. And Dad is a jerk. I spent all my babysitting money on their Christmas presents and they didn't even say thank you. Okay, so it wasn't ALL my babysitting money. I bought Aunt Bonnie a new bathrobe. She ripped her old one on the doorknob. She was going to mend it. Nope. I got her a new one. I also gave her some chocolate-covered cherries. Her favorite. She got me a birthstone ring. It's really pretty and elegant. She was very generous to give it to me. And I told her so. She almost cried. She gave me a pair of socks with little rainbows on them. I like them. Shhhhh. I tell myself BT gave me the ring. Wouldn't it be terrific if someone older like that gave me a ring? She's so smart and beautiful and kind. Shhhhh.

"Older, eh?" Stacy said. "BT is a girl and older. You're a junior so she must be a senior. The plot thickens." She smiled and turned the page.

We won districts!!!! Mrs. Stanley thinks we will absolutely win state. I'm going to review some chapters in the book. I hope I haven't forgotten anything from Accounting 1. Maybe I should review that textbook, too. Aunt Bonnie said she has no doubt we'll win. And she promised me $100 if we do. Damn, $100 for just answering a few accounting questions? No problemo!!!!

The word "Damn" had a line drawn through it.

"I remember Beverly Stanley said you were the only reason they won." Stacy nodded at the memory. "She said you answered every single question and in record time."

Junior-senior prom is next weekend. Josh invited me to go. He's a senior on the debate team. I guess he's nice and all but I don't want to go with him or any him. I'd rather go with BT, but she'd never ask me. Maybe I'll go to senior prom next year. Maybe. This is so hard. Why does it have to be so hard? Someday when I'm older and go to college and have my own place, maybe it will be easier. I hope so. Aunt Bonnie says it will.

"It's hard for everyone, Ros. Believe me. Being gay is not for wimps. Not when you're a teenager." Stacy heaved a sigh and turned the page.

SCHOOL'S OUT!!!!!!!!

Stacy laughed out loud at the statement written in bold letters in the middle of the page.

"We teachers agree with you. By May we need a break too."

Aunt Bonnie let me order a new bra from Sears. It was beige and had underwires and a little lace flower in the middle. It didn't fit and we had to send it back. It was way too tight. She made me let her measure my boobs so we could order the right size. That's embarrassing!!!! The difference between the rib cage and the boobs determines the cup size. Who knew? But they don't allow for fractions of an inch. Just whole numbers and you have to round up. That doesn't seem very accurate but she says that's how they do it. She says I won't like underwire but that's what Meredith wears and she said they make you look older. Somebody called her a boy at school just because she's flat chested and it made her cry. Stupid people. I told her not to let it bother her. They were probably jealous.

"Well, she isn't flat chested anymore," Stacy said and read on.

BT was wearing a Band-Aid on her finger. I wonder what happened. I hate having my period!!!

"Amen, sister. A-freakin-men," Stacy cackled. "Come on, tell me who BT is already."

This is my senior year and everyone is going to prom. I want to go but I don't want to go. Larry Collins asked me. Aunt Bonnie said I should go with him. How else am I going to get to go? You have to have a date. Well, you don't HAVE to have a date but people will make fun of you if you don't. That seems so sexist. Why should I have to go with a boy just to attend my senior prom? Maybe I'll go. Meredith said I should go with Larry. She thinks he's harmless. But he's a big goober. Aunt Bonnie said she'd take me shopping for a prom dress. I know what I want. And it ISN'T school colors. Orange or black? Oh, yuk!! I want purple. Or soft lavender. With matching shoes. I saw the most perfect high heels in the window. G-orgeous!! Rhinestones on the toe and on the straps. I could wear a rhinestone necklace and earrings. My pierced ears are almost healed. I'll be ready to wear something other than these training earrings by prom. BT noticed my pierced ears and said they looked nice. I about dropped dead right there in class. WOW!! I need to stop biting my nails. BT has the most beautiful hands. I bet she never bites her nails. I wonder what it would be like to hold her hand. They're probably extremely soft.

"I remember when you got your ears pierced, now that you mention it," Stacy said, rereading the section. "They did look nice. You kept fiddling with them all through class. And as I remember you did wear a lavender dress. Very captivating too. And yes, your date looked like a farmer. Every one of us chaperones noticed he was wearing brown work boots and a black tux. He also had a can of Skoal in his pocket until I confiscated it. And as I remember, he wasn't the only one." Stacy shook her head in disgust.

Jenny Milford and Shiner Williams were prom king and queen. We all voted for her. She SO deserved it after the accident. He carried her for the king and queen spotlight dance. Everybody was crying. Her mom was there to help with her wheelchair but we would have helped. Her dress was metallic gold lamé and she had gold sandals and she had flowers in her hair. She was so pretty. Shiner wore a matching gold bow tie and vest.

BT was at prom. She didn't dance with anyone. I would have danced with her if she had asked me. ALL NIGHT!!!!

"Sounds like a wallflower. Who was her date?" Stacy stretched and yawned. As much as she wanted to solve the mystery of who BT was, she was tired and she had a full day of painting ahead of her. She marked the page and went to take a shower before bed.

The next morning was forecast to be sunny and warm, but a surprise rain cloud meant Stacy wasn't going to be painting today, at least not this morning. She called Bonnie and gave her the news, then headed into town with the tree branches for Meade. She balanced the box on her hip as she opened the door to the flower shop.

"It's your neighborhood tree service," Stacy called to an empty front of the store.

"Be right there, tree person," Meade replied. She came striding through the doorway, carrying a bouquet of yellow and white carnations with sprigs of ferns.

"White bark birch," Stacy said, tipping the box so Meade could see the neatly cut pieces of wood, all of them about three inches in diameter and eighteen inches long.

"Perfect," she said, examining the contents while Stacy continued to hold the heavy box. "What do I owe you?"

"Nothing. I had a tree that needed trimming." She set the box on the counter and brushed the dirt off her shirt. "What exactly are you going to do with them?"

"The Sanchez wedding. They want log and gardenia centerpieces."

"I like the idea of gardenias, but I'm not so sure about the log thing."

"Actually they're going to be log, burlap, and gardenia centerpieces with sprigs of baby's breath. The bride's mother found a picture online of what they want. It's sort of a gaucho theme. By the way, if I had to cut a tree up for someone else, what would you charge them? I need to know."

"You decide. It doesn't matter to me."

"The truck stop charges six dollars for a bundle of nondescript firewood. This is probably three or four of those." Meade rummaged in the box, obviously trying to get Stacy to commit to a price.

"Whatever you'd like to charge is fine with me. I cut them. You decorate them."

"I'm tempted to not increase the price. They're going to pay enough for the gardenias. I do love the smell of gardenias. I planted two in pots for my patio. Acidic soil, right?"

"Yep. Stir in some coffee grounds every now and then and keep them well watered."

"How's the painting going?"

"Fine until it rained yesterday and today. Miss Bonnie is about ready to swallow her teeth over the delay. I should be finished in a couple days, though."

"I know you. You've probably been on the ladder by six in the morning."

"Five thirty. We've had some beautiful mornings. Not too hot. Fresh breeze. Birds chirping in the trees. Why not start early?"

"Of course, there's that other detail." Meade gave a wry grin.

"What detail?"

"Ros McClure. It was so nice to meet her the other evening. Very personable woman. I assume she's still in town."

"She is, but I'm not sure what that has to do with how early I start painting."

"It has everything to do with why you want to be there at all, my good person. Everything." Meade pinched her cheek.

"I have no idea what you mean. We're not back to that old topic, are we?"

"Ros McClure likes you. There! I've said it. I watched you two at the reunion. You were watching her and she was definitely watching you. And there was the dance. The slow dance." Meade did a little sashay behind the counter.

"You're reading way too much into that. Sure, she's a nice woman, but that's all there is to it. We have a common denominator. I'm painting her aunt's house."

"The common denominator is your past. Her aunt is just the convenient excuse to revisit that. Another convenient excuse was you leaving your phone at her house."

"I didn't do it on purpose," Stacy argued. "And I didn't tell her to bring it to me."

"Well, she likes you or she wouldn't have done it."

"She said she appreciates my help with her aunt."

"No, I mean she LIKES you. Really likes you. I can see it in her eyes. Why can't you admit you like her? I'll tell you what, how about I make a simple little bouquet, something nice and elegant, and you take it to her. Use whatever justification you think would work. Thank her for allowing you to be part of their lives. Apologize for some transgression you've committed."

Stacy started to interrupt, but Meade held up her hand and continued. "I'm sure you've done something you need to apologize for. Or just say Meade thought you'd like some flowers. Whatever works." All the while Meade was talking she was combining a few pastel flowers and lacy ferns and securing them with a yellow ribbon. Like magic, a little of this and little of that became an eye-catching bouquet.

"She wore yellow to the reunion," Meade added, adjusting the ribbon just so. "There. Take her this. Consider it payment for the birch branches."

"It's very nice, but I don't need to take her flowers."

"Of course you don't NEED to take her flowers, but how about you WANT to take her flowers?" Meade grinned and thrust the bouquet at Stacy.

Stacy stared at the bouquet. Only after a moment of hesitation did she finally take it.

"What if she doesn't like them? Or doesn't want them?"

"What woman wouldn't want flowers? Take it from me. Women's desire for flowers keeps me in business."

"I don't think so." Stacy took a deep breath as she felt her courage dissolving. She shoved the bouquet back at Meade and started for the door.

"Are you sure?" Meade called after her.

"Yes, I'm sure! Stop pushing it." The door slammed behind her as she headed out into the rain.

Stacy stopped at the grocery store for a few things, then at the hardware store for another gallon of white paint before heading home. By the time she emptied the truck it had stopped raining and the sun was out. It would take a few hours of warm sunshine before Bonnie's house would be dry enough to paint, but Stacy was hopeful she could do at least some of the trim work. While she waited for a can of soup to heat on the stove she sat down at the table with the diary, hoping she'd finally learn who this BT person was. It had to be someone important in Ros's life since the attraction seemed to last for two years. She had to know if Ros ever gets the courage to admit it. She opened to the second page of prom memories and began to read.

> *I was going to talk to BT but I didn't know what to say. Every time I got up enough courage there was Larry. He was being a real creep. I don't do what some of the other girls do but he thought I did. He's the last person I'd do that with. When I do that it'll have to be with someone really special. Someone I'm in love with. I told him I didn't want to go parking. He did anyway. He said it was too early to go home. I told him he was being a jerk. He tried to make me kiss him so I slapped him. Aunt Bonnie showed me how to defend myself. He's not so tough. I think I scared him. I hate kissing boys.*

"Okay, if BT was at your senior prom she wasn't a year ahead of you in school. Just a year older but in your class. Hmmmm." Stacy folded her hands across the pages and squinted off into space, trying to remember who was at Ros's prom. She had been a chaperone for so many it was hard to remember one from the next. She poured her soup in a mug and returned to the table to eat her lunch while she read.

> *I can't find my biology lab notebook. I've looked everywhere. I know I had it in my room. I know I did. I did all the drawings and the labeling. I only need to finish coloring and shading. I showed it to Aunt Bonnie and she liked the drawings of flowers. She thought I'd get a good grade on it. I can't find my colored pencils either. I don't want to buy a new pack. It's almost the end of the year.*

"Damn, woman. I hated to give you that grade. I sure wish you had found your lab notebook or come to talk with me about it." Stacy went to wash her lunch dishes before returning to the table for a few more minutes reading before she headed over to do some painting.

I got my acceptance letter from KU and one from Colorado State, but their accounting and finance degrees aren't terrific. Illinois, Michigan, and NYU are the best. I hope I hear from Illinois. Aunt Bonnie said she'd pay for my room and board if my grades are good enough to cover tuition. Straight A's and the honor roll should do it. I still can't find my lab notebook. It's starting to stress me out. One more week of school. DAMN!!!

This time the word damn didn't have a line drawn through it. Stacy turned the page to read what looked like the last entry.

Finals are over. Graduation is Saturday. It's supposed to rain. I didn't find my lab notebook. I'm so upset. We were supposed to leave it on the way out after we finished the lab final. I didn't have one to put in the box. What am I supposed to do? BT just looked at me as I walked out. She pointed to the box and asked where mine was. She said it was half my grade. I didn't say anything. She probably hates me. My biology teacher hates me.

Stacy sat motionless, staring down at the page in disbelief. She was the biology teacher. She was the BT of Ros's confessions.

"Oh my God. It's me," she gasped. She closed the diary and went to the window. It hadn't crossed her mind. She had been convinced BT was one of Ros's classmates.

As much as Stacy enjoyed being the object of Ros's infatuation once upon a time, twenty-five years had passed. Plenty of time to forget high school innocence and find new love. Stacy hadn't forgotten her attraction for Ros but surely Ros had forgotten those feelings for BT and moved on.

Even if she hadn't and if what Meade said was correct, Ros was going back home to Cincinnati in a few days and seemingly without regret. Their past had shaped a friendship. Nothing more. A friendship with a thousand miles between them. Stacy would have to settle for that.

She couldn't stay staring out the window all day. She had a house to finish painting. She collected what she needed and headed out to the truck. The day had warmed nicely, and it would be good painting weather.

Halfway to Bonnie's house she pulled to the side of the road and sat contemplating what she had read and her choices. She couldn't help it. She had to take a chance. She stomped on the gas, slinging dirt and gravel as she headed for town. She pulled to the curb and climbed out, striding into Meade's shop. Without saying a word, she opened the walk-in cooler and retrieved the bouquet with the yellow ribbon. She tossed Meade a don't-even-ask look and walked out of the shop to the sound of the door chime while Meade smiled approval.

Stacy wondered if she should call and tell Bonnie she was on her way over to paint. She didn't need to. Bonnie had said they didn't need to be home for her to work, and everything she needed was either in the barn or in the back of her truck.

It was a moot point, actually, she couldn't call. She was busy battling the swarm of butterflies in her stomach over bringing flowers to Ros. What should she say? How would they be received? How would she know the right moment to give them to her?

Stacy envisioned Ros offering a bright smile and a warm thank-you. Maybe a gleeful acceptance, after all they were yellow and white, like Bonnie's house. And yellow like the blouse Ros wore to the reunion that had had Stacy's eyes glued to it all evening, praying for a peek through the gossamer fabric.

She was still contemplating what to say when she turned into Bonnie's driveway. The front door was open and Ros was sitting in the porch swing reading something on her cell phone. She was wearing white capri pants and a baby blue sleeveless top, and she was barefoot. She looked fresh and radiant in spite of it being a hot summer day. Stacy didn't see Bonnie and assumed she was preoccupied inside.

This was the moment, Stacy thought. She had mustered her courage and tamed the butterflies enough to hopefully sound something less than stupid when she handed her the flowers. The exact moment she stepped out of the truck, however, bouquet in hand, Meredith and Bonnie came out the door onto the porch, laughing, arm in arm.

"You were right, Ros. My shoes were under the bed, right where I left them," Meredith said in Ros's direction.

"Hello, Stacy, dear," Bonnie said brightly. "Aren't those beautiful flowers?"

"Hello," Ros said, her eyes falling on the bouquet. "We didn't think you'd be painting today because of the rain this morning."

"I thought I could get a few hours in this afternoon, if that's okay with Miss Bonnie. But I can come back tomorrow. I see you've got company."

"I don't have company. Ros has company. You can go ahead and paint all you want," Bonnie encouraged.

"We'll stay out of your way," Meredith offered.

It was plain all three women were staring at the bouquet in Stacy's fist, like a pack of hungry dogs waiting for a biscuit.

"Who are the flowers for?" Meredith asked.

Stacy was at a crossroads. An awkward crossroads. How could she explain the flowers were for Ros? She'd barely summoned the courage to give them to her at all. It wasn't something she wanted to announce to a group of people. She didn't want to embarrass herself or Ros if they were unwelcome. And if they were, could Meredith be the reason? Was there more to their relationship than just their date to the reunion? Stacy hadn't considered that until now. And she felt foolish for not doing so.

"Oh, these?" Stacy cleared her throat. "I brought these for you, Miss Bonnie. Yellow and white, just like your house." She handed the bouquet to Bonnie. "Meade made it for you. She owns the flower shop where your flowers came from when you were in the hospital. She wanted you to have them."

"Aren't they gorgeous, Aunt Bonnie? So fresh and bright." Ros smiled sweetly, as if she genuinely admired the flowers and the thoughtfulness.

"Thank you, dear." Bonnie gave Stacy a kiss on the cheek. "Isn't that nice of her? I'll have to thank her next time I'm in town."

"You don't need to. I already thanked her. She enjoys doing things like that for people."

"Well, I will anyway. And I'm going to put them in some water. I know just the vase I'm going to use." Bonnie went inside with her flowers like a child carrying a new toy.

"That was very sweet of Meade to do that," Ros said with a curious look. "Very sweet. Very generous. Thank you for bringing them, Stacy. They're much appreciated." Ros's eyes met Stacy's and held them a moment.

"I'm glad she likes them." Stacy was reading way too much into Ros's smile but how could she not? She wanted those possibilities to be true.

"Meade is such a enchanting woman," Meredith said, taking a seat next to Ros in the swing. "You're lucky to have such a good friend, Stacy. And you two are a perfect fit. She's a florist and you're a biology farmer. Think of all you have in common. Just like Ros and I, on the other hand, are the quintessential odd couple. She's subdued, detail-oriented, and studious. I'm boisterous, extroverted, and flamboyant." Meredith flipped her hair as she leaned into Ros and laughed robustly.

"Yes, you are certainly all of those things." Ros nodded emphatically as they shared a happy moment.

"I better get to work. I'm burning daylight," Stacy said, turning on her heels. She had seen all she wanted of Meredith fawning all over Ros.

As she headed to the barn, she scolded herself. She had never been good at romancing anyone. Identify the genus and species of the butterfly perched on a woman's shoulder, yes. And its migration and mating habits, sure. But tell a woman she was as soft and delicate as a butterfly, no. And she hated herself for it.

She shook her head. It was time to paint. She suspected she would need lots of painting to block out the disappointment and humiliation for the botched gesture. Lots!!

CHAPTER EIGHTEEN

It was going to be a bright sunny day, welcome weather after a day and a half of rain. Ros started a load of laundry, changed the sheets on the bed, and baked some cookies while she waited for a call from Steve. His text seemed to indicate he was irritated at something or someone in the office and wanted her to be aware of the situation. She'd just as soon he didn't but as assistant chief auditor, she'd accept his call and discuss the matter politely.

"Don't change anything or we'll have to resubmit the entire report," Ros said sternly as Stacy walked through the back door and pointed to the sink with her water bottle. Ros nodded but continued her phone conversation. "I'll take care of it when I'm back in the office next week. Yes, I've looked at it. It looks fine to me."

Stacy filled her bottle, took a long drink, then filled it again. She looked hot and sweaty but had a smile on her face. She saluted and went back outside.

Ros finished the call amid a fresh flood of frustration. Steve was doing his best to handle things, but he wasn't listening to advice from her or the others in the office. She had a feeling she'd be busy once she got back, but she wasn't going to regret taking this vacation. She needed it and deserved it.

Ros took a glass of iced tea outside and sat down in the porch swing to answer some emails on her cell phone. It was hot but normal for June in western Kansas. She used to think the ceiling fan Bonnie had installed on the front porch was pointless but to the contrary the large blades were stirring the air just enough to make ninety degrees tolerable. Bonnie had gone to town for lunch with her friends. The heat even had Piano seeking shade and a breeze.

"Are you down there?" Stacy called. She was somewhere on the ladder on the side of the house.

"Yes. On the front porch. Do you need something?"

"My phone is ringing and I've got paint on my hands. Would you mind seeing who it is?"

"Where is it?" Ros asked, coming to the side of the house.

"In the grass at the bottom of the ladder."

Ros checked the screen for an ID.

"It's someone named Hank. There's a photo of an older gentleman."

"Answer it, please. He's one of my neighbors." Stacy looked down with interest.

"Hello. May I help you?"

"Stacy?" he said in a puzzled tone. "You don't sound like Stacy."

"No, I'm not Stacy. I'm answering the phone for her. She's busy right now. May I help you?"

"Tell Stacy she's got a cow out grazing about a quarter mile up the road. A branch from that big elm at the corner of the Varners' property came down and took out a section of her fence. All five strands. She'll have them all out if she doesn't do something. Does she want me to call someone?"

"Let me check," Ros said, holding the phone to her chest. "Hank says you've got a section of fence down and a cow out grazing on the road. He wants to know if he should call someone to fix it."

"Crap," Stacy replied disgustedly. "No. Tell him I'll take care of it. I'm almost done on this side. I'll be there in thirty minutes."

Ros relayed the message while Stacy quickly finished the spot she was painting and climbed down.

"Did Hank say if it's just one cow that's out?" Stacy stood at the hose, washing the paint from her hands and arms.

"Yes. And you've got paint on your face." Ros pointed to the spot.

"I'm not surprised. I kept getting buzzed by flies and I was trying to shoo them away. Probably in my hair too." She tilted her head so Ros could see.

"I don't see any but…"

"I know what you're going to say. White paint wouldn't show in my white hair." She continued rubbing at the paint on her arms.

"That's not what I was going to say. And I think your white hair looks nice."

"Nice, huh? That's a polite way of saying you're looking old."

"I didn't say that. In fact, in my opinion it looks stunning." Ros picked a piece of a leaf from Stacy's hair.

"Thank you but what were you going to say?"

"I was going to say you've got paint on your neck. It looks like a brush stroke all the way across the back."

"You're kidding." She wiped her wet hand across her neck, but the paint was still there.

Ros retrieved a rag from the sack on the tailgate of the pickup. She held it under the hose, wrung it out, and began rubbing at the paint smear on Stacy's neck.

"Hold still." She rinsed the rag and continued until she had cleaned away every trace of it. She ran her fingers up the back of Stacy's hair, checking for paint. "Close your eyes." She cradled her hand under Stacy's chin and dabbed at the paint above her eyebrow. Stacy did as she was told while Ros acted like a mother cat cleaning her young. "This rag looks familiar. I used to have a T-shirt like this."

"That's because Miss Bonnie gave me a bunch of old towels and clothes she was going to throw out. I go through a lot of rags when I'm painting."

"I see that." Ros gave one last dab, then smiled at her work. "There. All done."

"Thank you, Mommy," Stacy said childishly. She tapped the lid onto the paint can and carried the ladder to the barn. Ros did what she could to help clean up.

"By the way, do you need help getting the cow back in the pasture?"

Stacy looked up from loading tools in her truck with a surprised expression.

"I didn't know you knew how to herd cattle."

"Well, actually I don't, so I'd just be in the way. Never mind."

"No, no. You wouldn't be in the way. In fact an extra pair of hands would be very helpful."

"Even if I don't know what I'm doing?"

"I'll take my chances," Stacy said with a confident smile.

Ros sent Bonnie a text to let her know where she'd be and locked up the house while Stacy finished cleaning up the yard and climbed in the truck.

"Ready?" Stacy reached over and opened the passenger side door.

"Ready." Ros climbed in and buckled her seat belt.

"I'm sorry, but I'm all sweaty. You might want to open your window."

"It's summertime in Kansas. Who isn't sweaty? And there's a difference between sweaty and smelly. I remember you telling one of the boys in class that. Glen always smelled like dirty socks." Ros leaned over and gave Stacy the sniff test. "You're okay. You pass." She stepped out of her sandals and propped her feet up on the dashboard. "Is this okay?"

"Sure. Make yourself comfortable. I like the little ankle bracelet by the way." She pulled out of the drive and headed for home.

"A friend gave it to me for my birthday."

"Meredith?" Stacy asked cautiously.

"No. Someone at work. She's big on accessorizing."

"It looks nice."

"It would look better if I had a tan." Ros looked down at her pale legs.

"Not necessarily." Stacy hesitated, then reached over and brushed her finger up Ros's leg. "Time to shave again." She gave a little grin.

"I wondered when that was going to come up. Yes, I saw you watching me."

"I need to apologize for that, Ros. But I couldn't help it. I was caulking around the window and you were on the other side. How could I not see what was happening?"

"You're forgiven."

"Thank you. And since the trim on that side of the house is finished, you're safe. I won't be outside the bathroom window looking in."

Stacy drove down the road to get a look at the downed fence. Sure enough, a large branch from the neighbor's tree had fallen onto her property, crushing all five strands of fencing. She could see the cow up the road, lazily following its nose through the tall grass along the ditch.

"What do we do first?" Ros asked, slipping back into her sandals.

"Normally you fix the downed fence before more get out, but since I don't see any other cows close by we'll get her back in first."

Stacy pulled in the drive and circled up to the barn. "I'll be right back." She returned with a bucket carrying some grain, loaded some tools in the back of the truck, then drove back down the road.

"Tell me what you want me to do." Ros climbed out but remained safely behind Stacy as she walked toward the cow with the bucket of grain.

"This one is pretty tame. She'll follow the bucket. You stand over there and hold your arms out if she decides to mosey on up the road." Stacy positioned Ros across the road, then shook the bucket to get the cow's attention.

"Hey!" she shouted and shook the bucket again. "Come on. Let's go. Time to go home." She gave a sharp whistle and shook the bucket again. She allowed the cow to have a taste, then started walking up the road, holding the bucket out so the cow could see it. "Ros, you can follow in the truck but stay back a ways." She continued to walk and shake the bucket. The cow followed, plodding along.

Ros followed in the truck, keeping back a safe distance.

It took twenty minutes, but Stacy was finally able to escort the cow back through an opening in the fence, giving it a smack on the rump to hurry it along. Ros pulled off the road and parked next to the downed section of fence. Stacy went to work with a chain saw, cutting up the branch into usable lengths and stacking them in a neat pile. Ros came to help stack the wood, but Stacy waved her back, pointing at the sharp barbs on the wire fencing. When she was finished with the tree, she began repairing the fence while Ros watched.

"It's nice you and Meredith have stayed such good friends since high school," Stacy said, choosing a new topic of conversation, one Ros hadn't anticipated.

"To be honest, I haven't seen or talked to her in years. We kind of drifted apart. It's easy to do when you don't live in the same town or even the same state."

"So you've rekindled your friendship?"

"I guess you could say that. I invited her to come visit me in Cincinnati sometime. She has a conference in Cleveland in the fall so she'll be driving through."

"Cincinnati isn't exactly on the route from Colby to Cleveland, is it?"

"Well, no. But I invited her anyway. We've had a great time reminiscing about our high school days. She was a late bloomer, if you know what I mean. But she was there for me when I was coming out and needed someone to talk to."

Stacy looked over as if she had something to say but continued repairing the fence instead.

"I know. Meredith had a reputation in high school. But most of it was exaggeration. She was more of a tease and boys didn't like that. She wanted to be popular and that was the only way she knew to do it. She admits it."

"She's going to miss you when you leave."

"I'll miss her, too. And of course I'll miss Aunt Bonnie. And you," Ros added, leaning back against the truck. "I've had a good time. I forgot what it's like to be outdoors." She turned her face up to the warm sun and took a deep, cleansing breath.

"I assumed Cincinnati had outdoors," Stacy said with a chuckle.

"Nope. We have to import it."

"That's too bad. I'll have to send you some." Stacy began ramming the new post in the ground with a post driver.

"Please do. I'll have it mounted right outside my office window."

"Could you hand me the gloves on the tailgate?" Stacy wiped the back of her hand across her forehead while Ros retrieved the gloves.

"Shouldn't you be wearing these all the time when you're working around the farm?" Ros took Stacy's hand and examined the palm. "You need some heavy duty hand cream."

"I do, huh?" Stacy allowed Ros to rub her fingers over her rough skin.

"Yes. What's that stuff farmers use? Balm something?"

"Bag balm. I've got some."

"Then use it, woman." Ros scowled.

"I do, but not enough I guess." Stacy's fingers closed over Ros's and held them a moment before she went back to work on the fence.

"If the tree is on your neighbor's property, shouldn't they cut it up and fix your fence?"

"Yes, it's on the Varners' property, but if I wait for him to fix it my cows will be in Montana."

"Do you have names for your cows?"

"No. These aren't pets. They're livestock, bred and raised to be sold for a profit. I don't name them. Four-H kids name their project animals, then are heartbroken when they have to take them to the auction. One of the girls painted the hooves of her calf like fingernails then had to ride in the truck to take it to be sold."

"But the little ones are so cute. Not so much when they're older. Like puppies and kittens. I don't care what breed, animals are all adorable when they're young. Except snakes."

"Did you ever tell Miss Bonnie about the snakes in the barn?" Stacy asked.

"No. I don't plan to either. That'll be our secret. I don't want to worry her and I don't want a lecture on guns or snakes or nature's food chain."

"So I shouldn't lecture on the food chain?" Stacy grinned.

"No. Save that for Aunt Bonnie. She loves that stuff."

"Speaking of Miss Bonnie, has she tried to find that family church again?"

"No. I don't think so. I told her I'd take her one of these days before I go home, but she hasn't mentioned it."

"Aren't you afraid she'll drive off into northern Kansas and get lost again?"

"Yes. I am. But I can't stop her."

"Would you like me to take the two of you to find it? I think I know exactly where it is. It might be better to let her have the satisfaction of seeing it once and for all than wait for a call that she's lost."

"I couldn't find it on my GPS."

"I'm not surprised. It's at the intersection of two dirt roads out in the middle of nothing but farm fields. It's going to be in the nineties tomorrow so maybe it's a better day for an excursion than for standing on the ladder."

"You wouldn't mind taking us to find it?"

"Not at all. If we get lost you can blame it on the biology teacher, not the farmer. Of course if Miss Bonnie doesn't want to go, I can always finish up the painting."

"I bet she will. I'd like to see what my great-great grandfather built. A family legacy so to speak."

"Sounds like a plan." Stacy seemed pleased with the idea of going on an outing instead of painting in the sweltering heat. The idea sounded appealing to Ros as well and on several levels.

Stacy attached the last clip to the top strand of wire and checked to make sure everything was secure, then loaded the tools in the back of the truck and climbed in the driver's seat.

"Okay, now I'm sweaty and smelly," she said, wiping her forearm across the perspiration dripping from her chin. "I'll take you home, but then I really need a shower."

Ros put her window down and smiled but said nothing. There was something strangely appealing about Stacy's glistening skin and sweat-dampened hair, smell or not. And as much as she tried, the image of Stacy standing in the shower, ribbons of water rolling down her naked body, sent an electric jolt through her.

"Oh, my God," she whispered, gasping for breath at the thought.

"Sorry. Bad, huh?"

CHAPTER NINETEEN

Just before bedtime Ros reminded Bonnie about their trip to find the church. She seemed pleased about the outing. She didn't remember her recent failed excursion to find it but was happy to accompany Ros to visit a piece of family history. Bonnie was up early the next morning and busy in the kitchen when Ros finished her shower and came down to breakfast wearing khaki shorts and a white camp shirt. Bonnie was wearing navy blue pants and a long-sleeved gray sweater.

"Good morning," Ros said and gave her a kiss on the cheek. "Something sure smells good. What are you making?"

"Apple cake. I made it for our breakfast. My great-grandfather built the church, you know. Your great-great-grandfather."

"Yes, I remember you telling me." Ros wondered if this was going to be one of those days when Bonnie's memory struggled with reality.

"Shall I drive?"

"No, Aunt Bonnie. Stacy is going to drive. She knows where it is and volunteered to take us so we won't get lost. Her pickup has a backseat and plenty of room."

"Stacy's going?"

"Yes. Remember, I told you yesterday. Aunt Bonnie, don't you think you'd be more comfortable in a short sleeve shirt? Something other than a sweater. It's going to be in the nineties today and bright sunshine." Ros stroked her hand down the sleeve of Bonnie's heavy sweater. "Shall I go upstairs and get you something?"

"That warm?" Bonnie seemed surprised at the forecast. "I'll go change."

"Your light blue blouse would look nice." Ros hoped to guide the decision so she didn't come back downstairs in another sweater.

Bonnie returned to the kitchen as Stacy was pulling into the drive. She had indeed chosen the blue blouse but added a floral silk scarf around her neck.

"You look nice, Aunt Bonnie. A splash of color, as you used to tell me."

Bonnie arranged the scarf tails over her shoulder, then crumpled her hands in her short gray hair as if pushing curls into it.

"Your tour guide is here. Are you ladies ready?" Stacy stood at the back screen door. She was wearing faded jeans with a turquoise polo shirt.

"We are." Bonnie opened the door and waved her inside.

"Good morning, Ros," she said with a small smile Ros could swear was saying "I'm glad to see you again." "You look nice." Stacy's gaze drifted down and back up, lingering a moment as their eyes met. "Very nice." She turned to Bonnie and added, "You look nice, too, Miss Bonnie. Are you ready for an outing?"

"Have you ever been to the Rockford Church before?" Bonnie handed Stacy a piece of apple cake on a paper napkin.

"Yes, ma'am. I think so." Stacy finished the cake in three bites, being careful not to drop crumbs on the floor.

"Isn't it the Ash Rock Church, Aunt Bonnie?" Ros asked.

"Yes, the Ash Rock Church," Bonnie agreed, then followed Stacy out to the truck.

Ros closed up the house and climbed in the front seat.

"If you want to ride in the front, I don't mind riding back there, Aunt Bonnie."

"Nope, I've got plenty of leg room. You stay up there. If I get tired, I can always take a little nap. You sit up there and visit with Stacy. Do you need a map to find the church?" she asked, patting Stacy on the shoulder.

"No, Miss Bonnie. I think I know where we're going. We'll take Highway twenty-four east through Stockton."

"Are you sure? Shouldn't you take Highway 36 through Norton?" Bonnie insisted, leaning forward.

"No, ma'am. Highway 24." Stacy started the truck and offered an understanding nod in Ros's direction before pulling out of the drive.

"Stacy knows where she's going, Aunt Bonnie. Don't worry. We won't get lost."

"I remember my first car didn't have air-conditioning." Bonnie laughed at the memory. "It was a 1956 Ford. Two-tone blue. I wish I had a nickel for every time I drove that thing to Goodland and back. I thought the carry-out boy at Safeway was so cute."

"You never told me about that, Aunt Bonnie."

"I almost forgot. I only had the car a year or so. I blew the engine in it. No one told me I should check the oil every now and then." They all laughed.

"My first car was a 1986 Chevy El Camino." Stacy sighed dreamily. "I loved that car. Black with white leather interior. I thought I was hot stuff. I drove it all through college. Bucket seats and a chrome railing around the bed."

"And I bet you kept it polished and did lots of cruising."

"You bet. Mirror finish." Stacy pulled into the gas station and climbed out.

"Here. Use this." Ros quickly pulled out her credit card.

"No, I got it." Stacy scowled. Ros didn't argue.

The farther they drove the more anxious Bonnie seemed to become, looking out one window then the other with a worried expression on her face.

"Not too much further, Miss Bonnie," Stacy said, glancing in the rearview mirror. "We turn north on County Road 29 just past Woodston."

"This doesn't look familiar."

"That's okay. Our memories play tricks on us sometimes," Stacy said in an understanding tone.

"Yes, they do." Bonnie released a breath and leaned back in the seat. "Yes, they do."

Stacy turned onto a dirt road and headed north, slinging gravel behind the truck. Bonnie was staring out the window when Stacy turned at a crossroads and pulled to the side of the road across from a small white stone church.

"There it is," she announced, draping her wrist over the steering wheel. "Exactly one hundred miles."

"Ash Rock Congregational Church. Built 1883," Ros read on the front of the church carved in the stone.

"Yes! That's it," Bonnie declared breathlessly. She climbed out and slammed the door, never taking her eyes off the church.

Like a lush green oasis in a desert, the church sat on a corner lot in the midst of farm fields that stretched as far as the eye could see. It was a simple structure with a peaked roof and a small steeple and a divided set of stone steps that led up to the front door. The grass around the church was thick and recently mowed. Across the road, surrounded by a wrought iron fence was the Ash Rock Cemetery. The headstones, some weather-darkened and leaning, some newer granite, undoubtedly spanned over a century.

Bonnie stood in the grass, smiling up at the church as she clutched her hands to her chest.

"There it is, Aunt Bonnie. The church you've been searching for." Ros stood next to her. "The little church on the prairie."

"Yes," Bonnie gasped as tears welled up in her eyes. "I never would have found it." She turned to Ros and gave her a warm hug. "Thank you, dear."

"Don't thank me. Thank Stacy. She's the one who knew where it was."

But Bonnie was already heading for the front steps as if she expected the church to be open for inspection.

"It's probably locked," Stacy called. She was leaning against the truck, taking a few pictures with her phone. "That looks like a fairly new deadbolt lock on the door."

Bonnie tried the doorknob anyway. There was a small window near the top of the door, but it was too high to see in.

"All the windows are covered," Bonnie reported as she made her way down the side yard. Ros followed her, examining the details of the little church and imagining how long it must have taken to build it over a hundred years ago without modern technology. In the yard near the back corner of the church, she found a small white square stone. No bigger than a golf ball, it matched the stones of the church. Ros picked it up and held it in her hand, envisioning her great-great-grandfather holding it. He must have had help building the church, but she wanted to believe he touched this very stone and placed it just so. The stone was rough and left a chalky dust on her fingers.

Stacy had been making her way around the building, too. She looked over Ros's shoulder. "That's Fort Hays Limestone," she said. "It's a soft stone. Easier to work with. These older structures were usually built with two separate walls, an interior and an exterior, about eighteen inches thick. That little stone probably got blown off during one of our Kansas storms. Keep it as a souvenir. No one is going to come put it back up there."

"Look, outhouses." Bonnie pointed to adjoining wooden outhouses at the back of the property, one marked women and one marked men.

"I doubt those are original," Stacy said with a chuckle.

"I'm spoiled. I like indoor plumbing."

"Me too," Ros added.

"I'm sorry you can't see inside the church, Miss Bonnie. But at least you can see it from the outside."

They circled the building as the hot sun beat down on them and a dust devil danced down the road. Stacy returned to the truck and sat down on the tailgate. Bonnie continued to roam around the church as if reliving some past memory.

"I really appreciate you bringing her to see this," Ros said, crossing the road to where Stacy was watching. "It has made her very happy."

"No problem. She can take all the time she wants." Stacy opened a small cooler and took out two bottles of water. She opened one and handed it to Ros. "And so you know, I did it for you as much as for her."

"Thank you. You're very nice to Aunt Bonnie."

Stacy shrugged and said, "I never had an aunt. Or an uncle for that matter."

"Do you have any family?" Ros asked although she already knew the answer. Meade had told her.

"Nope." She took a drink, holding the bottle to her lips a long moment.

"No one?"

Stacy shook her head.

Ros looked at Stacy but didn't say anything, hoping she would offer some explanation.

"I was an only child," she finally said. "My mother was a single parent and she died when I was in college. Lung cancer." Stacy released a long resolute sigh. "So there's just me. Miss Bonnie fills a gap, I guess. I don't have any older relatives to check up on."

"I'm very grateful to have Aunt Bonnie in my life. She has always been there for me, even when my parents weren't or chose not to be. She taught me to drive and bought me my first car when I went off to college. She took care of me when I was sick. She listened when I was upset. She always had some pearl of wisdom that brought things into focus for me. When I finally decided to come out to her she just smiled and said she already knew. She said she knew I'd tell her when I was ready."

"She seems to be doing all right," Stacy said, watching as Bonnie crossed the road to the adjacent cemetery.

"I wish I shared your opinion."

"You don't think she is?"

"Sometimes yes. Sometimes no. It's the little things. Like forgetting the name of one of her best friends. Or thinking a winter sweater is appropriate on a ninety-five degree day. Leaving her car keys in the refrigerator. Buying more butter than she'll ever use because she forgot she already has several pounds in the fridge."

"Those are little things, Ros. Little things. She still seems rational."

"I know. But I worry." Ros watched as Bonnie meandered through the rows of tombstones, stopping to read each one.

"And you have a right to. She's your aunt and you love her and want only what's best for her."

"Sometimes we talk and it's like old times. She's lucid and reasonable." Ros took a deep breath and lowered her eyes. "But…"

"But what?" Stacy asked, looking over at her.

"She called me Sylvie the other day. Several times. I corrected her, but she kept doing it as if she wasn't aware she was saying anything wrong."

"Your mother, right?"

"Yes. How did you know?"

"Miss Bonnie told me. She doesn't have much regard for her, does she?"

"No, she doesn't. They are about as opposite as two sisters can be."

"How long has it been since you saw or talked to your mother?"

"Several years. She called. She wanted money. I sent her a little. Aunt Bonnie doesn't know and I don't want her to know. Good or bad, she is my mother. I've got a half-brother out there somewhere too. California or Oregon. I've never met him. I don't even know his name." Ros shook her head as she grappled with this bit of reality.

Stacy wrapped an arm around Ros's shoulder.

"I'm sure it was very hard for you. But Miss Bonnie loves you like a mother and provided you a stable home environment. And look at what you've become. A gorgeous, successful career woman with a stubborn streak a mile wide." She grinned and gave her shoulder a shake.

"I can't find anything that looks familiar," Bonnie shouted from deep in the cemetery. She wandered back across the road and circled the church again, trailing her fingers along the stones. It was a few more minutes before she seemed to satisfy her curiosity and came to the truck.

"I couldn't find anyone's marker that I recognize. But I don't need to. They're all resting peacefully in the hereafter. That's all that matters. As for me, I want to be cremated and my ashes scattered. I don't believe in occupying a piece of property for all eternity. That's just plain selfish. I was here. I did my best. I'll live on in people's memory. That's all there is to it." Bonnie gave an emphatic nod, took the bottle of water Ros handed her and climbed in the truck.

"That seems very profound," Stacy said.

"Profound and definite. That's been her wishes as long as I can remember. Every now and then she seems compelled to remind me."

It was after noon when they decided to stop in Stockton for a sandwich. It was a tiny farming town with a county courthouse on the square. There wasn't much to choose from, but they found a café on the square that was air-conditioned. They lingered over club sandwiches and tater tots. Bonnie entertained them with tales from her childhood. Her memory was clear and precise and she seemed to enjoy relaying bits and pieces of her youth.

"You were quite a mischief-maker, Miss Bonnie."

"Oh, yes, I was. I remember one time, I was about seven or eight, I took a dollar bill from my mother's purse and rode my bicycle to the store for chocolate milk and to ride the hobbyhorse out front. It cost a dime."

"Did you get in trouble?" Ros asked.

"Got my bottom paddled."

"Sounds like you deserved it," Stacy chuckled.

Sometime well after two they walked the square, window shopping at Bonnie's request, before starting for home and the hundred-mile drive.

"How would you like to stop for some ice cream at the Dairy Whirl? My treat," Stacy offered as they rolled into the outskirts of town.

"Not for me," Bonnie said before Ros could reply. "I'm tired and I need a bath. Just take me home, please."

"How about you, Ros? Do you see ice cream in your future?"

"I haven't been to the Dairy Whirl in years. Do you mind if I go, Aunt Bonnie?"

"Heavens, no. I don't mind. Go. Have a good time. Ice cream on a hot summer evening sounds wonderful. I just don't have the energy for it."

"Should I bring you back something? How about a strawberry sundae?"

"No, no. Nothing for me. I'll be sound asleep before you get back."

Stacy turned down Bonnie's street and headed for her house. It had been a long hot day and it showed on Bonnie's face.

"Would you like me to stay and help you, Aunt Bonnie?"

"NO," she declared adamantly. "I can take care of myself, dearie. A relaxing bath, maybe a little yoga and I'll be fine. I don't need pampering or supervision. I'm not a child."

Stacy opened Bonnie's door and she climbed out, tossing a stern look at Ros. She went inside without a goodbye wave.

"I see where you get your stubborn streak," Stacy said, stepping back into the driver's seat.

"Yes. She definitely lets me know when I've crossed the line. I shouldn't have been so persistent."

"Ready for ice cream?" Stacy headed across town.

"I wonder if they still have the volcano sundae."

"Chocolate ice cream with marshmallow cream, cherry, and caramel drizzle, right?"

"You've had one?" Ros asked.

"Sure, but I order vanilla ice cream."

"Where's your adventure?"

"I'm too old for adventure," Stacy teased.

"Oh, I don't know about that. You're never too old to try something new." Ros caught herself before she said "someone new" instead of "something new."

"I am, huh?"

Stacy pulled into the graveled parking lot in front of the Dairy Whirl. It was crowded with cars, trucks, and a few motorcycles. The umbrella-covered picnic tables on the patio were all occupied with families and couples enjoying a classic summer evening treat. A few were eating hamburgers and curly fries, presumably a late dinner. Unsurprisingly the walk-up window had a line of customers.

"I was going to suggest we eat at one of the tables, but it looks like everyone has the same idea," Ros said.

"You wait here. Keep the AC running and I'll get the ice cream. Chocolate volcano, right?"

"I don't know if I can eat all that. Maybe I should just have a cone."

"For old times' sake, you have to at least try."

"Okay, for old times' sake. My mouth is all set for it." Ros wiggled in her seat, playfully preparing herself.

"Patience, little girl. Patience." Stacy gave a little wink. Ros thought it was adorable, so was her good-natured humor.

Stacy stood in line to order, then waited in another for it to be filled. Ros watched, unable to take her eyes off Stacy and the way her jeans fit perfectly in all the right places. She wasn't a large busted woman but the breasts that had pressed against her during their slow dance at the reunion were firm and perky, as Ros remembered all too vividly.

Ros took in and released a long slow breath as Stacy turned, providing a perfect silhouette of her bustline. She adjusted the vent on the dashboard to blow cold air over her face. Perspiration was beginnng to form on her upper lip and Stacy Hagen was causing it. She was a gorgeous woman twenty-five years ago and was even more dazzling now.

"Here you go," Stacy said, bringing Ros's ice cream to her side window before she rounded the truck and settled into the driver's seat with her sundae.

"You got chocolate ice cream!" Ros leaned over to examine Stacy's sundae.

"I'm on an adventure." She took a big bite. "And proving I'm not too old to try something new."

"Good, huh?" Ros said with a soulful sigh as she gobbled down two big bites.

"Eat slowly or you'll get brain freeze." Stacy took another bite, slowly drawing the ice cream off the spoon with her lips.

"Too late," Ros said, panting and blowing frantically. "But thank you for the ice cream. It's the perfect ending of a perfect day."

They sat in the truck eating ice cream and watching the customers come and go. Stacy seemed content at just being in the truck with Ros. She finished first and dropped her cup in the trash barrel while Ros continued to pick and stir and eat hers.

"Where are we off to now?" Ros asked as Stacy started the truck and waited to pull out into traffic.

"If I was in my El Camino, I'd say we were cruising."

"I don't mind. I'm a slow eater and it's a nice evening for it."

Stacy took her time meandering through town as they chatted. Stacy related plans for the new school year and about the few women in town who occasionally sought her help perfecting their tennis game. Ros confessed how she had been overlooked for a promotion but optimistic the job would come her way eventually if she was patient. At least that's what she was promised. Stacy was a good listener and seemed to understand Ros's frustration at work. She drove past Bonnie's house but didn't turn in. Stacy circled by the park, the school, and the courthouse before heading out her country road.

"We used to drive this same route," Ros said, slipping out of her sandals. "I'd drive barefoot. I still do sometimes."

"We?"

"Meredith and I. Occasionally Neelie James would go with us but her mother didn't like her out after dark."

"Meredith, huh?"

"Yes. Tweedledum and Tweedledee. That's what Aunt Bonnie called us." Ros laughed. "When I told her we were going in search of the family church she expressed an interest in going with us."

"She's a nice person and probably a good friend but I'm glad she didn't come," Stacy said.

"I am too. I had a very nice time today. And I didn't get one phone call or text from the office. That doesn't mean I won't tomorrow, but today was a nice break."

"Can I ask a personal question?" Stacy said after a moment of thought.

"Probably."

"Are you dating Meredith Eason? I mean, is there a serious relationship blooming there?"

"That's a tricky question."

"Then never mind. Sorry I asked. I'm getting into your private life again."

"No, I just mean there are two sides to my answer. A serious relationship? Yes, if you mean we have rekindled our high school friendship. Dating? Other than attending the reunion together and her calling it a date, no. I have no plans to date Meredith Eason."

"I would have sworn Meredith had spent the night with you that day I brought the flowers to Bonnie."

"Spent the night?" Ros giggled. "No. She came by that morning to change her clothes. She was doing a story for the ag section of the newspaper and got a little too close to a cow with intestinal distress. She wore my robe while we washed her clothes. Twice."

"Boy, been there, done that." Stacy seemed both relieved and pleased at Ros's explanation.

"It's not like you and Meade. We don't live in the same town or even the same state." Ros was fishing for information and she couldn't hide it.

"Meade and I aren't dating," Stacy quickly asserted. "We attended the reunion together and she's a good friend, but we're not dating."

"Have you ever? My turn to be nosy."

"For a brief time. But it was several years ago."

"It didn't work out? I think she's a very charismatic woman."

"Yes, she is and no, it didn't work out."

"So you were just shoe shopping?" Ros asked with a cocky grin.

"Shoe shopping? What's shoe shopping?"

"Trying things on to see if they fit. You and Meade were trying out a relationship, but as much as you liked the looks of it, you just didn't fit."

"That's a good analogy. Yes, I guess we were shoe shopping. And at the time, I really wasn't in the market for new shoes," Stacy confessed.

"Before you ask, no, Meredith and I haven't done any shoe shopping."

"I wasn't going to ask. On the list of things that are none of my business, that's right up there at the top." Stacy slowed as they drifted out her country road past her house.

"Should we drive by to check to see if your fence is still standing?"

"It's kind of dark for checking fence. And besides, we just passed it. It looked okay."

"Well, I'm not through enjoying myself. I don't get to do this very often. Usually I'm in a hurry to get where I'm going and worried I'm going to be late."

"I'll drive slowly."

"I wasn't as wild a teenager as you might think. Sometimes I'd drive out in the country looking for a little peace and tranquility."

"Alone?"

"Yes. I can remember sitting out here on some deserted road without another soul in sight, listening to beautiful concert music on the radio. The music would swell and I'd close my eyes and let it wash over me. It was so relaxing and revitalizing at the same time."

Ros leaned her head back and closed her eyes, reliving the memory. She felt the truck slow, then stop. There was nothing but silence in the darkness. Ros was still drifting with her memory when Stacy caressed the back of her neck and pressed a kiss to her lips.

Was it real or was it an imaginary moment in time? She opened her eyes. It was real. Stacy laced her fingers through Ros's hair and placed another kiss on her waiting lips. Ros froze in her seat. Stacy's mouth was more tantalizing than she ever dreamed.

Stacy unhooked her seat belt and moved closer. She draped her arm across Ros's lap, resting her hand on her hip.

"That came out of the blue, but I'm not going to apologize for it," Stacy said as her fingertips stroked Ros's cheek.

"Then may I have another?" Ros found herself whispering.

Without a word, Stacy kissed her again, gently but passionately to sounds of Ros's soft moaning.

"You're going back to Cincinnati soon and I needed to do that. I couldn't help myself. I had to know."

"I don't need an explanation. It was perfect and I'm glad you did it. Well, maybe not perfect but very close," Ros said softly, drowning in Stacy's dark eyes. "Let me show you."

Ros wrapped her arms around Stacy and drew her into another kiss. This one was luscious and inviting. She parted her lips and allowed Stacy's tongue to invade her mouth. A spark rippled through Ros's body as she felt Stacy press against her in the seat, her breasts, her hips.

"Oh my God." Ros gasped for breath. She hooked a leg over Stacy's, holding on to her for dear life. There, in a pickup truck, on a dirt road, in the darkness, Stacy Hagen could have her if she wanted her. All she had to do was ask. Ros didn't consider herself easy. Never had been. But this wasn't just any night. And even if it was only one night, this wasn't just any woman.

Stacy climbed over the console, continuing to devour Ros's mouth and lips, and released the lever to Ros's seat back, holding it to allow it to recline slowly as she lowered herself upon her.

"Am I crossing the line here?" Stacy asked breathlessly.

"Yes, most definitely. But I love it." Ros clung to Stacy's body, pulling her down tight against her. She could feel Stacy's back muscles flexing beneath her shirt.

"I wish I knew how to tell you how special you are." Stacy looked down into her eyes with a sweet innocence.

"I think you just did," she whispered, smiling shyly.

"Well, I mean it." She combed her fingers through Ros's hair then lowered her lips to Ros's for another taste. With a flick of her fingers, she unbuttoned the top buttons on Ros's shirt, exposing her bra. "Damn," she sighed as she nuzzled down the pale valley of cleavage, her tongue licking gently.

Ros felt her nipples harden. Stacy slipped her hand inside the bra and cupped one of her breasts, rolling the nipple between her thumb and finger.

"Oh yes!" Ros panted. "Um, Stacy, I've never done this in a vehicle. Just so you know."

"Kiss?"

"I mean where I think this is going."

"Where do you think this is going?" Stacy continued to nuzzle Ros's neck.

"I'm not sure, but I hope we're not finished."

"No, we're not finished." Stacy slid her thigh up between Ros's legs, pressing it against her pubic bone.

"Forgive me if I'm awkward at this. I'm used to a bed."

"We'll call this a coachable moment."

Stacy plunged her tongue into Ros's mouth, kissing her deeply and commandingly, their bodies writhing against each other. She unzipped Ros's shorts and reached inside her panties.

Ros's heart raced with anticipation. She could feel her wetness begin to flow as Stacy's long nimble fingers massaged and probed.

"Coach me, coach me, coach me," Ros muttered as she arched her back, straining against Stacy's tender touch. She cupped her hands around Stacy's bottom, clinging to her as an orgasm ripped through her. Then another. Stacy had complete control of Ros's senses, guiding her to repeated rhythmic crescendos, her moans and shrieks echoing through the darkness. Ros grabbed Stacy's wrist and stopped her.

"You are an amazing coach," she said, her eyes closed tight as she gasped for air. "But I need to stop or I'm going to explode. I can't breathe." She released one long groan of finality.

Stacy teasingly inserted her hand into Ros's shorts again but before she could reach her curly patch of hair the reflection of headlights appeared up the road, coming in their direction. She shot back over the console and into the driver's seat, and Ros zipped her shorts and returned the seat to its upright position. She raked her fingers through the sides of her hair as if to hide any evidence it had been mussed. They both sat staring straight ahead as a flatbed farm truck roared past, a toot of the horn signaling a greeting.

"Did they see us?" Ros asked, checking over her shoulder.

"I'm pretty sure they did. It would be hard to miss another vehicle parked on this road." Stacy chuckled at Ros's naiveté.

"I meant do you think they knew who we are."

"Yep, I do. That was Frank. He lives up the road a few miles. He knows my truck."

Ros looked over at Stacy, panic-stricken.

"Don't worry about it. I won't." Stacy reached over and stroked Ros's face. "I wouldn't have given it up for the world."

"But you have to live here."

"Yes, and you have to visit here. What's your point?"

Ros didn't know what her point was other than protecting Stacy's reputation.

"Ros, I've lived in Colby most of my adult life. People here know me. Like I told you months ago, there are no secrets in a small town. Only small people. I'll probably get teased about it, but it'll be because I had someone out on a country road in my truck. Not because I'm gay."

"We should have gone somewhere else."

"Next time we will," she said with a tender smile and started the truck.

CHAPTER TWENTY

Ros woke early the next morning but was content to languish under the sheet while the ceiling fan lazily turned overhead. Remembering last night's tender moment with Stacy was far more appealing than anything else she had planned for the day.

She wondered what might have happened had they not been interrupted by the passing truck. What did Stacy's body look like? Was her skin soft and sensuous in all those secret places? Unlike the other women Ros had known, there was a maturity and respect to Stacy's lovemaking. And a tenderness like nothing she had ever experienced. Ros had fantasized about it, but the reality of it was better than she ever dreamed possible.

She moaned softly, closed her eyes, and stretched, the sheet exposing her naked breasts. Piano stuck her nose in the partially open bedroom door and meowed as if announcing her arrival. The cat didn't wait for an invitation. She jumped onto the bed and circled next to Ros's side, sculpting a nest.

"Good morning, kitty," Ros said, stroking her silken fur. "How about you bring me a cup of coffee, cream, no sugar."

The cat blinked, then burrowed its face in the sheet. "Fine. I'll get my own coffee. Soon. Maybe."

The rattle of the extension ladder against the house and voices outside told her Stacy was there to finish the painting. Bonnie was probably scouring the house, searching for places that needed last-minute touchups. Stacy was probably politely agreeing and reassuring Bonnie everything would be done to her satisfaction.

Ros imagined Stacy's long, nimble fingers wrapped around the paintbrush, pulling and pushing each careful stroke. The more Ros thought about it and about Stacy's taut muscles, the more she worked herself into a frenzy. And that wasn't something she wanted to do this morning and certainly not alone.

"That's it," she declared, flinging back the sheet. "I'm up."

She showered, dressed, and prepared to go downstairs to enjoy a glass of Bonnie's special peach iced tea and visit with Stacy while she finished the last of the painting. The visit with Stacy seemed the most appealing. But two phone calls and a text from the office occupied much of the morning.

"Yes, I'll be in the office Monday morning, regular time," she said for the third time. "I'm leaving day after tomorrow. I'll take care of it first thing. Those figures have to match the expense report from the library. They can't pay more salary for more employees than are on the payroll and receiving it."

She ended the call and went downstairs to see how the painting was going. Stacy was cleaning her brush and roller at the hose. Her face, clothes, and hair were speckled with white paint.

"What do you think?" Stacy asked with a welcoming smile. She used her sleeve to wipe the sweat dripping down her cheek.

"Are you finished already?" Ros crossed the yard to her, being careful where she stepped barefoot.

"All finished. Unless you find a spot I missed."

"I see one."

"Where?" Stacy snapped her head around.

"Right here." Ros pointed to Stacy's left cheek. "You have paint everywhere but there."

"I do, huh?" Stacy dipped her finger in the paint and smeared it down her cheek. "There. How's that?"

"Silly woman."

"You want some?" She held up her paint-covered finger, poised to rub it on Ros.

"No." Ros quickly stepped back.

"Ah, come on. Just a little." She swiped her finger through the air.

"I said no." She took another step back.

Stacy dropped the brush and took a step toward Ros, her finger extended.

"Don't you dare."

"Oh, now you're daring me?"

"I didn't mean I was daring you." Ros moved away, fearing she had started something Stacy planned to finish.

"I think you did, Ms. McClure." Stacy had a devilish gleam in her eyes.

"No, I didn't." Ros started running as Stacy began to chase her around the house. "No fair. You're an athlete. You can run faster. I'm just a numbers junky."

They were only halfway around the house when Stacy caught up to her, wrapped her arms around her waist, and prevented her from escaping while she dotted paint across her face. Ros wiggled and squealed but played along as Stacy tattooed her with white paint.

"That'll teach you to dare me," Stacy said, finally releasing her but only after tickling her.

"What's all the noise?" Bonnie shouted from the kitchen window.

"Nothing, Miss Bonnie. I was just explaining to Ros the various applications for trim paint."

"Yes, Aunt Bonnie. You have to be very careful with paint." She giggled.

"Ros, you need to stay back when Stacy's painting. You got it all over your face."

"Yes, I realize that."

"Come in here and wash it off," Bonnie instructed. "I'm going to the store for bread and eggs. Do you need anything?"

"No. Nothing for me."

"Stacy, you're welcome to stay for dinner. We're having hamburgers and onion fried potatoes."

"Sounds wonderful, Miss Bonnie, but I have an appointment. Another time."

"What kind of appointment, if I may ask?" Ros said following Stacy back to the hose.

"Tennis lesson. I've had to reschedule Haley's appointment twice already. I promised I'd be available this evening." Stacy seemed to read the disappointment on Ros's face, disappointment she was trying to hide. "I'm sorry. It's just one of those commitments I can't get out of this time."

"I didn't say anything. I understand commitments." They both watched as Bonnie pulled out of the drive on her way to the store.

"Come here. Let me wash off the paint," Stacy said, wetting a rag and wringing it out.

Ros could have done it herself, but she allowed Stacy to gently blot and wipe away the paint, their faces just inches apart. As soon as she was finished, Stacy gave Ros a quick peck on the lips.

"All's forgiven?" Stacy asked, giving one last wipe across her forehead.

"All's forgiven. But before you go, would you come sit on the porch with me for a few minutes?"

"I'm all sweaty and covered in paint."

"I don't care."

"I will if I can have a glass of water. I'm tired of drinking out of the hose. I think I swallowed a bug." Stacy tossed her brushes in the back of the truck.

"I'm sorry. I should have brought you some," she said, hurrying into the kitchen.

Stacy was already in the porch swing, enjoying the shade and breeze from the porch fan, when Ros returned with two large glasses of ice water and a handful of grapes.

"Here, eat these. They're excellent to help rehydrate you."

"Very good, Ms. McClure. You remembered my lecture on hydration." Stacy patted the seat next to her.

"Who remembers? I saw it on CNN."

They sat, leisurely swinging and sipping, as they stared off into space.

"So you're leaving Saturday?" Stacy finally asked.

"Yes."

"It's been nice having you back in Colby. I'm sure Miss Bonnie will be sorry to see you go."

"I don't have an endless number of vacation days. I don't normally take this many, but I was on a mission." Ros leaned her head against Stacy's shoulder. "I used to take naps in this swing. When I was a little girl my mom would bring me over for Aunt Bonnie to babysit. I'd lay here and go back and forth and listen to the birds. It seemed so perfect."

"You were communing with nature."

"I was enjoying a peaceful moment, just like I'm doing now. Even if it doesn't last, I will have the memory of it."

Stacy pressed a kiss into Ros's forehead, then stood.

"I better go. I'll need a shower before I meet Haley." She handed Ros her glass, their fingers lingering together for a brief moment. "Have a nice evening, barefoot girl."

"You have a nice evening too, Coach."

Ros continued to swing and watch as Stacy gathered her equipment and climbed in the truck. She put down the window and waved but said nothing. Her eyes were on Ros in the rearview mirror as she gradually pulled away.

Bonnie returned from the store and started dinner while Ros sat in the swing, replying to emails on her cell phone. The closer it got for her to return to work, the more frequent the messages. The only good thing she could find from it was the distraction it provided from constantly thinking about Stacy and their time together.

"Stacy did a very professional job painting the house, don't you think, dear?" Bonnie said as they stood together at the sink washing dishes.

"Yes. It looks wonderful. Very bright and cheerful."

"I have a check all ready to give her when she comes by tomorrow. I told her so. She didn't want to take it, but I insisted. I can most certainly pay to have my house painted."

"I'm not going to get in the middle of that. You both have your own ideas how that should be handled so you'll have to deal with Stacy directly. And yes, you can well afford to pay for your house to be painted."

"I think she likes you, Ros. She always asks if you're up yet when she comes to paint."

"I like her too, Aunt Bonnie." That was as much as Ros wanted to admit. She didn't want their private time together to be fodder for Bonnie's lunch group. Not that she would say anything malicious, but something might slip out to embarrass Stacy or her. The less said, the better. "What are your plans this evening?"

"I thought I'd do a little yoga. My shoulder always feels better after I spend a half hour or so on the mat. What about you? Would you like to join me?"

"I don't think so. I've got some things I need to do on my laptop." Ros put the last of the dishes back in the cupboard and wiped the counter. "There. All finished. Spic and span."

"Ros, when you have a minute, would you go through the stuff on the shelf in your closet? There's a box of your things there and I'd like for you to take what you want and we'll throw away the rest. I can't lift it down by myself. My shoulder just won't let me."

"I didn't know I had anything up there. I thought we cleaned all that out years ago. But I'll look before I head back to Cincinnati."

"No, no. Don't tell me that," Bonnie insisted. "I don't want to hear you're leaving. Lalalalala."

Ros took Bonnie's hand in hers.

"Please, Aunt Bonnie. Don't make me feel guilty about going back to my job and my home. I feel bad enough already," Ros pleaded, hoping to appeal to Bonnie's parental side. "I have to go. You know that."

"All right." Bonnie stiffened. "Not another word from me about it. But I don't have to like it."

"No, you don't." Ros leaned her forehead against Bonnie's. "You don't at all."

Bonnie walked out of the kitchen without another word. She wasn't happy and she wasn't doing a very good job of hiding it.

While Bonnie changed into her yoga clothes, Ros settled on the bed cross-legged for a few minutes of work on her laptop. But it was hard to concentrate with life pulling at her from so many directions. Her job was waiting and the possibility the promotion would soon be hers. And she was worried about Aunt Bonnie. She tried her best not to make Ros feel guilty about leaving, but it wasn't in her nature. Whatever Bonnie felt, she expressed. It was just her way. And then there was Stacy. She wasn't even sure where that situation was headed, but their time together was magical. And Ros wanted to savor it.

Ros set her laptop aside and flopped back on the pillow, staring up at the circling blades of the ceiling fan. Piano sauntered into the room and looked up at her, meowing insistently. Ros dropped her hand down the side of the bed and allowed the cat to rub against it.

"Kitty, is your life as complicated as mine?"

Piano meowed again, then left as slowly as she entered. Ros was tired of feeling sorry for herself. She climbed off the bed and brought down the box from the closet shelf, thinking whatever was in it would take her mind off everything else. She sifted through the box, taking out old shoes, a pair of winter boots that never fit quite right, a chess set she was sure she could learn to play, some sheet music from the few piano lessons Bonnie insisted she take, a small box of hair ties and barrettes from her days with long hair. And in the bottom of the box, covered by a Colby T-shirt, a notebook. *The* notebook. On the cover, written in Ros's script penmanship, were the words "Biology Laboratory Notebook, Ros McClure."

"No! It can't be." Ros snatched it up and opened it. Sure enough, this was the long lost lab notebook, the one that cost her an A in Stacy Hagen's biology class. The one she lamented for weeks, for months. What was it doing in her closet in the bottom of a box? She had a pretty good idea, but she had to know for sure.

"Aunt Bonnie, where did you get this?" Ros demanded.

"What, dear?" Bonnie was in the living room, holding a yoga pose with her arms gracefully extended.

"This notebook." Ros thrust the notebook at her aunt so she could plainly see what it was.

"I have no idea, dear. It isn't mine." Bonnie changed poses, maintaining a calm voice and deliberate moves while keeping her eyes straight ahead.

"No, it's mine." Ros opened the notebook and held out a page with a flower drawing on it. "This is my biology notebook. The one I couldn't find. The one I needed to turn in for a grade. I showed it to you. Remember?"

"When was that, dear?" Bonnie said quietly, holding the next pose.

"When I was in high school. When I was living here. Twenty-five years ago, Aunt Bonnie. Did you take it?"

"Ros, dear, I'm trying to create peaceful self-reflection here. You are not helping."

"Aunt Bonnie, please. Look at me. Did you take my notebook?"

"I have no earthly idea what you are talking about. I don't remember a notebook and I'm sure I didn't take it."

Ros was fuming at the thought Bonnie had taken the notebook and stolen her chances at straight As and a full scholarship. It was conceivable, she supposed, that she didn't realize what she was doing even back then. Nothing would be gained by badgering her about it now. The mystery of the notebook had been solved. Bonnie must have admired the sketches and colorings enough to want to keep it, so she did. Now she didn't even remember it. Nor did she care.

"I have to go out for a little while, Aunt Bonnie," she said stiffly. She needed an escape. She needed to get away from Bonnie and this house before she said things she'd regret.

She raced back upstairs, grabbed her keys, then headed out to her car. She wasn't sure where she was going, but the notebook lying on the seat beside her seemed to guide her down Stacy's road. She might not even be home. She could still be at the tennis lesson. She sought the comfort and security Stacy's property seemed to offer anyway.

"Please please please be home," she muttered as she turned in and circled up to the house. Stacy's truck wasn't there. Ros headed to the tennis courts at the park she assumed Stacy was using for her tennis lessons, but she wasn't there. She drove past the community college on the outside chance she was using their tennis courts, but she wasn't there either. Ros drove through town, up one street and down another, searching for Stacy's truck.

The more she searched, the more frantic she became. She was furious with Aunt Bonnie. Finding Stacy and explaining what happened all those many years ago seemed like the only way to deal with it. But if Stacy was anywhere in Colby, Kansas, Ros couldn't find her and it was almost dark. She pulled into the parking lot at the Dairy Whirl, wishing she had remembered to bring her cell phone. She still wasn't ready to go home and face Bonnie. She didn't want any ice cream, just a quiet place to decompress.

She leafed through the notebook, studying the drawings, remembering the lab classes and special projects Stacy had assigned. What would Stacy say about the found notebook? She was a practical woman. She would probably say forget it. It was water under the bridge. Don't waste your time upset over something you can't change. And remember, Bonnie didn't do it vindictively.

It was after ten when Ros returned home. Bonnie had left the lights on, but she was in bed, sleeping soundly as Ros made her way upstairs.

CHAPTER TWENTY-ONE

"What was it you were asking me yesterday? Something about a notebook?" Bonnie said as Ros came down to breakfast. She had a puzzled, almost confused look on the face.

"It was nothing, Aunt Bonnie. Nothing at all." Ros saw no reason to resurrect that topic. Bonnie had no memory of it. And the more Ros thought about it, the more she hoped to just let it slide.

"If you say so, dear. I made some nice hot oatmeal with cinnamon and cranberries for breakfast. Sit down at the table and eat it while it's still hot."

"Thank you. It looks delicious." Ros might not have considered hot oatmeal a perfect breakfast choice when the temperature was already in the eighties, but she ate it anyway. "By the way, Aunt Bonnie, I won't be home for dinner tonight. Meredith called and invited me out to JoJo's for barbecue. Some kind of two-for-one special."

"That sounds like fun. Well, I won't wait up for you then."

"It'll just be for dinner. She's coming by around four. She wants to go before it gets crowded."

"Do you need some money, dear?" Bonnie seemed serious.

"No, I don't need any money, Aunt Bonnie. I'm fine." Ros couldn't help but smile at her offer. It was the same one she used to make when Ros was going out with friends after school. On more than one occasion pizza or burgers and pop was Bonnie's treat for a carload of girls.

"I'm going to do some laundry this morning so throw down whatever you need washed, dear."

"I took care of it yesterday. I'll be good until I get back..." Ros stopped herself. Bonnie didn't want to hear about her leaving and Ros respected that.

Ros spent the day, packing what she could, replying to emails and wondering when Stacy was stopping by. There was still that matter of Bonnie's check for the painting and Ros had a feeling it was going to get testy. She might be needed as a referee.

Bonnie did laundry, worked in her garden and rearranged the pantry, chores that kept her busy most of the day as she cheerfully hummed to herself. Ros was about to call and ask Stacy when she was coming by when she heard her truck pull into the driveway. She hurried downstairs and met her at the front door.

"Hello," she said happily. "We've been expecting you."

"Did I miss something?" She was carrying two cans of paint.

"I thought you were finished painting."

"I am. This is an extra gallon of yellow and white just in case something needs a touchup later on. I'm going to put them in the barn. Do you think she'll leave them alone?" Stacy asked quietly.

"Your guess is as good as mine."

"That answers that question. I'm taking them back home with me. If she needs anything touched up, I'll bring them over." Stacy whirled around without losing a step and returned the cans to the back of her truck.

"Hello, Stacy dear." Bonnie came out on the front porch with an envelope in her hand. "I have your check ready." She handed it to Stacy proudly. "Paint and painting."

"Now Miss Bonnie, remember we discussed this last week. Do you remember what we decided?"

"Decided about what?"

"This check. We decided you would pay for the paint and I would do the painting." Stacy fixed her with an unyielding stare.

"Did we decide that? I don't remember."

"Absolutely we did. You wouldn't want to go back on your word, would you?"

"No, I wouldn't want to do that. If you say so, I believe you."

"I'll bring you an invoice from the hardware store for the paint after they figure my contractor's discount. We can settle up then, okay?" Stacy handed back the check.

"How did you get her to agree to that?" Ros asked behind her hand.

"I used my best teacher reasoning. I explained how it was a benefit to both of us to reach a compromise. I also told her that's what you would want."

"Well played, Coach. Well played."

Ros waited for Bonnie to go inside, then turned to Stacy.

"I need to talk to you when you have a minute."

"Sure. Go ahead. What's on your mind?"

"I'm going to bring up a subject I insisted was off limits but I recently learned something new and I wanted you to know," Ros said.

"The only subject I remember being off limits was your biology grade. And that's spilt milk. I won't ask you about it. I promise."

"I appreciate that, but I want to share this with you. For my own peace of mind, I need to share it."

Stacy put the tailgate down and sat on it, motioning for her to join her. Ros hesitated, then asked, "Would you wait here?"

"Okay."

Ros rushed inside and returned a minute later clutching a plastic grocery sack to her chest.

"I have something I want to show you. I found it in my room." She glanced over at the house to see if Bonnie was watching, then pulled the notebook from the sack and handed it to Stacy.

"You're kidding. This is your actual lab notebook?" Stacy glanced through the pages.

"Yes. It was in a box on the closet shelf. Who knows how long it's been there, but I can guess."

"Well, I'm sorry, Ms. McClure. This assignment is late and I'm afraid I can't give you credit for it now." Stacy closed the notebook and handed it back with a crooked grin. She seemed to take it as nothing more than a joke.

"That's not the point." Ros put the notebook back in the sack.

"I'm not sure I follow where you're going with this. Okay, you found your long lost notebook. You're relieved to have solved the mystery of where it was, but the school doesn't allow us to alter grades, Ros. Especially after twenty-five years. I wish I could. But what would it remedy? You know you completed it. I know you completed it. Of course, I always knew you did. That's what was so difficult about it."

"It's not that I found it or where I found it. It's who put it there? And who made it impossible for me to turn it in?"

"Who?" Stacy asked, playing along. Ros just stared at her until she seemed to follow her drift. "You don't think she took it, do you? Miss Bonnie? Why would she want your notebook? She was so proud of you and your accomplishments in school. I remember meeting her at parent-teacher conferences. She was so impressed with how you were doing. I can't imagine she'd take it and jeopardize your grade."

"I don't think she did it maliciously. I think she liked the drawings and wanted to have them. I asked her about it and she doesn't remember. I guess I shouldn't expect her to."

"You're saying it could have been one of the early signs of her dementia. A loss of contact with reality. Twenty-five years ago?"

"I think so. I'm sure I didn't understand such things as dementia back then even if I knew the word. I know it doesn't change things, but I had to let you know. I didn't want you to go on thinking I was irresponsible or negligent."

"Listen to me, sweet pea. I never thought you were irresponsible or negligent. Ever. I knew there had to be a legitimate reason I never saw that notebook. I'm happy you discovered what happened for your own peace of mind, but it doesn't change my opinion of you at all. You were and still are smart and funny and beautiful. Put the notebook back on the shelf and let it go." Stacy pulled Ros's hand to her lips and kissed it. "But thank you for wanting to share it with me."

"Gosh, you make it sound so simple. And practical. Find it. Then put it back."

"Hey, what would you want to do differently? You want me to grade it?" she said with a chuckle.

"Yes!" Ros suddenly said stoically. "I did the assignment. I want a grade."

"All right." Stacy took the sack and placed it on the front seat. "I'll look it over this evening."

"I'm going out to dinner, but I'll call when I get back. That should be enough time, shouldn't it?"

"You're serious, aren't you?"

"Absolutely. I'm stubborn and a stickler for details."

"You're leaving in the morning, aren't you?"

"Yes. I promised I'd be in my office bright and early Monday morning although I shudder to think what I'm walking into."

Ros had no sooner mentioned returning to work than the phone on her waistband chimed. It was Sue calling from her desk at the university. Ros hated doing it, but she allowed it to go to voice mail. She'd deal with it later.

"How early are you leaving?"

"Seven, hopefully. Aunt Bonnie will want to make breakfast before I leave. She always wants to send me off with a full stomach whether I'm hungry or not. I know it's early, but would you like to come to breakfast?"

"Sure, but don't you think you should ask Miss Bonnie first?"

"I'm inviting you." Their eyes met. "I can't ask you to spend the night, but I can ask you to breakfast."

"I could invite you to spend the night," Stacy said softly, hooking her finger in the waistband of Ros's shorts.

"Please don't." Ros stroked Stacy's cheek. "Things are complicated enough. Maybe next time."

Stacy leaned in as if ready to kiss her when Meredith's car came roaring up the driveway. She honked and waved.

"Hello," she called out the window.

"Is that your dinner companion?" Stacy asked quietly.

"Yes." She waved at Meredith.

"Hi, Stacy," Meredith said, climbing out of the car. She was wearing skintight western jeans and a loose-fitting ruffled blouse. "The house looks nice. I'm sure you're glad to have that big project behind you."

"Thanks, Meredith. And yes, it's good to have the job completed." Stacy turned to Ros and said, "I'll give you my report as soon as I'm finished. Probably no surprises but I'll look it over." Stacy climbed in the truck and started the engine, but it was clear she was giving Meredith the once-over before pulling away.

Ros waved, watching Stacy's truck until she was well down the street. Meredith came to her side and locked arms.

"I know, I'm early. But I was between projects so I thought I'd come over and we can visit until we go to dinner. I'm going to miss you, Ros." She hugged her warmly. "Are you sure you have to leave tomorrow? Couldn't you stay another week? Or at least a few more days? We've hardly had any time together. And remember, I'm the one who talked you into coming."

"I can't, Meredith. I have to get back to work before they fire me for being AWOL." They started for the front porch, but Meredith tossed a look back up the road.

"What was Coach Hagen doing here? Just painting stuff, right?"

"Yes. She brought over the extra paint." That was as much as Meredith needed to know.

"What are you wearing to dinner, Ros? Something sexy or just something gorgeous?" She giggled as they walked lockstep into the house.

Ros hadn't given her evening wardrobe much thought. It depended on what was left unpacked but clean. She assumed the shorts and top she had on weren't suitable although JoJo's Barbecue attracted everything from farmers right out of the field to prom dates.

Meredith flopped down on the bed while Ros sifted through possible clothing choices. Ros's phone chimed with another incoming call from Sue. And again she let it go to voice mail. Whatever catastrophe was looming at work could wait.

"How's this?" Ros asked, holding up a pair of black jeans with rhinestones on the pockets and a bright red shirt with Navajo detailing on the collar. She had planned on wearing them in the car in the morning, but who would care if she wore them tonight too?

"Oh, classy. I love the shirt." Meredith flashed a wicked grin.

"Since when does JoJo's require classy attire? Ralph Lauren and peanut shells on the floor don't exactly go together." Ros stripped out of her T-shirt and shorts. As before, Meredith's eyes were all over her as she changed. Ros stepped into the jeans, wiggling awkwardly as she pulled them up over the hips. As she began to button the blouse Meredith hopped off the bed and came to help.

"No, no, Ros. You have to keep the top buttons open. Show a little," she said, unbuttoning the top two and spreading the lapels. "Hey, what's that? Is that what I think it is?" Meredith parted Ros's cleavage with her fingers and looked deep in the valley between her breasts. "Is that a hickey?"

"It's nothing," Ros said, turning away and buttoning her blouse. "It's a birthmark."

"It is not. You've never had one there before. It's a hickey. An honest-to-God hickey," She laughed. "Who gave you that? Which one of your girlfriends back home?"

"Meredith, it's nothing. Don't worry about it." Ros stepped into her shoes, then went into the bathroom to comb her hair. Meredith stood staring at her, her brow deeply furrowed.

"Ros, who gave you that?" she repeated.

"Now you're just being nosy."

"Is it true? Have you been out with Stacy Hagen?" Meredith came to the bathroom door and scowled at her.

"Okay, yes. Once. We went out once."

"And she gave you that red badge of honor?"

Ros heaved a sigh and said, "Yes, Stacy gave me the hickey. She probably didn't even know she did it."

"Oh, she knew. You always know when you are giving or getting a hickey."

"We're not teenagers, Meredith. What's the big deal? And Stacy was right. It's hard to keep secrets in a small town."

"Ros, what were you thinking? Why in the world would you go out with Stacy?"

"Because I like her, if it's any of your business." Ros was becoming annoyed with Meredith's accusations and assumptions.

"First of all, she's too old for you. She's always been too old for you. She was your teacher, for God's sake."

"What does that have to do with anything now? I'm not her student and she's not my teacher. I never dated her back then. What's the harm in going out with her?"

"But you were going to go out with her back then. I know you were. You wanted to so bad you could taste it."

"Meredith, this conversation is getting way out of friendship territory. I suggest we end it before one of us says something we'll regret."

"If you weren't going back to Cincinnati tomorrow, would you go out with her again?" Meredith demanded.

"I have no idea. Maybe. We had a nice time. We went for ice cream. We cruised around town. We visited. There was nothing wrong with it. And whatever we did later is none of your business."

"I wish you had told me you were considering going out with her," Meredith said with a scowl.

"Since when do I seek your approval on who I do or do not go out with?"

"You used to. You asked my opinion on attending prom with Larry Happy Hands."

"That's different and you know it."

"I saved you from making a big mistake twenty-five years ago. I thought you'd have learned your lesson." Meredith bristled, her nostrils flaring.

"What do you mean you saved me from making a big mistake?"

Meredith turned to walk away, but Ros took her arm and stopped her.

"What are you talking about, Meredith? What did you do?" Ros had no idea what she meant, but she had a feeling she needed to know.

"Nothing." She stiffened.

"Meredith?"

"Okay, I'll tell you. You really want to know, I'll tell you. You were about to make a terrible mistake. You were going to go out with Stacy Hagen. You were going to date a damn teacher. You were always mooning over her. Watching her and smiling at her. Talking about her. I couldn't let you do that. It would have ruined your reputation in this town. And probably hers."

"I was not going to go out with her. I never was going to go out with her or any teacher. I'm not an idiot. I had a crush on her, I admit it. But that's all there was to it."

"As your best friend, it was my job to make sure nothing happened."

"Meredith, what did you do?"

"I took it. I took your goddamn notebook. The one you couldn't find. I took it so you wouldn't have one to turn in at the end of the semester. It was the only thing I could think of. Honey, I know it was wrong, but I was desperate. I was trying to protect you. In my warped little brain I figured if you didn't turn in a notebook, she'd think you weren't worth asking out. She'd think you were careless and immature."

"YOU took it?" Ros gasped. "You took my biology lab notebook?"

"Remember that night I was over so you could help me study for our geometry test. Well, I saw it on your desk and I don't know. I just grabbed it."

"Meredith, I found the notebook. It was in my closet. How could you have taken it?"

"I hid it under your mattress in the slats of your bed when you went downstairs to get us a glass of pop." She pointed to the spot.

"How could you do that? You knew how important my grades were to me."

"By the time I realized what a terrible thing I had done, it was too late. We graduated and the semester was over. Believe me, at the time I thought I was doing the right thing. I assumed it would just fade into history and be forgotten."

Ros's first thought was Aunt Bonnie. Bonnie had no memory of taking the notebook because she hadn't taken it. Ros owed her an apology, even if she didn't remember her harsh questioning yesterday. Ros instantly knew how the notebook made it from bed slats to the closet shelf. It must have fallen out of the bed frame when Bonnie had the new mattresses delivered. She had probably boxed it up with other stray items and assumed they'd be sifted through some time in the future.

Ros went to the window and looked at Bonnie working in her flower garden. She desperately hoped she hadn't done irreparable harm to their relationship. Meredith came to stand next to her, quiet gasps as if fumbling with what to say. "So now you have the hots for Stacy Hagen?" she asked meekly.

"I do not have the hots for her." As soon as Ros said it, as juvenile as it sounded, she knew she actually did.

"Why didn't you ever have the hots for me?" Meredith asked, her voice cracking.

The emotion in Meredith's voice caught Ros off guard. She knew what she was asking, but it never occurred to her to date her best friend, not back then and certainly not now. They were like sisters. Non-identical, occasionally incompatible and very different sisters.

"Oh, honey." Ros softened her tone.

"You hated me then and you hate me even more now, don't you?"

"No. I didn't hate you. We did everything together. We talked about everything and everyone. Yes, I'm not happy with what you did, but I'll get over it." Ros wrapped Meredith in a hug and added, "And I'm sorry, sweetie. No, I don't have the hots for you."

Meredith held on to Ros as they swayed back and forth.

"I'm so sorry, Ros. For everything." She straightened Ros's collar but left the buttons fastened. "I wouldn't blame you if you wanted to cancel dinner tonight. I was a bitch to steal your notebook. I was a bitch to think it was any of my business who you went out with. And I'm a bitch for sticking my nose in your relationship with Stacy now."

"A few minutes ago I was tempted to cancel, but I won't. And to show you there's no hard feelings, I'll let you buy me dinner," Ros said with a wink. "Just be my friend, Meredith. Not my warden."

"I can do that." She wiped away a tear. "I would have given anything for you to feel about me the way you felt about Stacy. But I can live with it if you don't."

"Good. Loyal friends are hard to find." Ros handed Meredith the lipstick from the dresser with a smile. "When you're ready, shall we go to dinner?"

As much as Ros tried, the dinner conversation was strained. Forgiving Meredith completely was going to take some time. She'd have a two-day, thousand-mile drive back to Cincinnati to wrestle with it. They had just finished their brisket sandwiches and cole slaw when her phone rang again, a third call from Sue. Her persistence caught Ros's attention, breaking through her reluctance to end her vacation. With a nod of apology to Meredith, she answered the call.

"Hello, Sue," she said cheerfully. "How are things in Cincy?"

"Where have you been?" she demanded. "I've been trying to call you all day. Did you get my voice messages?"

"I'm sorry, hon. I've been busy today. What have I missed?" Ros wanted to say what disaster has Steve caused, but she didn't out of respect.

"I wanted to get to you first, before anyone else had a chance to congratulate you."

"Congratulate me for what?" Ros noticed Meredith raising an eyebrow, obviously eavesdropping.

"Ros, the committee and the Board of Regents met two days ago and the decision was unanimous. You are being offered the job as chief internal auditor!"

"You're kidding!" Ros exclaimed. "But what about Steve? I don't know if that department can function with co-chief auditors."

"There'll be no co-anything. You will be the chief auditor. Steve is being shuffled into a supervisory role in student accounts until his retirement, which, if rumor is to be believed, won't be that much longer."

"Are you sure about this? No one has contacted me." Ros was dumbfounded. The job she always wanted and thought rightfully hers when Carla retired had finally come her way but she couldn't put words to her feelings.

"I'm sure. Carla told me. Her husband is doing much better and she was invited to sit in on the meeting. After all, she's the one who recommended you for the job. I'm so pleased that you're finally going to get the job you deserve. I think it became very clear how big a mistake it was to put Steve in a job he couldn't handle. Believe it or not, it took you going on vacation for them to realize it. Congratulations."

"Thank you, Sue. I'm pleased beyond belief." Ros felt her grin growing.

"No more picking up the pieces, Ros. No more fixing his mistakes. And I'm sure you'll see a very nice salary increase to go along with the job title. When you get back and all settled in, I'm taking you out for a congratulatory dinner at a place of your choice."

"That sounds wonderful."

"You'll be back Monday, right?"

"Yes. I'll have a pile of work waiting, I'm sure."

"You enjoy the rest of your evening and I'll see you when you get back. Call me."

"I will. Thank you."

Ros ended the called, clutching the phone to her chest and grinning like a kid at Christmas.

"What?" Meredith insisted, smiling at whatever good fortune had come her way.

"I'm being offered the promotion. I'll be the university's chief internal auditor." She heaved a relieved sigh. "I'm dumbstruck. This so came out of the blue."

"Congratulations. If that's what you want, good for you. You deserve it."

"Meredith, would you mind if we cut this evening short? I'd like to visit with Bonnie and let her know my good news."

"Sure, I understand. We can go." She agreed, but she didn't sound pleased. "Your aunt will be very happy for you. I am."

Meredith paid the bill and they headed back to Bonnie's.

"You can drop me off," Ros said, tactfully discouraging Meredith from inviting herself inside.

Meredith pulled to a stop by the front porch and turned off the engine.

"Thank you for dinner. It was wonderful." Ros patted her hand and offered a congenial smile but Meredith quickly wrapped her in a tight hug.

"It was so good to see you again, Ros. In spite of me being an idiot, I'm glad I talked you into coming to the reunion. I'm so very sorry for everything. I don't know if you can ever forgive me. I'm not sure I can." She gave a final squeeze, then released her. "Drive carefully and when you're ready, let's keep in touch."

"You take care of yourself, Meredith. And yes, we'll keep in touch." Ros wasn't ready to say more. As heartless as she knew it sounded, she wasn't ready to offer a blanket forgiveness. "Bye-bye." Ros climbed out and went inside to share her news.

Bonnie was sitting in her recliner, eating a sandwich and chips while watching the evening news.

"You're home early. Were they closed?" she asked, muting the TV. "Can I fix you a sandwich? I made tuna fish."

"No, we ate. They were a little crowded, but the brisket was good. Nice and moist."

"Oh, I hate dry barbecue."

"Aunt Bonnie, I have some good news I want to share with you." Ros moved the newspaper and sat down on the ottoman to face her.

"I can always use good news. What is it?" She turned off the TV and seemed to give Ros her undivided attention.

"I got a phone call while we were at dinner from a woman at the university. She called to congratulate me. The Board of Regents had a meeting and I am being promoted from assistant to chief internal auditor. Finally."

"That does sound like good news. Is this a job you can do?"

"Absolutely. I've been doing it since the head of our department retired months ago. She recommended me for the job."

"Then you are going to be the head of a department?" Bonnie seemed cautiously pleased.

"That's right. CIA is what they call it. It's taken years for something like this to come my way. It'll be hectic at first, but I'm confident I can do the job."

"Then I'm pleased for you, dear. I always knew you were the brightest apple in the bowl. But I have to confess I'm worried."

"About what?" Ros squeezed Bonnie's hand.

"If you're head of a department, you won't be able to come visit me as often. It's been so nice having you here." She seemed concerned.

"Don't worry, Aunt Bonnie. Even if I can't come here to visit, you can come visit me anytime you want. Stay as long as you want. Maybe you could come out in the fall. Whenever you're ready, you'll have a bedroom and a bathroom all to yourself. You could stay through the holidays."

Ros knew Bonnie wouldn't agree to that long a stay, but she wanted her to know she wasn't abandoning her.

"I know my memory is failing me, sweetheart. I know you're worried, but I'm doing okay. I know my limits. My doctor and I have a nice relationship. He's a very understanding man."

"Dr. Smithton?"

"Yes. Dr. Smithton. I like him. I trust him. And I'm pleased I remembered his name." She snickered. "Ros honey, don't worry about me so much." She pinched Ros's cheek lovingly. "I'm your crazy old aunt and I love you. I'll be here when you have time to come visit me."

"I love you too, Aunt Bonnie. You've always been there for me. And I appreciate it."

"That Stacy, she's a good egg. She looks after me when you aren't around."

"Yes, she's been very nice to you. But you can't expect her to do everything. She's a teacher and she has a farm to take care of."

"She's a teacher? I didn't know that."

"Yes, she's a high school science teacher. In fact she was my high school biology teacher. Don't you remember meeting her at parent-teacher conferences?"

"No, I don't remember her. The only one of your teachers I remember had long dark hair and she wore it in a braid. She had nice eyes too. Attractive woman, taller than average."

"Yes, Aunt Bonnie. That was Stacy Hagen. Her hair is short now and it has turned gray, but that's her."

"I like it better now. It suits her." Bonnie gave a knowing nod. "So, she was your teacher. What do you know? Small world. She's a nice lady, Ros. Very polite."

"Yes, she is."

"If you're still leaving in the morning, maybe you should share your good news with her. Why don't you run over there and tell her? It's not too late. It's not even seven. Take her some of those brownies on the counter. I made way too many."

"Would you mind if I run over there for a few minutes?" Ros asked, excited to share her news with Stacy as well.

"You go ahead. I'm going to watch *Golden Girls*. They're having a marathon this evening. I've seen every episode a million times, but it's better than the other garbage that's on these days. And, Ros, just so you know, a few years difference in age isn't that big a deal. You remember that." She patted Ros's hand and sent her on her way.

Ros slipped a few brownies in a baggie and headed over to Stacy's, hoping she was home and anxious to tell her the good news. She wasn't sure Stacy needed to know about Meredith's long-kept secret. She wasn't sure she even needed to know it herself. As Stacy had so succinctly put it, it was water under the bridge. Ros was even feeling a little foolish for insisting Stacy grade the notebook. It made no difference now. Ros had her promotion and she was satisfied Bonnie could live on her own, at least for now. Progress had been made. And she was going home with a sweet memory of Stacy's gentle touch. Would there be a next time? With every ounce of her being, she hoped so.

CHAPTER TWENTY-TWO

By the time Ros pulled into Stacy's drive and followed it around to the patio the few morning clouds had developed into an evening shower. The white pickup was parked next to the barn doors that stood open.

"Hello? Are you in there, Stacy?" she said, putting her window down and shouting. She wasn't sure she wanted to walk across the pasture to hunt her down in the rain. "Stacy?"

"Hey, I didn't expect company." Stacy came to the open barn door, smiling broadly. "To what do I owe this unexpected pleasure?" She pulled a rag from her back pocket and began wiping her hands but stayed in the shelter of the barn as the rain continued to fall.

"Aunt Bonnie sent you some of her famous walnut raisin brownies." She held up the baggie. "Plus I have some good news to share with you. What am I interrupting? It looks like you're doing something greasy."

"I was changing the chain on an old chainsaw. It needed cleaning and sharpening. Come on in while I put it back together. It shouldn't take very long. And you can tell me your good news." Stacy waved her in.

"Okay, but I don't need to know how to run a chainsaw." Ros hurried into the barn, carrying the bag of brownies.

Stacy stood at her workbench reassembling the chainsaw while Ros watched.

"So, what's the good news?"

"I got a call this evening from someone in administration on campus. I'm being offered the job as chief internal auditor. It seems the university and the Board of Regents, who we answer to, realized they made a mistake giving the job to someone without any experience or knowledge of the Auditor's Department."

"That's great, Ros. So you'll finally have the job title for the work you're already doing."

"Exactly."

"Took them long enough to figure it out."

"Apparently it took my going on vacation and being out of the office for them to realize he wasn't capable of handling things alone."

"That is wonderful news. Congratulations. Have you told Miss Bonnie?"

"Yes, she seemed pleased. But she's also a little worried we might not see each other as often. I reminded her she'd have a bedroom all to herself and can come visit whenever she wants. And I hope she does."

"She should. It'll be good for her to get out of Colby once in a while. But we'll see you from time to time, I hope. You'll have some vacation occasionally, won't you?"

"Yes, I'm sure I will, but if past is prologue, I'll be even busier than I am now. I'll have to hire and break in a new assistant. It might take a few months to get things running smoothly, but it's doable."

"I'm sure you can handle it. And congratulations again on attaining your dream job."

"Thank you." Ros glanced around the barn at the tools and equipment hanging on hooks and on shelves. It seemed well stocked with everything a farmer could possibly need. "I'm curious. Doesn't being a full-time teacher plus a part-time housepainter keep you busy enough? Do you really have time to be a farmer? Or is it rancher?"

"I like to think I can multitask. I raise a few head of cattle that I graze on my own acreage. And I enjoy it. I like being outdoors. Plus it's a good way to augment my income and plan for retirement. Teachers' salaries in small Kansas towns will never make you wealthy. Those of us who stay rural have a calling. I have no interest in living in a big city."

"Isn't that called finding your niche?"

"I think so. Like what you've done working at the university. You are good at what you do. Your promotion proves that."

"Twenty-five years as a teacher in the same school. That's commendable as well."

"Twenty-eight years. I was there three years before you graduated."

"Is it tacky if I ask how old you are?" Ros asked.

"Fifty-three. And according to my rapid mental calculations, you're forty-three."

"Yes, I am."

"The house is unlocked and I'm almost finished here. Why don't you take those brownies inside? We can have a glass of milk and a brownie for dessert." Stacy nodded in that direction.

Ros rushed across the yard and in the patio door, dashing through the rain. It was the first time she had been in Stacy's home. She wasn't sure what to expect, but it was surprisingly bright and airy for a berm house.

Stacy was a tidy housekeeper. There were no dirty dishes in the kitchen and no clutter. Her living room had a couch, two recliners, and a large screen TV. All the floors were either hardwood or ceramic tile and all were spotlessly clean. Two framed pictures hung on the wall, one of an amber sunset over a green pasture, the other of a field of sunflowers with morning dew on the petals. Several fishing rods stood on a rack in the corner; some of them looked like antiques.

It was a warm home with soft tones and welcoming accents, Ros thought. She was tempted to look in the bedroom, but she would respect Stacy's personal space and wait for an invitation into that part of the house. She carried the brownies back into the kitchen, ready to serve their dessert whenever Stacy finished in the barn. She opened the cupboard and reached for a plate, but something caught her eye. Something standing in the corner of the shelf. Something that took her breath away.

"Well, I got it back together. Tomorrow I'll see if I assembled it correctly," Stacy said, hurrying in out of the rain. "Where's dessert?"

Ros spun around and glared at her, holding up what she'd found in the cupboard.

"Where did you get this?" she asked, her voice strained.

Stacy stared at her, her mouth open and her eyes wide.

"This is my diary. Where did you get it?" she repeated with a clenched jaw.

"Ros," Stacy started but stumbled over her response.

"Where did you get it?" she demanded.

"Miss Bonnie asked me to carry some boxes out of her attic. It was in the bottom of one of the boxes. I don't know if she even knew it was in there. She was adamant she wanted it all thrown away. I agreed to take it so she wouldn't try to carry it down the stairs."

"So you rifled through the boxes and took whatever you wanted, right?"

"There were some old towels and rags I could use painting. I saw no harm in taking them. She said I could have them."

"This is NOT a rag. It's my personal private diary. I lost the key to it, but I see that didn't stop you." Ros flipped her finger under the locking strap and folded it open. "You read it, didn't you?"

"Ros, I thought it was Miss Bonnie's. I wanted to make sure I shouldn't return it to her instead of throwing it away."

"So you read it?"

"Yes." Stacy swallowed hard.

"All of it?"

"I won't lie to you. Yes, I read it all."

"You had no right. Do you have any idea how embarrassing this is? You must not or you wouldn't have read my diary."

"There's nothing to be embarrassed about."

"Those flowers you brought over, they were intended for me, weren't they? You thought that's what I wanted. Flowers from the teacher?"

"Yes, no," Stacy stammered, growing more flustered by the second.

"And what was last night in your truck? Did you think you were doing me a favor when you kissed me? Fulfilling some teenage fantasy? Well, thank you very much, but I don't need to be the teacher's pet. And I don't need your pity."

"Last night had nothing to do with what you wrote in your diary. It was spur of the moment. It was spontaneous." Stacy frowned, seemingly aggravated with her reply.

"You have no idea how violated I feel," Ros said angrily. "Here. You wanted to read it. You keep it. Put it with the notebook and burn them both." She tossed the diary at Stacy and pushed past her, hurrying out to her car.

"Ros, wait." Stacy ran after her but slipped on the wet grass and couldn't catch her. "Please, come back inside. Let's talk about this." Stacy placed her hands on the window as Ros started the car.

"I'm not in your class anymore, Ms. Hagen. We don't need to talk. Now please move. I'm going home." She turned on the wipers and roared away, flipping mud on Stacy as she stood in the rain.

"Ros, wait," Stacy shouted, her words barely audible through a clap of thunder.

Ros pulled into Bonnie's drive and sat in the car while rain pelted the roof. She leaned her head back against the headrest, her mind swimming with confusion. How could this day and this visit have gotten so bizarre? One revelation after another. Some pleasantly satisfying, some horrendously disappointing. Tomorrow she would head back to Cincinnati and the security of her new job. It was the only way she knew to deal with the chaos. She hadn't intended to develop feelings for Stacy, but she had. And with time, she prayed, they would fade. She certainly didn't need Stacy to feel sorry for her.

She went inside to finish packing. Thankfully Bonnie was busy with yoga and Ros didn't have to explain why she was upset. Bonnie had had no idea what was in the boxes she asked Stacy to haul away. The less said about it, the better.

Ros was up early and loaded the car while Bonnie made breakfast. Stacy didn't show up. And Ros was grateful. They ate a quick breakfast, said their goodbyes, and Ros was on the road by seven, as she planned. She slipped out of her shoes and began her two-day road trip east. She played music on the radio, listened to an audio book, and counted the small farm towns as she sailed across the interstate.

It was late Sunday afternoon when she finished unloading her car. She gave Bonnie a quick call to let her know she was home safely, reassuring her they would see each other again soon. At that moment, though, Colby, Kansas, was the last place she wanted to be.

When she arrived at work the next morning, a few minutes early to intercept whatever mayhem awaited her, she was greeted by cheers and rounds of applause from her coworkers. A large bouquet of flowers and a muffin basket were waiting on her desk, provided by the university. Steve's office was vacant. Even the desk had been removed.

"They ordered a new desk for you, Ros," Laurel announced. "And a new chair. They're even going to repaint the office as soon as you decide what color you'd like."

Ros burst out laughing at the thought of going through the ordeal of picking paint.

"What's so funny?"

"Nothing. I just didn't think I needed my office painted."

"Not this one. You get the bigger office." She pointed across the hall.

"Seems unnecessary, but okay."

Ros plugged in her laptop and began to work. She knew exactly what needed to be done, but a parade of visitors stopped by throughout the day to congratulate her on the promotion. It was Tuesday before she accomplished anything meaningful.

Little had changed. She had been doing the work for months and it was easier now without Steve's constant interruptions. As busy as she was, though, it didn't preclude occasional thoughts of Stacy and what might have been.

The rest of the month was one detail after another. Ros interviewed several prospects to fill her old slot, knowing exactly what she was looking for in an assistant. Her occasional calls to Bonnie were brief. Either she was busy or Ros was. But she kept in touch anyway. The subject of Stacy never came up.

The first weekend in July was rainy in Cincinnati and humid. Ros spent her days off catching up on household chores. It was after ten in the morning when she called Bonnie to check on how she was doing.

"Hello, Aunt Bonnie. I heard on the Weather Channel that Colby had a pretty nasty thunderstorm yesterday. Are you okay? Is the house okay?"

"Oh, I'm fine." She laughed. "It wasn't that bad. A little lightning and maybe pea-size hail but nothing outrageous. We've had a lot worse."

"Good. I was worried you might have trees down in your yard."

"I had a few branches down, but they were all small, so I bundled them up for the trash. You know, I can't find my chainsaw. I thought sure it was in the barn. But I didn't need it. Stacy called to see if I needed help."

"She did? That's nice."

"I told her it was nothing I couldn't handle. I told her if she'd stop by I'd give her some of my ambrosia salad."

"Did she?"

"No. I think she's been sick. She sounded strained. She didn't have time to talk. She never used to be like that. She was always so friendly and outgoing."

"Did she say she was sick or just busy?"

"She didn't say." Ros heard a car horn in the background. "I have to go, dear. My ride is here. We're going to the park for a picnic. Talk with you soon."

Bonnie hung up before Ros could ask why she thought Stacy was sick. As skewed as things had become, she still worried about

Stacy. It was painful to think she might be ill with no one to care for her. She wasn't interested in a relationship built on pity and patronage. She couldn't put herself in that kind of vulnerable position again. But she had to know if Stacy was all right.

She stared at her phone, poised to make a call. If she needed an excuse she could thank Stacy for checking on Bonnie after the storm. Or she could call Meade at the flower shop and order some kind of plant for Bonnie. She loved living things and maybe, by the way, she could ask if she'd heard how Stacy was doing.

She didn't want to make a difficult situation worse. She decided it would be less awkward to send Stacy a text.

Thank you for checking on Aunt Bonnie after the storm. She appreciated it. I'm glad she didn't have major tree damage. Fortunately she couldn't find her chainsaw. That's a relief. By the way, Aunt Bonnie thinks you're sick. Are you?

She received an almost immediate reply.

I have her chainsaw. It's the one I was cleaning. I removed it so she wouldn't be tempted to use it and hurt herself. And I'm fine.

A few minutes later Ros received another text from Stacy.

Are you all right?

Ros thought a moment, deciding how best to reply. She took the easy road.

Yes, I'm fine.

* * *

"Gifts? For me?" Meade said as Stacy walked through the shop door carrying a box of clinking glassware.

"Yes, if you can use them. Miss Bonnie left these on her porch with strict orders to haul them away to someone who can use them. They're bud vases, of which she has dozens. She's thinning the herd, I think. Can you use them?"

"Let's see." She patted the counter for Stacy to set down the box. "I use a lot of bud vases. Most of them end up in people's trash or in garage sales."

"Help yourself. Toss what you don't want." Stacy stood fiddling with the leaves of a potted plant.

"Will you please leave that poor lily alone?" Meade scolded. Stacy grumbled but obeyed.

"What's wrong with you? You seem like there's something on your mind," Meade said, giving her a sideways glance as she unpacked the bud vases and lined them up along the counter.

"Nothing is wrong," she snapped.

"Wow, sorry I asked." Meade continued unpacking and examining the vases. "That bad, eh?"

"I'm kicking myself for doing something stupid." Stacy groaned and shook her head.

"Do you need to share?"

"No, I don't."

"It must be pretty bad if you won't confess what it is."

"Yep, bad. The really brainless thing about it is I knew it was bad when I was doing it, but I did it anyway."

"Involving who?" Meade raised an eyebrow. "Ros McClure?"

"Yes," she finally said with a smirk.

"Did you apologize?"

"I think I even screwed that up."

"Do you need to send flowers?" Meade offered.

"No, that isn't the panacea this time."

"I wish I could help."

"I got myself into this mess. I'll have to get myself out." Stacy heaved a sigh. "I'm not very good at this."

"She's important to you, isn't she?"

"Yes," Stacy said without hesitation.

"My advice. Just be yourself."

"That could be what got me in trouble in the first place," she said as she walked out the door.

CHAPTER TWENTY-THREE

Stacy sat down in the grass on the bank of the pond and stared across the water at the setting sun. She held her cell phone in her hand, distractedly rubbing her thumb across the screen as she spent another evening thinking about Ros and how much she missed her. She wished she could steer her thoughts to something more serene, more joyful. But she couldn't. How could she have been so stupid? Why was it so difficult to explain her feelings for Ros? And how on God's green earth did she fix it?

Fortunately there were only a few weeks left before the school year started. That was always a busy time; hopefully it would take her mind off Ros. She tossed a rock into the pond and watched the ripples grow. No, it wouldn't. Nothing would take her mind off that beautiful woman with the twinkling eyes and soft lips.

She flipped through the contact list on her phone and stared at Ros's number. She was tempted, so tempted, to call and just say hello. But she wasn't sure her call would be welcome or even answered.

As the sun melted into the horizon it cast an orange glow that made the puffy white clouds look like hot burning coals reflected in the water. Mother Nature at her best, Stacy thought. She wished she could share it with Ros. She'd appreciate the simple beauty of it. Stacy watched as the brilliance grew and consumed the entire pond. She snapped a quick picture with her phone. It was too breathtakingly gorgeous not to share; she instantly sent the picture to Ros. As soon as she sent it she wished she hadn't. It was silly. Just a photograph of a pond at sunset. She closed the cover on her phone and started across the pasture toward the house. She didn't expect a reply. But she had just closed the barn door and latched it when she received one.

Beautiful!!

Stacy smiled at the text. It wasn't much, but it was something. And she treasured it.

It was well past midnight, but Stacy was still staring at the ceiling, unable to sleep, with thoughts of Ros running rampant in her mind. She considered herself an intelligent enough woman, someone capable of figuring out most problems and coming to a rational solution. The scientific method provided logical steps to solve a problem. Formulate a hypothesis. Run experiments. Collect data. Make observations.

"Now you're just being stupid," she muttered as she threw back the covers and went into the kitchen for a drink.

She was standing at the sink in her underwear and tank top, drinking a second glass of water when she remembered the diary still tucked in the cabinet, right where Ros had found it. She pulled it out and opened it, her fingers tracing the words written on the page. This Belongs To Ros McClure.

"I should have stopped right there," she said out loud. "I should have closed it and never read it."

She carried the diary back into the bedroom and crawled into bed. She was tempted to read some of it again, but she couldn't. Not in good conscience. She tossed it on the other side of the bed, turned out the light, and closed her eyes, hoping sleep would finally come. It didn't.

The next morning she sat at the kitchen table, drinking her second cup of coffee just after seven thirty. She was exhausted, but there were chores to do. The brown leather diary was on the table too. She turned it so it was staring straight at her, ready to be opened. Even the strap was folded back. Stacy opened it again to Ros's name on the title page, then went to refill her cup. She stood at the counter, sipping coffee and staring across at the little book, its innocence so palpable yet inviting. Stacy sat down at the table, opened the diary to the last entry, and read it. Then read it again.

* * *

"Ms. McClure, they're waiting for you in the conference room downstairs," Mia said from the doorway. She was the latest graduate student assigned to the department to answer the phone and run errands. She seemed efficient and polite. Ros had no complaints.

"I'm headed that way in three minutes." Ros stood at her desk hurriedly typing out an email while she waited for her printer to finish spitting out pages. She didn't like being late, but they couldn't start without her. She was the boss, something she was still getting used to.

"You'll be back in the office before you leave for the day, won't you?" Mia asked.

"I assume so. Why?"

"You've got a package, Priority Overnight Express. It just arrived. Should I open it?"

"No. Leave it on my desk. I'll take care of it later. Whatever it is, it can't be that important. I didn't order anything." Ros gathered up the papers she'd need and headed down to the meeting. She was halfway out the door when she ran back in her office and slipped into the shoes, aggravated at herself for forgetting them.

The meeting ran late. Ros returned to her office as the rest of the department was leaving for the day.

"See you in the morning, Ms. McClure," Mia said as she passed her in the hall.

"Good night, Mia. Have a nice evening."

"You have three phone messages. They're on your desk. So is that package."

"Thank you, Mia."

Ros looked over the messages, determining if anything needed immediate attention or could wait until the morning.

"You can wait," she said, dropping the first slip of paper in her in-basket. "So can you." The third message was from Aunt Bonnie. It looked like it had been transcribed exactly as dictated.

This is your Aunt Bonnie. Just calling to check up on you. I miss you, dear. I'm going out with the gals for cards and dessert tonight, but call me tomorrow when you have a minute. Nothing drastic. I just like to hear your voice.

"I miss you, too, Aunt Bonnie," she muttered as she picked up the Priority package and examined the return address. It was a P.O. box number and a zip code, nothing else. "Well, it's from Colby but I don't recognize the P.O. box," she said. She plucked a letter opener from the coffee mug on her desk. Meredith? Bonnie's bank? Her doctor's office? The choices were endless. When she opened the package and pulled out her brown leather diary, though, she knew exactly who sent it. "Why are you sending me this? I thought we settled this."

The diary was locked, the strap buckled securely. There was no letter or message with it. Just the diary. Ros searched the package again, looking in vain for any possible explanation or note from Stacy. That didn't make it easier to accept. Her feelings for Stacy hadn't faded. She still got a chill up her spine at the memory of her kiss and her soft touch. She still found herself lost in a daydream when she remembered their night in the truck. She still prayed that someday, somehow they'd see each again.

And, as much as Ros hated to admit it, she knew she had made a mistake. She had been childish and stubborn and she had overreacted. She didn't give Stacy a chance to explain. Stacy shouldn't have read her diary, but like the long lost notebook, that was water under the bridge. Was it so terrible Stacy had read how she had felt all those years ago? What Stacy didn't know was Ros still felt the same way. Every word of it.

Ros slipped the diary into her desk drawer, locked her office, and headed home. Tomorrow was another day, maybe even one during which she wouldn't constantly obsess over Stacy Hagen.

* * *

"Good morning, Mia," Ros said as she unlocked her office. "How was your evening?"

"It was okay. My boyfriend took me out for pizza, but I got a migraine."

"I'm sorry to hear that. I hope you're feeling better. Did the pizza cause the migraine or did the boyfriend?" Ros replied with a cautious smile.

"I think a little of both."

"Can you find me some printer paper, Mia? I'm almost out." Ros sat down at her desk and picked up the phone, ready to place those calls she had put off yesterday. But when she opened her desk drawer to retrieve a pad of paper she noticed the diary. She was still staring at it when Mia set a package of printer paper on her desk.

"Are you okay, Ms. McClure? You look pale."

"What? Oh, yes. I'm fine," she said and closed the drawer.

"I'll be back," Ros announced as she walked out the door. She didn't say where she was going or how long she'd be gone. It was no one's business but hers. And she wasn't sure herself. She just knew she needed to think and she needed a sounding board or she was going to scream. She found a secluded bench in the shade and placed a call to Bonnie. Her aunt was as good a person as any when she needed to talk.

"Hello, Ros," Bonnie said, answering on the first ring.

"Hello, Aunt Bonnie."

"It's so good to hear your voice. I miss you, dear."

"I miss you too, Aunt Bonnie. How are you feeling?"

"I have a little bit of a cold or maybe it's allergies. Who knows? My herbal tea seems to help."

"I'm sorry you're sick."

"I'm not sick. I just have a runny nose." She chuckled. "How are things in Cincinnati? Are you enjoying your new job?"

"Cincinnati is fine, and yes, I'm enjoying my job. Busy, but I enjoy it." Ros hesitated a moment, waiting for Bonnie to offer something else. It was a long silence.

"Ros, dear, is everything all right?" she asked in her mothering tone.

"I don't know, Aunt Bonnie." Ros swallowed, hoping the catch in her throat wasn't noticeable.

"What is it? What's wrong?"

"I guess I just miss you."

"Oh, honey. You don't miss me that much. It has to be something else. So tell me what it is," Bonnie asked.

"Aunt Bonnie, do you ever hear from Stacy?"

"Stacy?"

"Yes, Stacy Hagen."

"I know who you mean, Ros. I'm just wondering why you asked." When Ros didn't reply right away Bonnie added, "Is Stacy who you miss, Ros?"

"Yes," she admitted softly.

"Then why don't you call her up and talk to her?"

"I'm not sure she wants to hear from me. We didn't part on the best of terms."

"Oh, dear."

Ros heaved a sigh. She wasn't sure what to say or how much to admit. The details were long and involved and more than she wanted to confess to her aunt.

"I'm going to give you some sage advice, Ros. Don't waste precious time. Time is a gift you shouldn't squander. Life is too short to spend it wondering what you should have done. Do what you know in your heart is right. And in case you want my opinion, I think Stacy is a nice person. A very nice person."

"I think so too," Ros said, choking back the tears.

"Now you go think about what I said. We'll talk later." Bonnie's voice was steeped in wisdom and kindness. Exactly what Ros needed.

Ros returned to her office after a walk around campus so the tears could dry and her head could clear. It took some doing, but she squeezed an hour or so worth of work out of the day. She composed and deleted several texts to Stacy. She wasn't sure how to tell her she was sorry. She didn't know how to seek forgiveness for her accusations.

She gathered her things into her briefcase, adding the diary, and headed down the hall. She'd work on a text tomorrow. Maybe a simple "I'm sorry" was all she needed to send. Maybe that was all Stacy could or ever would accept.

She stepped into the elevator and pressed the button for the lobby. The door closed, but the elevator didn't move. She pressed the button again, but the lights went out and didn't come back on.

"Not again," she groaned loudly. She tapped the buttons one at a time but the numbers didn't light up. "What's going on out there? I'm not amused," she shouted. "I'm stuck in here."

"Is someone in there?" she heard a male voice call.

"Yes! I'm in here and I want out."

"Who is it?"

"It's Ros McClure. I closed the door and pressed the button, but the lights went out and the elevator doesn't move."

"Ros, this is John from Accounting. There's a power outage in the building. All the lights are out. Are you okay?"

"I am if the power comes back on soon."

"I'll call maintenance and get them up here right away. Hold on. I'll be right back."

"I can't believe this happened again. What is it with this elevator?" She kicked the wall angrily. "Don't you like me either?" She slid down the wall and sat on the floor to wait in the darkness. She wasn't afraid of the dark, but she was glad her cell phone had a flashlight feature. She turned it on, also glad she had recently charged her phone. She shined the light into her briefcase, hunting for a lozenge or a piece of gum or anything to occupy herself. She pulled out the diary, wondering why she decided to take it home. It was a reminder of things she'd rather forget.

She fiddled with the lock, as she had done years ago after she lost the key. She searched through her purse and found a safety pin. She inserted it into the lock and was instantly rewarded. The strap fell open. She didn't need to read it; she knew what it contained. She fanned the pages and was ready to close it when she noticed a small piece of yellow ribbon marking a page near the back of the book. She opened the diary to that page and read the entry. It wasn't her handwriting.

BT loves Ros McClure. Always has and always will. It's been a secret far too long. Now she can shout it for all to hear. BT LOVES RM!!!!!!

A row of tiny hearts colored in red were drawn across the bottom of the page.

"Oh, my God," she gasped as tears rolled down her face. "She loves me."

She was still sitting on the floor, hugging the diary and crying when a pry bar was inserted through the crack and the elevator door opened. Two men stood in the doorway staring down at her.

"Are you all right, ma'am?" one of them asked.

"Yes, I am now," she replied, grinning up at them through her tears. "I am now."

* * *

Ros placed a call to Stacy and slipped out of her shoes to wait for her to answer.

"Hello," Stacy said happily.

"Hello. Stacy, could you stop by Aunt Bonnie's house this afternoon?" Ros asked.

"It's nice to hear from you. It's been two weeks since I sent back the diary and we've only had three conversations. I was getting worried I screwed things up again somehow."

"We talked for over two hours each time," Ros giggled. "I was getting hoarse. Anyway, could you please stop by her house? She's got something you need to pick up."

"Ros, I'd love to see her and I'm always happy to haul away whatever she needs me to take, but I'm really, really busy right now. Could it possibly wait until the weekend? We've got teachers' meetings all week. And I'm the freshman class sponsor this year. It was last minute, but Mrs. Glover is pregnant and asked to be replaced. As if that wasn't enough, my barn roof has a leak I'm going to need to repair."

"Wow, and I thought I was busy. The beginning of the school year is always hectic."

"I'm glad you called, though. I miss hearing from you. Are we okay? Are we making progress?"

"I'd like to think so. Do you want me to let Bonnie know you aren't available?"

Stacy groaned.

"Nooooooo, don't tell her that. I'll find the time to come by. I can fit in a couple minutes somewhere."

"She'll appreciate it, I know."

"I'll swing by about four. Oops, gotta go, Ros. Here comes the principal. Another meeting. Bye-bye," she said, then added softly. "Love you."

"Love you too." Ros smiled and clutched her phone to her chest.

"Is she coming by?" Bonnie asked, coming out onto the front porch.

"Yes, about four."

"You didn't tell her, did you?" Bonnie grinned mischievously.

"I want to see her face when she gets here." Ros looked up at Bonnie. "I hope she'll be pleased."

"Honey, she'll be pleased. I'm sure of it." She patted Ros's hand and went back inside.

It was after five and Stacy still hadn't been by. Ros was beginning to wonder if she was too busy for a visit. She hoped not. The surprise she had waiting was too big to ignore. She prayed it would be well received.

"She hasn't been here, has she?" Bonnie asked from inside the screen door.

"No, but she will," Ros said, content to swing and wait.

"Maybe you should come in and have a bite of dinner. I made hamburgers."

"I'm not hungry. I want to wait out here."

"Come get your plate and you can eat out here on the porch," Bonnie insisted.

"All right." Ros climbed out of the swing and went inside. She was in the middle of stacking lettuce and tomato on her hamburger when she heard a pickup pull into the drive.

"I'm here, Miss Bonnie," Stacy called and the door to the pickup slammed.

"And you're late," Ros said, stepping out onto the porch.

"Oh shit! What are you doing here?" Stacy exclaimed as a smile grew across her face.

"I'm doing some paperwork here in town. I thought I'd surprise you."

"You have, woman. You definitely have." Stacy vaulted up the steps, gathered Ros in her arms and kissed her. "You should have told me you were coming."

"It was all pretty last minute trying to get the details ironed out." Ros draped her arms around Stacy's neck and smiled into her eyes. "I came all this way. I think I deserve more than just one kiss."

Stacy obeyed and kissed her again.

"That's much better."

"How long will you be in town?" Stacy asked, the unmistakable sound of hope in her voice. "Please don't tell me it'll only be a few days and you'll be busy the entire time."

"It kind of depends. I need a reference on an application. I was wondering if you'd mind signing it."

"Reference for what?" Stacy was busy running her fingers through Ros's hair and nibbling her neck.

"The Northwest Kansas Educational Service Center in Oakley needs an administrative auditor. They need someone who can develop and implement the protocols for the schools' new tax regulations."

"Oakley, Kansas?" Stacy suddenly raised her head as she realized what Ros had said.

"Yes. It's twenty-three and a half miles away," Ros said innocently, grinning up at her. "Is that very far, Coach Hagen?"

"You're taking a job here, in Kansas?" Stacy gasped.

"Yes, if I can find a Kansas teacher willing to sign as my reference."

"Absolutely I will but what about your job in Cincinnati? The position you wanted."

"Somehow it didn't seem as important as I thought it would be. I spoke with the Board of Regents and explained I was needed elsewhere. They were very understanding. The question is, am I needed?"

"Oh my God, yes. You definitely are needed." Stacy kissed her passionately and completely. "My barefoot farm girl is definitely needed."

Bonnie smiled proudly and nodded, then slowly closed the front door.

Bella Books, Inc.

Women. Books. Even Better Together.

P.O. Box 10543
Tallahassee, FL 32302

Phone: 800-729-4992
www.bellabooks.com